THICKER THAN WATER

A DCI JACK LOGAN THRILLER

J.D. KIRK

CRIME

Thicker Than Water
ISBN: 978-1-912767-13-7
Published worldwide by Zertex Media Ltd.
First published in 2019.

5

www.jdkirk.com
www.zertexmedia.com

CHAPTER ONE

THEY WERE GOING TO GET IN TROUBLE. SHE WAS CERTAIN of it.

She was sure she could feel her parents' eyes on her as she slid clumsily down the embankment. Sure her dad would shout after her as she sprackled through the heather. Sure she would hear the rustling of the tent being unzipped, and see the beam of a head torch sweeping across the campsite towards her as she stumbled the final few rocky steps to where the water met the land.

But, she didn't. Instead, she stood there shivering at the shore of the loch, listening to the gentle lapping of the waves and the faster crashing of her own heart.

Nathan was a pace or two ahead of her, the moonlight bathing him as he hopped on one leg and wrestled off a shoe.

"We're not actually doing this, are we?" Lolly asked. They were a good hundred yards from the campsite, tucked out of sight, but the fear of getting caught turned the question into a whispered giggle.

She'd only known Nathan for a day and a half, but he'd

quickly turned a tedious family camping holiday in Scotland into much less of a soul-crushing ordeal. He was two years older than her—almost in Sixth Form—and she had immediately taken a shine to him.

He was funnier than the boys back home. Smarter, too. He'd been able to tell her all kinds of stuff about the history of the area. Yes, her dad had told her almost exactly the same information during the drive up, but the difference was that Nathan had explained it in a way that didn't make her want to self-harm. He managed to make it *interesting*.

Mind you, she would quite happily listen to him reading the entire GCSE Maths curriculum, she thought.

He was from just outside Oxford, less than a hundred miles away from where she lived. They'd already made plans to meet up back home the night before, arranging the details via Snapchat. Lolly had lain awake in her sleeping bag for hours, listening to her parents snoring through the dividing canvas wall as she and Nathan swapped messages and photos.

His GIF game was top-notch, and when he'd sent a version of the 'distracted boyfriend' meme to her with one of her own photos superimposed over the face of the attractive passing woman, she'd felt her heart skip half a dozen beats.

It had been momentarily concerning, in fact, before she realised that she wasn't about to go into cardiac arrest and that instead this—*this*—was what love must feel like.

"Yes, we are. But it's freezing!" Nathan yelped, placing a bare foot in the water then immediately yanking it back out again. He kicked off his other shoe and tugged on the end of his sock. "Come on, hurry up before I get frostbite!"

"You're not exactly making it sound appealing," Lolly told him, but she pressed the toe of a trainer against the heel of the other shoe and prised it off.

The rocks were smooth and rounded, and she was able to stand on them in her bare feet without too much discomfort. Nathan already had his t-shirt off, and she spent a moment just staring at his exposed top-half, partly in admiration but mostly in shock.

Was this actually happening? She glanced nervously back in the direction of the campsite, still expecting to see that lighthouse-beam of her dad's head torch sweeping out over the water. When she didn't, she wasn't sure if she felt relief or disappointment.

Nathan covered his nipples with two fingers of each hand and fluttered his long eyelashes. Lolly laughed despite her nerves. Or perhaps precisely because of them.

"Don't laugh! You'll make me all self-conscious," he told her.

She stifled the giggles, and he saw the look of uncertainty that moved in to replace the smile on her face.

"You OK?" he asked, dropping his hands to his sides. He reached down for the t-shirt he'd discarded on the rocks. "Want me to put this back on?"

Lolly took a moment, then gave a shake of her head. Her fingers went to the buttons of her shirt and she fumbled with them, her hands shaking through cold and nerves and... something else. Anticipation, maybe. She couldn't give a name to it, but she liked it, she thought.

Mostly.

Her skin goose pimpled along her arms as she folded them across her chest and wished that she'd brought a nicer bra with them on holiday, or that she better filled the one she had on.

Nathan didn't seem to mind, though. She heard his breath catch in his throat and hoped that he wouldn't notice her blushing in the darkness.

"Wow," was all he said, then he set to work unfastening his jeans and wrestling his way out of them.

Once he had struggled his way free, he tossed the jeans down next to his t-shirt and held his arms out, presenting himself like a gameshow prize.

"Ta-daa!"

He grinned at her, showing none of the embarrassment or self-consciousness that Lolly felt. His underwear was tight enough to reveal a bulge that turned Lolly's anticipation into something more apprehensive.

Was she really going to do this?

Nathan noticed where her gaze was pointed and shifted awkwardly. "It's cold out here, alright?" he said, still smiling. "That's my excuse, and I'm sticking to it."

He flicked his gaze to her lower half. "Your turn," he said, indicating her cut-off cargo pants.

She kept her arms folded, hugging herself in an attempt to stop the shaking. Her mouth felt dry. She felt like she should say something, tell him this was a mistake, but the words wouldn't come.

What was wrong with her? She liked him. *Really* liked him. And he liked her. So, it was fine, wasn't it? This was how it was supposed to happen. Better here with him, than back home at some party with someone she had no interest in six months from now.

Right?

He stepped in close, derailing her train of thought. The heat of him warmed her. Melted her.

"Hey, it's OK, it's OK," he soothed, placing his hands on her shoulders. He looked so calm, so serene in the moonlight. Angelic, almost. His skin, unlike her own, was smooth and near-flawless. She felt an urge to run her hand across it, to check if it was real.

"It's just swimming, that's all," he assured her.

Lolly's voice came as a series of unsteady breaths. "Is it?"

"If that's what you want, then yeah," Nathan promised. "I'm not going to do anything that makes you uncomfortable, OK?"

Lolly swallowed. Nodded.

"OK, then. Good." He leaned a little closer until she could feel his breath on her skin. "Trust me, alright?"

She shivered as his fingertips trailed delicately down her arms. Almost spasmed as they tickled down her ribcage, his palms brushing the sides of her covered breasts.

He kissed her. His lips were soft, but the shock of them suddenly pressing against her own hit her like a sledgehammer. She ejected an, "Umf!" of surprise right into his mouth, which made him draw back, a puzzled expression furrowing his brow.

"Sorry," she whispered, flushed with embarrassment. "I was just... You just... I wasn't expecting..."

She tensed and closed her eyes as he kissed her again. This time, to her relief, she was able to avoid making any involuntary sounds of surprise, even when she felt his tongue pushing its way into her mouth.

His tongue. His tongue was in her mouth.

On purpose.

Was this nice? She wasn't sure. Probably. It wasn't *not* nice, exactly. Strange, definitely. It wriggled around like a worm in there, brushing against her own.

She wished she'd brushed her teeth before coming out.

She was so focused on the tongue-waggling, and so worried about her dental hygiene, that she didn't notice him working the buttons of her shorts until they dropped down around her ankles.

He was kissing her neck now, less tenderly than he'd kissed her lips. She felt his hand on her bum, kneading one buttock through the thin cotton of her underwear.

Another hand pushed one side of her bra up, briefly exposing her breast before his fingers clamped over it, concealing it again to everything but his touch. He grunted and pressed himself against her, the bulge in his boxers making its presence felt.

"Wait," Lolly said. "Stop."

He paused just long enough to whisper an, "It's fine," in her ear before he brought his hand around from her bum and moved it between them. She felt it press against her belly, felt the fingers slide down inside her underwear, stalking down through her pubic hair.

"No, I said *stop*," she objected, more forcefully than she'd intended. It got the message across, though.

She pushed back from him and saw a flash of frustration screwing up his face. It lasted only a moment, before he masked it behind something kinder and gentler.

"What's wrong?" he asked. "What's the matter?"

Lolly repositioned her bra and pulled up her shorts.

"What are you doing? Come on," Nathan said. "It's just a bit of fun."

"I don't want to," Lolly said, not meeting his eye. "Sorry."

"What? Why not? I go home tomorrow," Nathan told her, struggling to hide the impatience in his voice. "This is our only chance."

Picking up her shirt, Lolly pushed an arm through the sleeve. "We can meet up back home. Get to know each other a bit before... Before we... You know. Before we do anything."

"For fuck's sake. What are you, *twelve*?" Nathan spat, and

the tone of it hit her like a slap to the face. "We live a hundred miles apart. We're not going to meet up. This is it."

"But, I thought we said..."

"Jesus Christ, you actually thought we were going to... what? Become boyfriend and girlfriend? Have a *long-distance relationship?*" Nathan said. The scorn in his voice made Lolly's cheeks sting with shame. "I hate to break it to you, but that's not going to happen. This is it. This is our only chance. It's now or never."

Lolly swallowed down her embarrassment and began buttoning her shirt. To her surprise, her hands didn't shake this time. Not one bit.

"Never, then," she told him.

The firmness in her voice surprised her. From the look on Nathan's face, it surprised him, too.

"Hey, wait. Come on," he said, his voice softening again as he moved to close the gap between them.

"I swear to God, come near me and I'll cave your head in with a rock," Lolly warned.

"OK, OK! Jesus," he said, raising his hands in surrender. "I'm sorry. Honest. I got carried away. I overstepped the mark. It's just..." He motioned to her. "I mean, look at you. You're beautiful."

Lolly said nothing. The breeze coming in across the water toyed with her hair.

"Of course we'll meet up back home. I can get the train over," Nathan told her. "We can get to know each other, like you said. Or you can come to me. I'll introduce you to my mates. They're all dicks, though. I feel I should warn you."

"What, like you?"

"Worse than me," Nathan said. "If you can imagine such a thing."

Lolly sighed. She should be walking away by now, she knew, and yet her feet hadn't found their way back into her trainers.

"Just come swimming. That's all. Just swimming," Nathan pleaded.

"No thanks," she said, although not with the same conviction as just a few moments before.

Nathan backed into the water. He was all smiles again, back on the charm offensive. "But what if Nessie gets me?" he asked. "You're not going to let me face a big scary monster alone, are you?"

Annoyingly, Lolly felt herself smirk as Nathan kicked back through the waves, his eyes and mouth widening into three circles of surprise.

"Shit! It's cold! How can it be this c-cold?"

"It's Scotland."

"But it's July!" Nathan said, slapping at his bare arms.

"But it's *Scotland*," Lolly reiterated.

"I know, but s-still," Nathan continued through chattering teeth. The water sloshed around him as he forced himself back a few more icy-cold steps. "You'd think that it'd at least be a *little bit—*"

He went down suddenly, arms flailing, face twisting in panic. There was a yelp, then a splash.

And then silence.

And then nothing.

"Very funny," Lolly said, watching the spot where he'd gone under.

Ripples expanded lazily across the loch's surface, moonlight dancing across each undulating peak as they steadied back into stillness.

"Nathan?" she said, as loudly as she dared. "Nathan, this isn't funny."

She took a step closer to the water, then cried out in shock when he exploded up from below, eyes wide, breath coming in fast, frantic gasps. He grabbed for her. At first, she thought he was trying to pull her in with him, but then she saw the fear on his face and the panic in his movements.

"What? What's the matter?" Lolly yelped, her voice becoming shriller as Nathan's terror awoke the same response in her. "What is it? What's wrong?"

Slipping and stumbling, Nathan dragged himself clear of the water, clawing his way up onto the rocks on his hands and knees, coughing and wheezing. Lolly saw a dark shape following, sliding out of the water right behind him. He kicked out at it, squealing now like an injured animal, but a long blue tendril was tangled around his foot, attaching him to the shapeless mass.

No, not shapeless. Not exactly.

As the dark water fell away and the moonlight played across the thing, Lolly saw a hand, fingers curling upwards like the legs of a dead spider.

She saw an arm, cold and blue.

She saw a face. Eyeless, yet somehow staring at her from within the folds of a bright green tarpaulin shroud. Begging. Pleading.

Accusing.

With the dark water lapping around her feet, and the cool night air swirling around the rest of her, Lolly screamed and screamed and *screamed*.

CHAPTER TWO

DCI Jack Logan sat in a pokey wee Dumbarton café, nursing a disappointing cup of coffee and briefly glancing up on the rare occasion that the front door opened.

He didn't like waiting. During his time in the polis, and the last few years in the Major Investigations Team in particular, he'd become known for many things. Patience was not one of them.

"You sure I can't get you a menu, son?"

Logan looked up from his two-thirds empty mug and found the café's owner smiling down at him. Standing, she wasn't much taller than he was sitting. Her big square glasses magnified her eyes to bug-like proportions as she watched him expectantly, a laminated piece of A4 held between both hands.

"I'm fine, thanks. I'm just waiting on someone."

"Are ye, aye?" asked the owner. Her voice had the rasp of a lifelong heavy smoker. Her fingers, starkly yellow against the white of the menu, were a giveaway, too.

She looked to the door, then across to the clock on the wall. "It's just it'll be the lunchtime rush soon, son. It gets busy."

Logan cast his gaze across the dozen or so empty tables. Aside from himself, the only other customer in the café was a young woman with a baby.

"You've only got one other customer in here," Logan pointed out.

"Two," she corrected.

"What? The wean?" Logan said. He thumbed in the direction of the baby. It was currently gulping down milk from a bottle. "Hardly going to be ordering up a cheese and ham panini anytime soon, is he?"

"She," said the owner. "That's my granddaughter."

"So, she's not even a real customer, then?"

"We'll need the table, is what I'm saying," the owner said, getting snippy now. "I'm not chucking you out, son, but we'll need the table. For people eating."

Logan sighed. Through the window, he saw a woman in a blue jacket, but she continued on past the door without stopping.

Not her.

"Aye. Fine. I suppose I'd better take a menu, then," he said, holding a hand out.

The owner smiled and nodded, then passed him the laminated sheet. Logan took it and placed it face-down on the table without so much as glancing at it. The old woman's smile faded.

"Are you no' going to look at it?"

"In a minute, aye," Logan told her. "Eventually."

She opened her mouth to reply, then clamped it shut again, the puckering of her wrinkled lips conveying her displeasure before she turned and began noisily clearing some dirty cups from a neighbouring table.

The door opened. Logan's eyes went to it as a couple of workmen entered, newspapers tucked under their arms.

Council boys, going by the logo on their high-vis vests. Lunchtime on a Friday. Traditional knocking-off time.

"Alright, hen?" said the older of the two as they both took seats. "Couple of rolls and square sausage when you get a minute."

"No bother, pet," the café owner said, drawing Logan a look that managed to say both, 'I told you so,' and, 'you'd better bloody order something, sharpish,' at the same time. "I'll get that for ye's now."

Logan's gaze followed her to a door at the back of the café, spent a few seconds getting the measure of the council boys, then went back to the door.

Waiting.

He hated waiting.

He especially hated it when he was waiting for something he suspected wasn't going to happen.

He'd first suspected it wasn't going to happen about forty-five minutes ago, when she was a mere twenty minutes late. Now that it was an hour past their arranged meeting time, he was more or less convinced of it.

He'd give her five more minutes.

Ten, maybe. Traffic might be bad. It had been nose to tail across the Erskine Bridge on the way out here, and while she wasn't coming in from the same direction, there was no saying she wouldn't be stuck in a queue somewhere. It was tourist season, after all.

He took a gulp of his coffee, then grimaced. Cold.

He daren't order another without having something to eat, too. It didn't pay to get on the wrong side of a wee Glesga granny, and he reckoned he'd probably pushed his luck far enough as it was.

He turned the menu over and was just considering the

Stornoway black pudding with caramelised onions when his phone chirped at him. He knew what it was going to say before he looked at it.

Running late. Cant make it. Sry.

He read the message four or five times before tapping out a reply.

Heading north today. Don't know when I'll be back down. Be good to see you.

He typed it all out properly. He wasn't one for all that '2CU' shite.

Logan re-read the message a couple of times, then deleted the last sentence.

Then, he added it back in again and hit 'Send.'

He waited, his eyes fixed on the screen.

He was still waiting when the owner delivered the rolls to the council boys, then crossed to his table.

"You ready?" she asked.

Logan looked up. "What?"

She pointed to the menu still held between the finger and thumb of his left hand. "You know what you're after yet?"

Logan looked first at the menu, and then at his phone. The screen was dark, the speaker silent.

"Just the bill, please," he said.

The old woman peered at him over the top of her glasses. "What's the matter? Date stand you up?"

"Daughter," Logan corrected, pushing back his chair as he stood. "But aye. Something like that."

Logan opened the boot of his Ford Focus and tossed his coat in on top of his bags. He'd bought three cases, thinking that would be enough for everything he wanted to take with him. In the end, he'd filled one, half-filled the other, and put the third into the storage unit along with the boxes, bags, and general clutter that he'd emptied out of his flat over the course of a few weekends.

He checked his phone again, just on the off-chance.

Nothing. She'd well and truly dinghied him.

Not that he could blame her, he supposed. God knew, he'd done it to her and her mother often enough over the years.

Sliding the phone into his pocket, he opened the driver's door and stood there for a while, staring at the seat and considering the road ahead. And the one already travelled.

It had been four months since he'd finally been able to close the file on the Owen Petrie case, and put the whole *Mister Whisper* thing behind him.

Or try to, anyway.

The reality of it was, he hadn't got anything like the closure he'd been hoping for. The opposite, if anything. Aye, he finally knew what had happened to Petrie's first victim. He'd got an ending of sorts. It just wasn't the one he'd been expecting.

In hindsight, he'd almost rather not have known.

But still, it was over, and as the weeks passed, Logan had found himself liking Glasgow less and less. He'd grown up in the city, spent most of his adult life there, too, but increasingly it began to feel like a gallery of his greatest failures, filled with reminders of the people he couldn't save, or the cases he'd never been able to crack. Murderers gone unpunished. Victims gone unavenged.

The whole place was filled with everything he'd lost, and crisscrossed by all the lines he'd had to cross to get the job done. A graveyard of bad memories.

Six weeks, almost to the day, since he'd closed his file on

Petrie, he'd put in for the transfer up north. The Gozer—or Detective Superintendent Gordon Mackenzie, if you were talking to his face—had objected, of course, and the Assistant Chief Constable was originally having none of it, either. But Logan had too much dirt on both of them, and when he gently reminded them of that fact, their resistance had soon crumbled away.

Besides, DCI Grant had been crying out for a transfer to the Central Belt for years, so it was simple enough to sort out a handover and do a straight swap.

"It'll be quiet up there," the Gozer had said when Logan stood in front of his desk for what would probably be the last time. "You'll crack up."

"Quiet sounds good," Logan had said. "I'll risk it."

They'd shaken hands, then Logan had been on his way, sneaking out through the back to avoid the smiles, well-wishes, and pats on the back from the rest of the team. They were a decent bunch, but that sort of thing had never really been his cup of tea.

Here, now, standing in the ASDA car park, staring at the driver's seat, he gave a single nod.

"Right, then," he said. Then he climbed into the car, closed the door, and fired up the engine.

He was barely five minutes up the road, still on the dual carriageway stretch before the Stirling roundabout, when a call came through from an Inverness number.

"DCI Logan," he said, after tapping the big green icon on the screen.

"Jack. It's Ben. You on the road?"

Logan had known DI Ben Forde for a long time. He knew right away that there was something up.

"Barely, why?"

"You're going to have to make a wee detour on the way to Inverness," Ben said, his voice resonating through the car's speaker system. "Take the back road from Fort Augustus. There's a campsite in Foyers, right down by the loch. We'll meet you there."

Logan shot a glance in his mirror then pulled out into the right-hand lane, powering past a line of slower-moving traffic.

"Something come up?" he asked.

"Aye," said Ben. There was a faint *pop* as he sucked in, then spat out his bottom lip. "You could say that."

CHAPTER THREE

DETECTIVE INSPECTOR BEN FORDE PICKED HIS WAY ACROSS the rocks, muttering to himself about slipping, and hips, and men of his age. It was a typical summer's day in the Highlands, and so Ben had his jacket zipped right up to the neck.

The loch side had been a hive of activity for the past several hours, and this section of the bank had positively heaved with white paper suits as the crime scene team did their best to gather up what evidence they could. Which, by all accounts, hadn't been much.

"That's where they found her," Ben said, before rounding off the sentence with an, "Ooh, shite," when he almost lost his balance on a wobbly boulder. He took a moment to compose himself before continuing.

"She'd been wrapped in tarp and tied with rope. The lad, Nathan, got it tangled around his legs."

"And what were they doing out here?" asked Logan.

He put a hand on the back of his neck and moved his head around, easing the stiffness that had been building there on the drive up. It had been a long trek, and although he'd turned on the lights and siren to get past a few convoys of camper-vans and meandering sightseers, it had still taken him the best part of four hours to get here.

The last stretch along a winding single-track road had seemed endless, with more time spent manoeuvring past or pulling over for oncoming vehicles than making any sort of onward progress.

His body was not thanking him for the experience, and he suspected that it'd be even less happy with him when he woke up tomorrow morning.

Something to look forward to.

"Swimming, apparently. Well, the boy was. The girl didn't go in the water."

"Ages?"

Ben checked three jacket pockets before finding his note-book. "He's sixteen, she's fourteen."

Logan's eyes narrowed a fraction. "And we're sure it was just swimming?"

"That's what they're both saying," Ben wheezed. "No funny business as far as we... Jesus, it's further than you think."

He stopped, his face pained as he struggled for breath. "This is close enough, isn't it?" he asked, gesturing ahead to a taped-off area down by the water. There were a couple of uniforms standing guard, but the Scene of Crime team had long since departed.

Logan's eyes went to the cordoned-off spot, then traced a route across to the grassy banking that ran down to the rocky section they were standing on. A row of conifers, badly in need of a tidy-up, stood to attention at the top of the slope.

"Campsite's up there?"

"Aye," Ben confirmed. "The boy's family are going home today. We've interviewed him and got everything useful out of him, I think, but we asked them to hang around in case you wanted a chat."

Logan nodded. "Good. And the girl?"

"They're here for another couple of days. At least, that was the plan. A lot of folk are packing up and shipping out. I expect they'll do the same."

Logan shot the DI a questioning look. Ben raised his eyebrows in surprise.

"*Obviously*, we got names and addresses," he said. "Although, one of the bods from SOC reckons the body's been in the water a few days, so if it was someone at the site then chances are they didn't hang around. No saying it was dumped here, though. Could've drifted in from somewhere else. Currents, and what have you."

"Right. Aye."

Logan cast his gaze across the surface of Loch Ness to the shore on the other side. He could see cars meandering up the main road between Fort Augustus and Inverness, but they were too far away for him to hear anything over the lapping of the water and the wheezing of DI Forde.

His mind wandered back to another stretch of water much like this one. Him kneeling by the shore, prodding away at a disposable barbecue, trying to get the bastard to light. Vanessa knee-deep in the water, a squirming Madison in her arms, pudgy hand grabbing for the water well out of reach below. Barely toddling yet, but desperate to get down and investigate the wet stuff swooshing around her mother's legs.

The sun had been beating down that weekend, and half of Glasgow seemed to be camped out along the banks. But Vanessa had known a spot tucked away out of sight, a little bay just thirty feet across, hidden by a curve of trees. They'd had to wade for a few seconds to reach it, but once they had... Bliss.

With the sun shining, Madison giggling, and the water licking the smooth rocks on the shore, you could almost tune out the thunder of traffic winding along the A82 just fifty or sixty feet up the banking behind.

Loch Lomond. Almost... what? Twenty years ago? Christ, had it been that long?

He never had managed to get that barbecue going.

Across the water, a procession of traffic was being led by a couple of caravans and a timber lorry. He pitied the poor bastards stuck behind that lot. They may have been too far away for him to hear the engines, but they were close enough that he could sense their frustration and misery.

Bloody tourists.

The sky was a shade of grey-blue that suggested it hadn't quite made its mind up, weather-wise. The clouds rolling in from the top end of the loch begged to differ.

"I want to talk to the girl first," Logan announced. "What's her name?"

Ben consulted his notebook. "Lolly."

Logan frowned. "Lolly? What's that short for?"

"Nothing," Ben told him. "Just Lolly."

Logan continued to frown as he tried to process this. "What? That's no' her actual name, is it? *Lolly*? Who names their child *Lolly*?"

"That's her actual name," Ben told him.

Logan shook his head. "Well, at least we know that stumbling upon a mutilated corpse isn't the worst thing that's ever happened to the poor lassie. I mean... *Lolly*. Jesus Christ, what were they thinking?"

With a final glance at the cordon tape, he turned and started towards the grassy bank.

"Come on, we'll go talk to her," he said, leading away across the rocks. "Try not to fall on your arse, if you can possibly avoid it."

"No promises," Ben muttered, then he picked his way after Logan, muttering once more about his hips.

UPON MEETING THEM, Logan realised that Lolly's parents were *exactly* the sort of people he'd expect to saddle their child with such a name. If anything, she'd probably gotten off lightly. Under different circumstances, she might've been a Petal Blossom, or a Lily Boo, or some other nonsense. Lolly, on reflection, was a lucky escape.

Mr and Mrs Montague were minted. *Proper* minted. That much was obvious. Sure, they were on a camping holiday in the Scottish Highlands and not, say, swanning in the sunshine of Dubai, but this was clearly a choice, and not something they had done through necessity.

The camping gear was all top of the range stuff and looked brand new. Their car, which was parked right beside their pitch, was a private reg Range Rover. One of the ones with the waiting list, Mr Montague had said, dropping that little titbit into the conversation at the earliest possible opportunity.

Neither of the parents were dressed for camping in Scotland. Not really. They were dressed for what rich people imagined camping in Scotland to be like, all fancy fleeces, tweed bunnets, and three-hundred-quid hiking boots that barely had a mark on them. They could've stepped off the pages of *Horse & Hound*, were it not for the miserable looks on their faces.

Given the circumstances, Logan couldn't really blame them.

They sat either side of their daughter on a PVC couch in

the on-site café, which the Major Investigations Team had commandeered for the interviews. The site manager had offered up his office, but as there was barely room to swing a cat in there and the ceiling was black with damp, he'd reluctantly agreed to let them use the café instead, on the understanding that he was reimbursed for any tea and coffee consumed.

Dead woman or not, he wasn't running a bloody charity, and the arrival of a mutilated corpse right on the site's doorstep wasn't exactly going to do wonders for business, so he needed every penny he could get.

"First of all, you've got nothing to worry about," said Logan. He was sitting across from the family on a slightly unsteady wooden chair that wobbled whenever he shifted his centre of gravity. "You're not in any trouble, and I know you've already answered a lot of questions today, but I just have a few more for you, alright?"

"Alright, poppet?" asked Mr Montague, before Lolly had a chance to answer.

"Alright," Lolly said. She was pale, her eyes ringed with concentric circles of red and black from tears and exhaustion.

"Alright," said Mr Montague, looking up from his daughter and beaming at the DCI.

"He heard her, William," said Lolly's mother, practically hissing the words through her teeth. "You're not a bloody translator. She doesn't need you repeating everything parrot-fashion. Do you, darling?"

Lolly shook her head.

"No."

"No," echoed Mrs Montague, shooting her husband a triumphant look. "Precisely."

Logan shot a sideways glance to Ben, who was sitting in an

armchair to the side of the family, notebook open, pen poised and ready.

"So, Lolly," Logan began. He felt faintly ridiculous addressing her by that name but tried not to show it. "What time did you leave the tent last night?"

Lolly had pulled her hands into the sleeves of her shirt so only the tips of her fingers were visible. She fiddled with the cuffs, her eyes not quite meeting Logan's own.

"Quarter to one."

"And you met..."

"Nathan Powell," said Ben.

"Nathan. Right. Where did you meet him?"

Lolly's eyes went to the window, then onwards to a row of conifers that marked the edge of the site. "By the trees."

"She had no business being out at that time. We had no idea," said Mr Montague.

"William!" his wife scolded.

"Well, we didn't!"

"It's not about us," Mrs Montague hissed, her face a picture of contempt. "It's about Lolly."

Logan liked her. More than he liked her husband, at any rate, although that wasn't exactly saying much. He was getting the distinct impression, though, that she hadn't been altogether in favour of a camping holiday in the Highlands, even before a mangled corpse had emotionally scarred her daughter for life.

"So, you met Nathan by the trees, then what?" Logan continued.

"We went down to the water," Lolly said.

"Why?"

Lolly shrugged. "To swim."

"And whose idea was that?" Logan asked.

"His, of course," Mr Montague snapped. "He led her astray. She'd never have done anything like this back home."

"William!"

"Well, she wouldn't? Would you, poppet?"

Logan fixed Lolly's father with a look. It wasn't a particularly stern look, but it was one that suggested there was real scope for it to become much sterner at any moment, and implied that this probably would not be an enjoyable experience for anyone who found themselves on the receiving end.

"Mr Montague, this will all be over much quicker if you just let Lolly answer. She's been through quite enough for one day, and I'm sure she just wants to put it all behind her."

He kept the look fixed on Mr Montague for a few moments, then turned to Lolly, his face softening into a smile. "Right?"

Lolly nodded. "Yes."

"OK. I just have a few more questions and you're done, alright?"

Lolly nodded again.

"So, who suggested you go swimming?"

Lolly glanced at her parents, just briefly. "Both of us. We both thought it would be a laugh. We arranged it on Snapchat."

"It's a phone thing," Ben chimed in.

"Aye. I know what Snapchat is," Logan said.

"You're a step ahead of me, then. I had to ask."

Logan leaned in a little and spoke conspiratorially to Lolly. "He's only just figuring out email. He still says, 'all small letters, no spaces,' when he's giving out his address."

"Well, it is all small letters with no spaces," Ben pointed out.

"See?" said Logan.

Lolly smiled at that. Or her mouth did, anyway. Her eyes didn't really get involved. Still, she relaxed a little, and that was the main thing.

"So, you both decided to go swimming. You met up, went down to the water. Then what?"

"Nothing," Lolly said.

"Nothing?" asked Logan.

"I mean..."

Lolly's gaze flitted left and right. It was body language Logan understood all too well. She was about to tell him not the truth, but a version of it. She was carefully selecting a few events from all those that had actually happened to craft a narrative. She wasn't about to lie, exactly, but she wasn't going to be completely honest, either.

"Nothing much. It was cold. I changed my mind about going swimming, but Nathan went in, anyway."

"He didn't... try anything?" Logan pressed.

"I beg your pardon?" blustered Mr Montague. "What are you saying?"

Both parents looked down at their daughter. From their expressions, this thought had not yet occurred to either of them.

"He didn't, did he, poppet?"

"No. No, he didn't try anything," Lolly said. "It was just swimming, that's all."

"Oh, thank God for that," said Mrs Montague. She gave her daughter's shoulder a squeeze.

"Right. OK," said Logan. He didn't believe that, but there was no point dwelling on it. Instead, he shot Ben a glance. The DI's pen scribbled a note on the page.

"So, he got undressed," Logan continued.

"Not all the way," Lolly interjected, her cheeks reddening.

"OK. He got partially undressed, went in the water, and then...?"

The girl's breath caught in her throat. Her eyes glazed over a little as the memory replayed in her mind's eye.

"He fell. He was just... One moment, he was complaining about how cold the water was, and then... He just fell. He went right under," she said, her voice becoming hoarse. "He went right under, and I thought he was joking, but then... But then..."

Mrs Montague's arm tightened around her daughter's shoulders.

"Is this strictly necessary, Detective Chief Inspector?" the girl's mother asked.

"We're almost done, I promise," Logan said. "How long was he under for, Lolly?"

Lolly shrugged. "I don't know. A few seconds, maybe. It felt like a long time, but... A few seconds."

"And then what happened?"

Lolly's expression had become distant again, but her eyes were fixed on a spot somewhere behind Logan, as she recalled—or relived—the memory.

"He... He came back up," she said, hesitantly feeling her way through the words like Ben had picked his path across the rocks. "Just, like, *whoosh*. All of a sudden. He came up, gasping for air. He looked scared. *Really* scared. And then he crawled out. He crawled out of the water and onto the rocks. He was screaming and crying. And then... And then..."

A tear cut a track down her cheek. She was shaking, and if it hadn't been for her parents squashing in on her at either side, she may well have vibrated right off the couch.

"You're doing so well, Lolly," Logan assured her. "And then...?"

"It came out behind him," Lolly whispered. "It was wrapped around his legs. I didn't know what it was to start with, but then I saw..."

Her face crumpled. She wedged both hands between her knees and squeezed them together.

"She was looking at me. It was like she was looking right at me."

The girl's voice was barely audible now, a knot in her throat trying to silence her.

"I think that's quite enough, don't you?" said her father. "Surely you have everything you need? This is the fourth time she's been through all this."

For once, his wife didn't try to shut him up. Instead, she glared at Logan, almost daring him to argue.

"I think you're absolutely right, Mr Montague," Logan said. "Lolly's been through enough."

He stood. After a few false starts as he tried to get himself up out of the low armchair, Ben joined him.

"You've been a big help, Lolly. Thank you. I'm sorry you had to see what you saw."

Lolly sniffed, wiped her eyes on her shirt sleeve, then looked up. "Will you catch him? Whoever did it?"

Logan gave a nod, then reached for his coat, which he'd draped over the back of the chair.

"Aye," he assured her. "We'll do everything we can."

CHAPTER FOUR

THE INTERVIEW WITH NATHAN WENT MUCH THE SAME AS the conversation with Lolly, with a few minor differences. Only one of the boy's parents were present. He was a little bit mouthier and less helpful. That sort of thing.

The biggest difference came near the end of the interview, when Logan gave the teenager a lengthy explanation of what Statutory Rape was and detailed the dire consequences that might befall a sixteen-year-old who pressured a fourteen-year-old into doing things she wasn't comfortable with.

"And the things they do in prison to kiddie-fiddlers," Logan had said, sucking air in through his teeth. "Isn't that right, DI Forde?"

"Oh God, aye," Ben had agreed, nodding gravely. "Turns the stomach just to think about it."

Funnily enough, a lot of the boy's defiance had deserted him then, and he'd suddenly become much more forthcoming with information.

Essentially, though, the stories were the same. Nathan

elected to miss out the part where he was screaming and crying, but otherwise the stories matched.

He went in the water, fell, then got himself tangled in the rope. He'd caught a glimpse of the body when he'd first gone under, the face floating right next to his in the murky darkness. It was a miracle the boy could speak, let alone be a mouthy wee arsehole.

After the interview, Logan had told Nathan's mother that they could go, but that he might be in touch for more information in the next couple of weeks, so not to leave the country.

"Thoughts?" asked Ben, as they watched Nathan and his mother hurry across the rapidly-emptying campsite towards their car. A Mercedes, this time, brand new plate. Was it all bloody toffs who went camping these days?

"The mother's alright. The boy's a thoroughly horrible wee shite. Tried to get his end away, but don't think he got anywhere. Otherwise, he's telling the truth."

"Aye," said Ben, having come to the same conclusion.

His phone rang. Logan continued to look out of the café's window at the campsite while Ben took the call.

"That was Caitlyn," he said, once he'd finished. "DS McQuarrie."

"I remember her."

"We've identified the vic. Mairi Sinclair. Primary school teacher. Aged thirty-one, going on thirty-two. Birthday's on Sunday. Reported missing five days ago."

"By who?"

"Now you're asking," said Ben, his eyes narrowing as he tried to recall. "Sister, I want to say. It's been on the news."

Logan shook his head to indicate that he hadn't seen it.

"There's more. Pathologist wants to see you to go over a few things about the body. Apparently, it's... odd."

"Odd?"

"That's all she's saying. 'Odd.' Make of that what you will."

Logan nodded. "Right, then. Make sure your man here turns over his records. We need details of everyone who was here over the last—"

"Aye, aye. Done," Ben said. He was smiling, but there was a suggestion of reproach colouring the lines of it. "It's no' my first spin around the block, Jack. This is my job, would you believe? They actually *pay me* to do this sort of thing."

"Someone clearly has more money than sense, then," Logan remarked. "I mean, you're no' as young as you used to be."

The DCI didn't rattle off any more instructions, though, which Ben knew was as close to an apology as he was likely to get.

Ben flipped his notebook closed, shoved it into a randomly selected jacket pocket, then drained the final dregs from a mug of coffee. It had been cheap and unpleasant-tasting to start with, and now that it was stone-cold, it had not improved. Still, he'd paid for it, and he was bloody sure he wasn't letting it go to waste.

"Right, then," he said, after a full-body shudder of displeasure. He set the mug down on the café counter, then gestured towards the front door. "Shall we?"

———

THEY WERE CROSSING the car park when Logan heard the shout. It was loud and piercing, more like a wail of despair that had somehow been formed into words.

"Just tell me! Just bloody tell me what happened!"

"Aw, shite," Ben muttered, as he and Logan both looked in the direction of the sound. A wiry-looking man with salt-and-pepper hair was gesticulating angrily at a uniformed officer. "That's Malcolm Sinclair."

"Who's Malcolm...? Wait. Sinclair? Victim's father?"

Ben nodded. "Aye. He and his wife—Mairi's mother—were informed earlier that her body had been found."

"Did they identify?"

"No. Dental records," Ben said. "We didn't tell him exactly where she'd washed up, but it's not hard to find out. News like this travels fast up here."

"Look, just... get out of the way. I want to see, alright? I want to see where she was found!" Malcolm ranted, the pitch of his voice rising. It was still a couple of octaves below 'fingernails down a blackboard' stage, but it was heading in the right direction.

A woman in her mid-twenties was doing her best to calm him down, but it was clearly a losing battle.

"Dad. Dad. Just... Please. Come home, alright? Come home to Mum," she said. She was smiling, but the effort was visibly taking its toll on her.

"You want to handle this, or will I?" Ben asked. "And, just a reminder, only one of us here is the Senior Investigating Officer. And it's no' me."

Logan sighed. Ben gave him a pat on the back. "Attaboy."

The gravel of the car park surface crunched beneath Logan's feet as he strode over to where the uniform was trying her best to defuse the situation. At the sound of his approach, Malcolm's head snapped towards the DCI, the other officer immediately forgotten.

"You. Are you a detective?" he demanded.

"Mr Sinclair," said Logan, giving the older man a nod. The woman who'd been trying to calm him down shuffled over to join them, but hung back a few paces. "Yes. I'm Detective Chief

Inspector Jack Logan. I'm the Senior Investigating Officer. I'm very sorry about your daughter."

"Finally! Someone with a bit of clout," Malcolm said. "I want to see. I want to see where she was found. I want to see where my little girl was found."

"I understand, Mr Sinclair," Logan said.

"No! No, you don't! How can you? *How can you?*"

Logan said nothing. He knew better than to engage. Better to just let the man's anger burn itself out.

"She was my—" Malcolm began, but he choked on the rest of the sentence. Clenching his fists down by his sides, he tried to compose himself.

The woman behind him—another daughter—slipped a hand onto his shoulder and gave it a squeeze. He seemed to deflate, as if the pressure had opened some sort of valve and released whatever had been driving him on.

"I just want to see. I want to see where they found her. That's all. I'm not... I don't..."

He looked down. Logan watched the muscles in his jaw tighten and relax, tighten and relax, over and over.

When he raised his head again, his eyes swam with tears. "I just need to see."

Logan glanced at the uniformed constable, who looked enormously relieved that she no longer had to deal with this situation, then around at DI Forde. Neither one offered anything in the way of suggestions.

"In my experience, Mr Sinclair, it won't help," Logan said. "It'll only make it worse."

"That's what I said, Dad," his daughter said.

"Worse? *Worse?* How can it be worse?" Malcolm demanded. "How can it *possibly* be worse? She's been bloody murdered! It doesn't get any worse!"

Logan knew better. It could always get worse.

Still, the man was grieving. Desperate. And Logan got the impression he wouldn't back down without a fight.

"Very well, Mr Sinclair," he said. "It's against my better judgement, and it's still an active crime scene, so we can't get too close, but if you'd like to follow me I'll show you the spot where Mairi's body was discovered this morning."

He gestured towards the conifer trees that lined the edge of the campsite. The loch stretched out beyond them, deep, and dark, and riddled with secrets.

Malcolm Sinclair didn't move. His gaze went in the direction that Logan had indicated, but his feet remained planted on the ground.

It was the wording that was important. *Mairi's body*. It solidified the idea of it in their minds. Forced them to confront a finality they almost certainly weren't yet ready to accept.

"Mr Sinclair?" Logan asked. "Would you like to see where the body was found?"

Malcolm's bottom lip trembled. His breath whistled in and out through his nose. He shook his head, the sudden movement sending a tear cascading down his cheek. His daughter stepped in closer, sliding an arm around his waist.

"Probably for the best," Logan told him. He put a hand on the older man's shoulder. "We're going to do everything we can to catch the person responsible for this, Mr Sinclair. We're going to make sure whoever did this is brought to justice."

Malcolm nodded, but said nothing.

"Do you have someone to drive you home?" Logan asked.

"I'll take him," the daughter said. She shot Logan a brief smile. "Michelle. Mairi was my sister. Sorry about this. He just... When he heard..."

Her voice failed her. She cleared her throat, then tried

again. "We can leave his car here. I'll get it picked up somehow."

"I'm sure we can help with that," Logan told her. He raised his eyes in the direction of the uniformed constable. "Can you take Mr Sinclair's car home for him?"

"Yes, sir. Not a problem."

"Hear that, Dad? They're going to bring your car home. You can come with me," Michelle said.

Logan watched as Malcolm allowed himself to be led away. He moved slowly and unsteadily, but most likely through shock and grief than any ailments or old age.

The gravel crunched as Ben walked up to stand at the DCI's side.

"Nicely done."

"Poor bastard," Logan muttered.

"Aye," Ben agreed, as they watched him be helped into the passenger side of a royal blue BMW hatchback. "You can say that again."

Logan was first to arrive at Raigmore Hospital, but by the time he'd spent a full twenty minutes circling the car park trying to find a space, Ben had beaten him to the front door.

"Did I no' tell you about the parking?" the DI said, feigning innocence. "They keep a spot for us."

"No, you didn't mention," Logan replied through gritted teeth.

"Shite. Sorry. Must've slipped my mind," Ben said. "Still, you can't blame me. It's no' like I'm as young as I used to be."

With that, he about-turned and led Logan through the sliding doors into the hospital.

"The problem is the free parking, you see?" Ben explained as they passed a little coffee shop. Logan's stomach rumbled, and he realised it had been a long time since he'd almost-but-not-quite eaten lunch.

Still, considering what he was on his way to look at, he thought it maybe best not to go putting anything in his stomach quite yet.

"They run a bus service into town from here," Ben continued. "And, because people are—by and large—a shower of arseholes, anyone working in town uses it as a Park and Ride, hence no bugger can get parked."

"Fascinating," Logan told him.

"It's bloody outrageous, if you ask me," Ben continued, not letting the subject drop.

They took a right at the end of a corridor, then immediately hung a left. Logan hadn't seen any signs for the mortuary yet, but the DI seemed to know where he was going.

"You've got folk coming in for an appointment, or to visit family, or what have you, and they can't get parked. They've to go to Tesco across the road and walk over." He shook his head. "It's not right."

Logan kept quiet, choosing not to get involved. He was relieved when they finally reached an area with 'ZONE 6' plastered across the walls, and saw a sign indicating that the mortuary was nearby.

"I'll wait out here," Ben said, stopping when they reached the doors. "I've a few phone calls to make, and the stomach's no' what it used to be."

Logan patted the older officer on his ample belly. "Aye, you can say that again."

"All bought and paid for," Ben told him. He reached over and pulled open one of the double doors that led through into the morgue. "Enjoy."

CHAPTER FIVE

"I'M LOOKING FOR THE PATHOLOGIST," LOGAN SAID, addressing a woman who sat behind a desk, hoovering the contents of a *Pot Noodle* into her mouth.

She was dressed in a lab coat, but had fashioned herself something that might have been a napkin, but could equally have been considered a giant bib, out of part of a surgical gown.

"'Mmsec."

Logan took in the room, trying to ignore the hurried *slurping* as the woman wolfed the noodles down.

He'd entered into some sort of office area, with a couple of cheap desks, two chairs that belonged in a skip, and a range of filing cabinets of assorted makes and models. Nothing in the room looked like it was supposed to be there, with the possible exception of the woman herself, who looked right at home as she guzzled her way through the last of her *Bombay Bad Boy*.

She was average height, average build, with hair that was neither one thing nor the other. At first, Logan had thought it was blonde, but there was some auburn in there, too, and maybe a wee touch of ginger when she tilted her head back to drain the sauce dregs from the bottom of the pot.

She was about his age, maybe a year or two either way. The eyes that peered at him over the rim of the pot were a blue that fell a little short of 'brilliant,' but were pretty striking, nonetheless.

"Sorry. Famished," she said, setting the container down on the desk. She pulled the homemade bib off, drew it across her mouth, then wiped her hands on it before scrunching the whole thing up and tossing it into a waste paper basket down behind the desk.

Or, she might've just dumped it on the floor, Logan couldn't really tell from that angle.

He'd been right about the lab coat, although hadn't been expecting the *Batman* t-shirt she wore underneath it. Logan wasn't really up on his superheroes, but that was one of the few whose logos he did recognise.

"Awful bloody things," she said, shooting the *Pot Noodle* tub a dirty look. Her accent had a suggestion of Irish about it. The lilting twang of the republic, rather than the more guttural tones of the north.

"Aye, you can say that again," Logan agreed. It was not unknown for him to partake of the odd *Pot Noodle* himself after a long shift, and he was usually burdened by the same sense of regret that was now painted across the woman's face.

"Shona Maguire," she said. "I'd shake your hand, but I'm all sauce."

She looked him up and down, idly picking at her teeth with the nail of a pinkie finger. "You must be the new fella. DCI Logan, wasn't it?"

"Jack," Logan told her.

She rolled the word around inside her mouth, as if testing it out. "Jack. *Jack.* I knew a Jack once. Another one, I mean. A different one. Not you."

"It's not an uncommon name."

Shona wrinkled her nose. "Wasn't a fan, to be honest. For a number of reasons." She shrugged and stood up. "Still, I'll try not to hold that against you."

Logan had a feeling she expected him to show gratitude for that. He didn't.

There was a little sink in the corner. Shona crossed to it and washed her hands, watching Logan over her shoulder the whole time. "So, you're taking over from DCI Grant, then?"

"As of today, yes."

"Those are some big shoes to fill," Shona said. She shook the water from her hands, then looked around for a towel. "Literally. He was huge."

"Aye. We'd met," Logan said. "Big fella."

"Thick as pigshit, mind," Shona continued. She gave up looking for a towel, and wiped her hands on her coat, instead. She smiled encouragingly in Logan's direction. "Maybe you'll be better."

"You *are* the pathologist, aye?" Logan asked, increasingly doubtful.

The pathologist he'd worked with down the road had been of the classic 'grey-haired-auld-fella' variety, with a plummy Morningside accent and a neat line in tweed waistcoats. He was a million miles away from the woman standing before Logan now.

"I am. I've got a certificate and everything," Shona told him. She glanced briefly around them. "Somewhere."

"I'll take your word for it. DI Forde said you've had a look at the body."

"I have," Shona confirmed.

"And?"

"And, at first I thought it was a bit odd." She raised a finger. "I stress *at first*."

"So... what, then? You don't now?"

"No." Shona shook her head. "Upon closer inspection, in my professional medical opinion, it's not odd, no."

Her eyes widened, betraying her excitement. "It's *bizarre*."

Logan glanced in the direction of another set of double doors that presumably led through to the morgue proper.

"Bizarre in what way?"

"Tell me, Detective Chief Inspector," said Shona, adopting a somewhat mysterious tone. "Do you believe in monsters?"

"No," said Logan.

Shona laughed. "No, fair enough. That would be mental," she said. "But, make no mistake, it was a monster who did this."

She gave a little sigh, audibly expressing her disappointment.

"Just a predictably bog-standard human one."

She fished around on one of the desks until she found a cardboard box around the size of a small shoe box. She tossed it to Logan, and when he caught it he turned it over to reveal a hole in the top, and a layer of blue latex inside.

"Stick some gloves on," Shona instructed. "Do you want a mask?"

"Will I need one?" Logan asked, peeling a couple of surgical gloves out of the box.

"I don't know. How strong's your stomach?"

"I've been doing this a while. It's pretty cast iron by this point," Logan told her.

She looked him up and down. "Right," she said. There was a *cluck* sound as she clicked her tongue off the roof of her mouth. "I think I'd best get you a mask."

CHAPTER SIX

LATER, WHEN RECALLING WHAT FOLLOWED, LOGAN WOULD be grateful for the mask.

Nobody looked their best after being in the water for a few days, and Mairi Sinclair was no exception. Most of her body was covered by a sheet, but the aroma of death lingered around the table she lay on and clung to the very fabric of the room.

The sight of a corpse didn't bother him. God knew, he'd seen enough of them, and often in a rawer, more visceral tableau than the one before him now. He'd been first on the scene at an RTA his first week in uniform, and his life had been an endless parade of horror ever since.

The smell, though? The smell still got him. Dark and bitter, yet somehow cloyingly sweet. It got in about the mucus lining of the nostrils and set up camp there, somewhere near the back where it was best placed to trigger the gag reflex.

It had been years since Logan had last heaved at the smell, but he never ruled out the possibility of it.

He did his best to ignore what he could smell now, and concentrated on what he could see.

The victim's face was a blueish-white, aside from a dark and raw area around her mouth and down over her chin. Having heard the statements made by the teenagers who'd found the body, Logan had been braced for the whole no-eyes thing, but he evidently hadn't been braced enough, as the sight of those sightless black hollows made his breath catch behind the mask.

The skin on her nose and forehead had started to come away in uneven strips. Logan could make out some darker marks around her temples and some relatively fresh scarring on her left cheek.

Logan was so fixated on the body that it took him a while to register the music. Actually, 'music' was a generous description of what he was hearing. It was a strangely rhythmic computerised beat that played through a Bluetooth speaker in the corner of the room. It wasn't dance music, exactly, but shared the same repetitiveness. Just a few seconds after first registering it, Logan could feel it getting right on his tits.

"What's this?" he asked, indicating the speaker.

Shona followed his hand-gesture, frowning like she had no idea what he was talking about.

"Oh, that," she said, once she realised. "It's for concentration."

"Concentration?" asked Logan. The only thing it was helping him concentrate on was the growing headache it was giving him.

"You know binaural beats? Well, this is computer generated *non*-binaural audio," Shona explained. "It's designed to enhance neural synchrony."

"Is it?" asked Logan, as if he had any idea what any of those words meant.

"Yeah. Focuses the old brainwaves," Shona told him, rapping

a knuckle on the side of her head. "I find it useful for concentration."

Logan shrugged. "I'm more of a *Come On Eileen* man, myself," he said.

"Want me to stop it?"

"God, aye. Please," the DCI said, rubbing his temples to add a bit of urgency to the request.

Shona depressed a springy button on top of the speaker and it popped up. Blessed, merciful silence fell across the mortuary.

"It's an acquired taste," Shona said, joining him again beside the victim's head. "They do a great one for sleeping, though. It'll help with your insomnia."

"What makes you think I've got insomnia?" Logan asked.

"Because you've all got insomnia," Shona replied. "Must come with the job. You should give the audio a go."

"I'll keep it in mind," Logan said, knowing full well he definitely wouldn't. He looked from the pathologist to the body, then very deliberately back again. "So?"

"Hmm? Oh! Right, yes," said Shona, springing into life. "So, the big headline first. She didn't drown."

"You're sure?"

"Positive. No frothy gunk in the airways, which is a big indicator."

"Could've been washed away."

Shona looked pleasantly surprised. "That's right. It could! Well done. You're doing better than the last one, already!" she told him. "But there are other indicators, too. There's very little in the way of pleural fluid accumulation, and no sign of any subpleural haemorrhaging. Investigation of middle-ear and sinuses both back up—"

She burped, then immediately clamped a gloved hand over

her mouth, her eyes widening. "I am *so* sorry," she said. "It's that *Pot Noodle*. I knew it was a bad idea."

"It's fine," Logan told her. "Honestly."

He turned his attention back to the body. "I always thought it was difficult to say for certain if someone did or didn't drown."

"It is. Notoriously," Shona agreed.

"So, then how can you be so sure she didn't?"

"Well, all that stuff I mentioned. Those were big pointers," Shona said. "Also, someone force-fed her a caustic substance, gouged her eyes out, knifed her through the heart, and drilled four dirty-great holes in her skull. So, you know, those were all indicators, too."

"Jesus," Logan said.

"It's worse than it sounds," Shona told him. "Hard as that is to believe."

"What? How?"

She began to count on her fingers. "Caustic, eyes, drill, heart," she said. "As best as I can tell, at least. And the stab wound is the one that killed her."

"What are you saying? She was *alive* for the rest of it?"

Shona produced a pen and indicated the bruising on the side of the dead woman's head.

"See this? I think it was some sort of clamp, holding her head in place. One of the drill holes is messy, like she was moving. The other three are neater, like the clamp was applied or possibly just tightened before those were drilled."

"So, you're saying she was *conscious*?"

"Probably just barely at that point. Not that that's much of a consolation," Shona said. "I can't be a hundred-percent, but from what I can tell it all happened quite quickly. She was likely still choking on the caustic substance when her eyes were removed.

Blunt instrument jammed in at the bottom of each eyeball. A spoon, possibly. Clumsy, but effective enough."

She gestured with the pen again. "There's some lateral tearing at either side, suggesting a number of violent head movements."

"She was thrashing about," Logan concluded.

"Aye. Poor cow," Shona muttered. She exhaled, her earlier energy deserting her for a moment before she rallied herself again. "Two of the holes failed to puncture all the way through the cranium. The other two went deeper, but not enough to damage the brain itself."

She stepped around to the other side of the victim's head and raised her eyebrows at Logan. "Want a look?"

'Want' wasn't the right word, he thought. There was little he *wanted* less. But he nodded, then joined her in leaning in closer to examine the top of the victim's skull. Sections of her hair had been carefully shaved off, to reveal four holes spaced symmetrically across her scalp.

Two were close to the front, just back from her hairline, several inches apart. These were the shallower of the four, and the one on the left was visibly less precise than its opposite number on the right.

The other two holes were a little back from the top of the skull, and much closer together. They reminded Logan of nostrils, complete with two snot trails of a viscous fluid that seeped out of them.

"Any thoughts of these?" Logan asked.

"What, besides, 'Ooh ya bastard, that looks sore?'" said Shona. She shook her head. "No. Can't say I've seen anything like it before. You?"

"No."

"Well, brace yourself, because it gets weirder," said Shona. "Kind of. I mean... Yeah. Weirder. See for yourself."

She pulled back the sheet. Logan had just half a second to brace himself for the full horror of a post-mortem in progress and was relieved to instead see that the body had been sewn back together. The careful suture work was the first thing he noticed.

The second thing he noticed was the pattern of symbols. They were etched—no, *carved*—into the victim's skin, the wounds slicing deep into the flesh. There were maybe a dozen that he could see on her stomach and breasts, with a couple more on each thigh.

"Ta-daa," said Shona.

Logan flicked his eyes in her direction, and she cleared her throat. "Sorry, that was inappropriate," she admitted. "Crazy, though, right? There's one on the sole of each foot, too."

"You recognise any of these symbols?" Logan asked.

"Recognise them?" Shona gave a snort. "What do I look like, a witch?"

She held a hand up. "Don't answer that. No, I don't. I can't tell you what they say, but I can tell you that they were carried out both pre and post-mortem. The left side a short time before she died, the right soon after."

She went back to counting on her fingers again. "So, in case you haven't been keeping up, that means we've got, slicey-slicey, caustic mouthwash, eyes out, head drilled, stabby-stabby, and then back to the slicing again," she said. "The only two I'm not certain of are the eyes and the drill. I'm pretty sure that's the order, though, and from her point of view I doubt it made a lot of difference."

"And time of death? Can you tell when she was killed?" Logan asked.

"That's the big question, isn't it? Short answer is 'not with any great degree of accuracy.' Long enough for the water to start taking the skin off her extremities, so... four days? That's rough, though. Could be a day or two before, or a day after."

"She was reported missing five days ago," Logan said.

Shona made a weighing motion, then nodded. "Yeah. That would fit. The water's a bit warmer at this time of year, which is why I said four, but five isn't a stretch. Even six wouldn't be impossible."

"So, she could've been taken on Sunday and kept somewhere for a day or so," Logan said, thinking out loud. "Alive."

"Potentially, yeah. There's some bruising on her wrists and ankles that would back that up."

She took hold of one of the dead woman's hands and held it up enough for Logan to see. A thin purple weal ran across the back of the wrist.

"Cable tie?" Logan guessed.

"I'd say so. But check it out," said Shona. She turned the arm over to show the line didn't continue along the wrist's underside.

"Hands tied together?" Logan guessed.

Shona looked non-committal. "Maybe. But I'd expect the lines to be running diagonally then," she said. She set the victim's arm down, then placed her own hands together with the wrists meeting. Her clenched fists and forearms formed a cross-shape. "Most people are tied like that."

She adjusted her arms so the fists were together. "Not like that. And, if it's behind the back, the angle of the marks on the wrist is even more pronounced. So, I'm thinking—"

"She was tied to something. A chair, maybe," Logan concluded.

"Bingo," said Shona. "Anyone would think you'd done this before, Detective Chief Inspector."

"Once or twice. You got anything else for me?" Logan asked.

He was keen to get out of the room. Now that he had some idea of what the victim had gone through, the smell of death seemed more pungent than ever. It forced its way in through the mask, pushing up his nostrils and snagging at the back of his throat.

"Not yet. Anyway, I reckon that's probably enough to be going on with," Shona told him. "I've got some other tests to run, so I might have more for you later. I took some scrapings from under the fingernails, but it'll be a day or two before I start getting any DNA results back. After a few days in the water, though, I wouldn't go holding my breath for anything overly useful."

"I won't."

Logan gave the body one more quick look over. That's how he'd learned to think of them over the years. This wasn't Mairi Sinclair. She was long gone. This was a clue to who had killed her. A piece of evidence. That was all.

And yet, he had to resist the urge to reach out and squeeze her hand. To tell her he was sorry for what had happened to her. To promise he'd make it right.

"Right, then. Good," he said, pushing the thought away. "Can you put together a report on—"

"Already emailed it over. That's what I was doing when you came in."

"You were eating a Pot Noodle when I came in," Logan reminded her.

"I was multi-tasking. It's a thing women do. You should try it," Shona told him. She checked the clock on the wall. "Now, I'd like to get home at some point tonight, so are we done here, or do you want to hang around for a bit and help me weigh a spleen?"

Logan regarded her curiously for a moment, then jabbed a thumb in the direction of the door. "I'll probably leave you to it."

"Good call. It's not nearly as much fun as it sounds," Shona told him.

Logan backed towards the door. "If anything else does come up..."

She pointed at him, then drew back her thumb and turned the gesture into a finger gun. She mimed firing it in his direction. "You'll be the first to know," she promised.

She smiled. It was not, Logan thought, a wholly unpleasant smile.

"Nice to meet you, Detective Chief Inspector."

"You too," said Logan and he reckoned that, all things considered, he probably meant it. "Enjoy your spleen."

He bumped against the swing doors that led out into the cluttered office, opening them.

"I always do," said Shona. "Oh, and... Jack, was it?"

Logan stopped. "That's right."

"Do me a favour, will you? Catch this sick bastard."

"Funny, you're the second person to suggest that today," he said. He gave her his word with a single nod. "Aye. Will do."

And then, he retreated from the mortuary, bringing the clammy odour of death out into the corridor with him.

"How did it go?" asked DI Forde, folding up a copy of the *Highland News* that he'd procured from somewhere while he was waiting. He grunted audibly as he eased himself up off the moulded plastic chair he'd been trying unsuccessfully to get comfortable on, then pointed to his mouth. "You've still got the mask on, by the way."

Logan glanced down, then removed the paper mask. The gloves *snapped* as he pulled those off, too.

"What did you think of Dr Maguire, then?"

Logan shrugged, non-committal. "Fine. Seems to know what she's doing."

Ben wrinkled his nose. "Bit weird, though, eh?" he said.

"Aye. But, aren't we all?" was all Logan had to say on the matter. "She's emailed over the report. We'll swing into base and—"

"Whoa, whoa. Not so fast there, Jack. Hold your horses," Ben said, raising his rolled-up newspaper like a stop sign. "Alice was expecting us at the house..." He checked his watch. "Eighty-seven minutes ago. And she's no' a woman you keep waiting."

Logan frowned. "Maybe you haven't noticed, but we're investigating a murder here."

"Aye, but we're hardly in the Golden Hour, are we? The liaison's talking to the family, Tyler and Hamza are following up on a few things, and there's hee-haw else we can do at the moment."

"Hamza?"

"Aye. He's back up and about. We're trying to get him to take it easy, but he's no' one for lying down to it."

"Good on him."

Logan wanted to argue about heading into the station. He could think of a dozen things that he could be getting stuck into. Avenues he could be exploring in the hope of dredging up some useful leads.

But, Ben was right. Alice was not the kind of woman you kept waiting. Besides, he was a guest in their house until he could move into his rented flat on Monday, and Alice hadn't exactly been his biggest fan to begin with.

He made his annoyance felt with a sigh, then nodded. "Right. Aye. Fine. We'll pick up in the morning, then."

Ben tapped the DCI on the chest with his paper. "Good lad. She's doing us a curry," he said, setting off along the corridor. "I mean, technically it's just a sort of stew with some curry powder in it, but it's nice enough, and I don't have the heart to tell her."

"Sounds delicious," said Logan, following along behind.

"Was that sarcasm?"

"Aye."

"Just grin and bear it," Ben told him. "Thankfully, she's no' exactly generous with the portions."

They stepped aside to allow a couple of nurses to pass them in the corridor, then turned the corner that led to the exit.

"She forgiven me yet?" Logan asked.

"For Harry?"

Ben stopped and chewed his bottom lip while he considered this.

"Aye. Aye, she has," he said.

He tilted his head from side to side a couple of times.

"Mostly," he said. "Ish."

"That's a no, then."

"Aye," said Ben. "That's a no."

CHAPTER SEVEN

LOGAN'S FORK *CLINKED* ON HIS PLATE AS HE STABBED AT something lumpy, drawing an irritated glare from the woman at the end of the table.

Alice Forde was two years older than her husband, but a regimen of gym sessions, copious amounts of make-up, and some rumoured Botox injections had kept her looking maybe eighteen-months younger than he did.

Given that Ben did very little exercise, regularly drank to excess, and subsisted on a diet predominantly made up of pastry products, Logan was sure that the relatively minimal returns on her efforts must be a constant source of frustration for the poor woman.

She sat at one end of the tile-topped dining table, across from Ben who sat at the other end. Logan was between them, his seat edged closer to Ben so he was just beyond Alice's reach. He wasn't expecting her to take a swing at him, but better safe than sorry.

He'd been in DI Forde's house a few times over the years.

He knew the dining room better than he knew most of the other rooms, because this was where it had happened.

This was where Logan had murdered Harry Pricklepants.

He glanced up briefly from his plate, his teeth working their way through a lump of something gristly. His eyes alighted on the spot on the display cabinet where Harry had once stood with his wee hedgehog face beaming as he tipped his colourful little hat at the world.

Alice had left a space where the ornament had been. The rest of the shelves were practically overflowing with a menagerie of similar porcelain monstrosities, but not that space. That was Harry's spot, and Alice wasn't going to let Logan forget it.

He clocked her watching him, her chin resting on the hand that held her fork. She chewed, teeth working their way through a substance Logan was confident was meat, but which he'd need the help of the forensics team to identify further.

"This is lovely, Alice," said Ben, in an attempt to ease the tension. "First class. What do you think, Jack?"

"Aye, it's delicious," said Logan, arranging his expression into something he hoped was convincing enough. "Can't beat a good curry. That's what I always say."

"It's not curry," said Alice, still chewing.

Logan looked down at his dinner. Lumps of the mystery meat lay sprawled in a thin, watery gravy that pooled around an island of mashed potatoes. Of course it wasn't curry. It was nothing bloody like curry, and if Ben hadn't told him that's what it was going to be the thought wouldn't even have crossed his mind.

"That's what I was saying," said Logan, thinking on his feet. "I always say that you can't beat a good curry, but I'm going to have to stop doing that in future."

He motioned to the plate with his fork. Something rubbery went *twang* between his teeth. He grimaced briefly, then pushed right on through. "Because this is better."

Amazingly, that seemed to do the trick. The atmosphere around the table relaxed a fraction, the temperature in the room raised a degree or two above freezing, and over the next few minutes the conversation began to flow just a little more freely.

"How do you think Snecky's going to get on down the road?" Ben asked. He was tackling the mystery meat with a gusto Logan had been unable to summon, and had almost polished off the lot.

"God. Now you're asking," Logan replied, taking a sip of water. He'd been chewing the same piece of meat for the past five minutes, and while it was now a suitably mushy paste, he couldn't swallow it. It was as if his stomach had ordered his throat not to accept any more of *whatever that shite is*, and his mouth was being left to deal with the consequences.

DI Grant had been Christened 'Snecky' years ago, mostly on account of there being little noteworthy enough about him other than his strong Invernesian accent. He was a fairly big fella, and had made his way up the ranks more through dogged perseverance than by demonstrating any natural aptitude for the job, so there had been nickname potential in those. But, the accent—in particular, the way he formed his As somewhere between the top of his nose and the back of his throat—had superseded everything else, so 'Snecky' was what he'd ended up with.

"He's got a good team," Logan said. He was really starting to get the hang of this diplomacy thing, he thought. "If he makes use of them, he'll be fine."

"He won't," Ben said, mashing his mound of potato into the gravy with the back of his fork. "He hasn't the brains. I'm amazed you got the Gozer and the high-heid-yins to agree to the swap. They must've known what they were saddling themselves with."

"I can be pretty persuasive when I want to be," Logan said, and left it there.

"How's Vanessa?" asked Alice, cutting in.

Logan couldn't help but see the warning look Ben shot across the table at his wife, but it bounced off her without her noticing.

"You still keep in touch?"

"Not really," Logan said, trying his best to keep it light and breezy. It was still a sore subject for him. Probably always would be. "Not since the divorce. The odd message here and there."

"Christmas and birthdays?" Alice guessed.

Logan puffed out his cheeks. "House stuff, mostly. And once when her dad was sick. Nothing for a year or two now."

"Oh. That's a shame."

Ben finally managed to catch his wife's eye. A series of looks passed between them that Logan pretended not to notice.

"I'm just making conversation," Alice eventually protested.

"You're being bloody nosy, is what you're doing," Ben told her. "He doesn't want to talk about it."

"How do you know? Have you asked him?"

"Alice..."

Logan knocked together something that resembled a smile. "It's fine. It's fine, honestly," he said.

"See?" Alice said, shooting daggers along the length of the table. "He says it's fine."

Ben muttered something, but was careful to be quiet enough about it that his wife didn't hear.

"Well, next time you're talking to her, tell her I said hello,"

Alice said. She finished eating, set her fork down, and dabbed at her mouth with a napkin. "And how's your daughter doing these days? What is she now? Twenty?"

There was a loud *clink* as Ben dropped his cutlery onto his plate. Propping his elbows on the table, he turned to Logan.

"So. What did you find out?" he asked. He flicked a look along the table at Alice. "*About the body*."

"Oh, God, do you have to?" Alice groaned. "I've only just finished my dinner. I don't want to hear about... *dead bodies*."

She pulled a face and spat out the last two words, like even saying them aloud was turning her stomach.

"Sorry, sweetheart, has to be done," Ben said. "Big case, and all that."

There was a clattering of plates as Alice stood and began to gather up the dishes. "Well, I don't have to listen to it," she decided. "I'll take these to the kitchen, but you can do the dishwasher later."

"You sure you don't want to join us?" Ben asked, knowing full well what the answer would be. "I'm sure it's not all *that* gruesome."

He locked eyes briefly with Logan.

"It's pretty grim, actually," Logan said.

"Ah. Right." Ben said. He smiled apologetically at his wife. "Maybe not, then."

Both men sat in silence while Alice finished collecting the dishes. She paused at the door of the dining room to remind Ben that he was on dishwasher duty, then elbowed the door closed behind her.

"Thanks," Logan said.

"Sorry about that. She can be a right nosy cow when she wants to be."

Ben got up from the table, patted his stomach a few times,

then crossed to a little oak cabinet that stood against the back wall. It was an ugly, old-fashioned thing, with Mother of Pearl handles and scuffs in all the wrong places. Ben had picked it up at an auction in Motherwell a decade or so ago. Logan remembered how excited Ben had been about the find, and how misplaced that enthusiasm had seemed at the time.

Now, with the benefit of hindsight, Ben shared Logan's opinion that the thing was a fucking eyesore, but Alice loved it, so it had followed them north when Ben had transferred up the road.

"It's fine," Logan said, waving Ben's apology away. "I broke her wee hedgehog man. She's just getting her own back."

Ben had opened the cabinet and was just producing two glasses and a large bottle of amber-coloured liquid when he stopped.

"Shite. Sorry. Wasn't thinking," he said, wincing. "You still off it?"

"Aye," Logan confirmed. "Mostly. You go ahead, though."

"You sure? I don't mind."

Logan shook his head. "It's your house, Ben. Don't let me stop you."

He rose to his feet, stifling a yawn. "I think I'm going to turn in, though. Long day, and tomorrow's only going to be worse."

"You think?"

"After seeing the state of that body? Aye."

Ben unscrewed the lid of the bottle and poured a glug of whisky into one of the glasses. Logan's eyes followed it.

"Rough one then, is it?" Ben asked.

Logan tore his gaze from the glass. "I'll fill you in tomorrow. Otherwise you'll never get to sleep."

"Shite. That bad?"

"Maybe worse," Logan confirmed.

He stole another glance at the glass. Something stirred deep in the primal parts of his brain, but he wrestled it into submission and turned away.

"But that's tomorrow's conversation. Good night."

"Night, Jack," said Ben.

He waited until Logan had left the room before picking up the glass and raising it to his lips. He jumped when the DCI's head appeared around the door frame again, spilling a third of the glass's contents down his front.

"And for fuck's sake, don't forget the dishwasher," Logan warned him.

And with that, he was gone.

CHAPTER EIGHT

"HEY, BOSS! WELCOME TO THE MADHOUSE!"

Logan gazed impassively at Detective Constable Tyler Neish. The younger detective stood with a hand raised, poised to do one of those best-bud handshake slaps with the interlocking thumbs that Logan had never had any time for. He regarded the hand, the irritatingly groomed appearance, and Tyler's cocky grin for a moment, then turned to Ben.

"Don't tell me he got *more* annoying."

"You wouldn't have thought it was possible, would you?" Ben sighed. "And yet..."

Tyler laughed it off. "Funny stuff." He lowered his hand. "Seriously though, boss. Good to see you."

"Thanks," said Logan. He offered up a handshake. A proper one. Tyler accepted it. "You too."

The team had been assigned the largest of the Incident Rooms at Burnett Road station, and Logan had been pleased to see plenty of activity going on when he'd first entered. It had all come to a halt almost immediately after he and Ben had arrived, though, with the team stopping what they were doing to come over and say hello.

"Good to see you up and about, Hamza," Logan said, shaking hands with a darker-skinned man with a neatly trimmed beard. The last time Logan had seen Detective Constable Khaled, the DC had been in the Intensive Care Unit at Glasgow Royal Infirmary, recovering from a series of stab-wounds to the back.

"Well, it was touch and go for a while they tell me, sir," Hamza said, his Aberdonian accent momentarily taking Logan by surprise just as it did every time the man opened his mouth. "But no real lasting damage."

Ben patted him on the shoulder. "It'll take more than some bastard wi' a dirty great knife to keep Hamza down. Right, son?"

"Well, aye. But I'd rather not put that to the test by having another go," Hamza said.

"No, maybe best not," Logan agreed. "Any pain still?"

"Only when I laugh, sir," Hamza replied.

"That's why we sat him next to DC Neish," said Ben.

It took DC Neish a moment to pick up on the slight.

"Hey!"

Logan turned to DS McQuarrie next. She was only half invested in Logan's arrival, and was the one member of the team who hadn't yet put down the paperwork she was holding. Even now, when Logan was talking to the others, her eyes were darting left and right as she read over the top page of a report.

This was more like it.

"DS McQuarrie," Logan said.

Caitlyn looked up and they briefly shook hands.

"Sir."

"What have we got?" Logan asked, seizing this opportunity to get down to business.

He'd lain awake in Ben and Alice's spare room, unable to flick the switch in his head that would've let him get some sleep.

Whenever he'd closed his eyes, he'd come face-to-eyeless-face with Mairi Sinclair, and his nostrils had been filled with her death-stench again.

Or he might just have been smelling the lingering after effects of Alice's cooking. He hadn't been able to tell for sure.

At five o'clock, he'd concluded that he wasn't going to get any more sleep, and had dug out Dr Maguire's report from his phone's email inbox. The picture the report had painted of the victim's last few hours had done nothing to set him at ease, and by the time Ben had risen at seven, Logan was up, dressed, and ready to get going.

"Just looking it over, sir," Caitlyn said, indicating the report. "Can you give me five minutes?"

Logan nodded, appreciating the lack of time-wasting waffle. "Five minutes, then."

"By the way, case made the papers, boss," Tyler said. "Further back, though, nothing major. Got a few days until the local goes out, too, so with a bit of luck this one should be more low key than the last one."

"Hopefully," Logan agreed. He'd never really seen eye-to-eye with the press, and the circus that surrounded the kidnapping case in Fort William had done his blood pressure no favours whatsoever.

While Caitlyn continued to work her way through the report, Ben gave Logan the official tour. It lasted just a few seconds, beginning with, "Toilets are that way," and finishing again almost immediately after with, "and this is your office through here."

Logan had seen plenty of Incident Rooms over the years, and they were all much of a muchness these days. He'd also visited the Burnett Road station enough times that he could find his way around it without too many problems, so Ben hadn't seen the need to dwell too much on any of it.

Logan's office was a decent enough size, with a window looking out over the rest of the Incident Room, and a clean desk that was positively crying out to be covered in paperwork, Post-Its, and coffee mugs. There were In and Out trays on a smaller table that ran at right angles to the main desk. The Out tray was empty, while the stack of paperwork in the tray beside it was already displaying some structural integrity issues.

"Alright?" Ben asked. "They were supposed to give it a lick of paint after Snecky left, but..." He flicked his gaze around the room. "They didn't."

"No, I see that," Logan said, picking at a chip in the magnolia paintwork with a fingernail. "It's fine, though."

"For all you'll use it," Ben said. He had worked with the DCI enough to know that separating himself from the rest of the team wasn't really his style.

"Somewhere to put the coats, though," Logan said.

Ben chuckled. "Aye."

He glanced back over his shoulder, then quietly closed the office door behind them. Logan crossed his arms and leaned against the desk, recognising the incremental change to the atmosphere in the room.

"What's up?"

"I've been meaning to ask..." Ben began.

Quite what he'd been meaning to ask, he didn't go on to say.

But then, he didn't have to.

"Petrie," said Logan.

Ben nodded.

Owen Petrie. *Mister Whisper*. The serial child-killer who

had haunted Logan's life for years, and whose shadow had loomed large over the recent Fort William case.

Logan puffed out his cheeks. "I went to see him in Carstairs," he said. "Afterwards, I mean."

He spoke slowly, either because he was carefully picking his words or because he was having to force them out of his mouth. "I wanted him to know what had happened with... You know. The abduction case."

"Aye. I know."

"I showed him a front page about the aftermath," Logan said. "And he reacted. I saw it in his eyes."

Ben's expression turned doubtful.

"I know, I know, he's meant to be..." Logan tapped himself in the centre of the forehead a few times. "But he's not. He's faking it, Ben. I'm sure of it."

"Well, he's managed to fool all his doctors, then," Ben said, trying not to make it sound like the opening salvo of an argument. "But you got closure, though?"

Logan shrugged. "As much as I'm ever likely to," he said. "But aye. I'm done with him. Hence me wanting to get out of Glasgow. Too many bad memories."

Too many failures.

"And here was me thinking you just missed me," Ben said.

"You should be so lucky," Logan replied, then Caitlyn caught his eye through the window and he gave her a nod. "Looks like she's ready for us."

Ben put a hand on the door handle, but didn't open it yet. "You'll be doing a wee speech first though, aye?"

Logan frowned. "Wasn't planning to, no."

"Ah well," said Ben, grinning. "The best laid plans, and all that..."

LOGAN STOOD with his back to the Big Board, looking out at the rest of the team. There were only the four of them, so it wasn't exactly a sea of faces. More of a puddle, really.

He wasn't one for speeches. Aye, he could carry them off if he had to, but that had never really been his leadership style. He'd much rather inspire through action than by spouting off a few half-arsed words of encouragement here and there.

Still, it was his first day in a new patch, and the team apparently needed a bit of a boot up the backside after serving under Snecky for the past few years, so Ben had talked him into it.

"Unlike my predecessor, I'm here entirely of my own free will," he said. As openings went, it wasn't exactly *'I have a dream,'* but it was good enough, and raised a couple of weak chuckles from the tiny audience. "I asked for a transfer here because every single one of you impressed me on the kidnapping case we worked back in March."

"What, even DC Neish?" asked Ben.

"Well, not so much DC Neish, no. But the rest of you."

"Cheers for that, boss," said Tyler.

"The fact is, I'm here because I can see the potential of this team. You might not be able to tell from my face, but I'm excited by it," Logan continued. "And so should you be. You've all done some good, solid work in the past, even with... certain parties potentially holding you back. But you could do *great* work. *We* could. Together. And, we will."

He tapped a photograph on the Big Board with the back of his hand. It showed Mairi Sinclair, smiling and vibrant and very much alive.

"We're going to start by finding the bastard who killed this lassie," Logan said. "We're going to do it quickly, we're going to do it efficiently, and we're going to get her family the justice they deserve."

He looked from face to face. "I'm assuming no one has any objections to that?"

"No, sir," said Caitlyn, amid a more general murmur of agreement from the others.

"Good."

Logan clapped his hands and rubbed them together.

"Then somebody get the kettle on, and let's see where we're at."

CHAPTER NINE

DS McQuarrie had replaced Logan in front of the Big Board, and was going through everything that had been pinned to it. It was mostly for the DCI's benefit, although a recap wouldn't do the others any harm, either.

"Mairi Sinclair. Aged thirty-one at estimated time of death," Caitlyn announced. There was occasionally a hint of her Orcadian heritage in her accent, but she was always quick to suppress it for reasons Logan hadn't yet been able to fathom. "Last seen Sunday morning by her son, Stuart, aged fourteen, when she left the house to go to the shops. A small cashline withdrawal was made from her account around eleven-twenty, and that's the last trace we have of her until her body was discovered in the early hours of yesterday morning."

"Where was the money taken out?" asked Logan.

"A Spar on Montague Row. About quarter of a mile from the house, sir."

"Any CCTV?" asked Hamza. The others were standing through the presentation, but he'd taken a seat and was scribbling notes in an A4 notepad he had open on the desk.

Caitlyn shook her head. "Cameras inside the shop, but the machine's on the outside. Doesn't have built-in surveillance. It's one of those ones you pay a fee to take money out, so not your typical ATM."

"I hate those," Tyler remarked. "It's my money, why should I have to pay to get it out?"

"You're paying for the convenience, aren't you?" Ben told him. "It's a penalty for being a disorganised bastard and not getting the money out somewhere else."

"No, I get that, it's just—"

He felt Logan's stare burning into him before he saw it. Tyler smiled sheepishly, then motioned to Caitlyn.

"Sorry. Continue."

"*Thank* you," she replied, with a degree of sarcasm that impressed Logan no end. "No CCTV between her house and the shop, although we're still checking for private cameras."

"What about dash cams?" Logan asked. "Have you put out a call for people who might've been in the area to check those?"

For the first time since beginning the presentation, Caitlyn glanced down at her sheet. "I'm not... No, sir. We haven't."

"I'll get onto MFR and the papers," said Hamza, jotting it down. "Put a call out."

"What's MFR?" Logan asked.

"Oh. Sorry. Moray Firth Radio, sir," Hamza explained. "Local station."

"Right. Good," Logan said. "Anyone remember seeing her in the shop?"

"No, sir," Caitlyn reported. "We've spoken to staff and put notices up for customers, but no one has come forward. Internal CCTV shows no signs of her on the day, either, so it doesn't look like she went into the shop itself."

"The question is, where did she go?" Tyler wondered.

Ben tutted. "Aye, we know that's the question, son. That's why we're all standing around here, isn't it?"

Tyler shifted on his feet. "No, I mean... Aye, but—"

"Kind of the entire point of our job, really," said Hamza, enjoying his fellow DC's obvious discomfort.

"No, I know. I was just saying."

"Maybe only say something if it's worth us listening to next time, eh?" Ben suggested. There was no real malice to it, though, and while Tyler's face had reddened in embarrassment, he gave a nod and a thumbs-up, before surreptitiously giving Hamza the finger behind his back.

"Is that normal behaviour for her?" Logan asked, getting back to the matter at hand. "Using that cashline, I mean?"

"Not as far as we can tell, sir. She usually just swipes everything. Last time she used an ATM was..." Caitlyn checked her notes. "...over eight months ago. She withdrew a grand over three transactions. She was buying a car, her sister tells us. That checks out. Which reminds me, we haven't found her car yet, either. It's a light blue Citroen C3. Been missing all week. Everyone has their eyes open."

"Mark that as a priority," Logan said. "It could tell us a lot."

"How much did she take out on Sunday?" Ben wondered. "From the cash machine, I mean."

"Ten pounds."

Logan frowned. "A tenner? That's it?"

"Aye, sir. That's it. A tenner."

There was a moment of silence as they all contemplated this small, yet potentially telling, detail. It was broken only by the sound of Hamza's pen nib on his notebook page.

"What else have we got?" Logan asked. "Anything on the material she was wrapped in?"

"Forensics is working to identify it at the moment, but the

water will most likely have washed away anything useful," Caitlyn said. "Early indicators are that the plastic probably came from a building site. Bright green, so pretty distinctive, which is good. It was tied with climbing rope. We're trying to pin down the make to see if we can find a local supplier. But, you know, it's the Highlands. There are a lot of places to buy climbing rope."

"Any building sites in the area?" Logan asked.

"Aye, a few, sir," said Caitlyn. She turned to a map that took up a full third of the board, and indicated six blue pins. "Three new house builds, two extensions, and some repair work on a path. There's roadworks, too, but we haven't included those at the moment."

"That's in the immediate area around where the body was found?" Ben asked.

Caitlyn nodded. "Aye."

"But the body could've drifted in from somewhere else on the loch," the DI continued. "That's a big stretch. How many construction sites are there along both sides? Must be dozens."

"We've been able to identify over forty within a mile of the water," Caitlyn said. "There's a bit of a boom on, they tell me."

"It's not tidal, though, is it?" said Tyler.

Logan turned to him, an eyebrow raised.

"The loch, I mean. It's not flowing in and out, so the body probably hasn't moved that far. Right?" He looked around at the others, his cocksure swagger replaced by something a little less certain. "I mean, I'm no expert, but that makes sense, doesn't it?"

"Aye. Makes sense," Logan agreed, and the relief was immediately evident on Tyler's face. "Let's stick with those closest for the moment. Anyone been to look at them?"

"Not yet, sir. Didn't want to send uniform trampling in until we had a better idea of what we were dealing with," Caitlyn said.

Logan approached the map and considered the blue pins. One in particular caught his eye. It was closest to the water. Almost right on the edge.

"What's this one?" he asked, tapping the end of the pin.

"Repair work on the tourist path. Pretty minimal presence. Mostly just a couple of lads with spades and cement, I'm told."

There was a red pin along the shore next to the campsite, identifying the spot where the victim's body had been discovered. A green pin a mile or so along the road struck Logan as unusual.

"What's this one for?"

"Boleskine House, sir," said Caitlyn, which prompted a quick blast of the theme to *The Twilight Zone* from Tyler.

"What's Boleskine House?" Logan asked.

"It's a ruin now, mostly. Burned down a few years back," Ben explained. "Used to be owned by Aleister Crowley."

Logan's face suggested the name meant nothing to him.

"Big occultist, sir," said Caitlyn. "Black magic, devil worshipping, all that stuff."

"Is he worth bringing in?" Logan asked.

"Well, considering he died in the nineteen-forties," Ben said, smiling smugly. "He's not high on our list of suspects, no."

"It's not technically a building site, but there are some construction materials on the grounds," Caitlyn said. "And people with an interest in that sort of thing travel from all over to see the house, so I thought with the markings on the victim's body..."

"Worth looking into," Logan agreed. "Anything on the symbols themselves?"

"Not yet," Hamza volunteered. "I've got some people looking into it."

"CID?"

"No, sir," said Hamza, shifting a little uncomfortably in his chair. "Reddit. I did some drawings and posted them on a few Subreddits. Anonymously, like. No details. Thought that was our best chance of getting a quick hit on them."

"Subreddits?" Logan said, repeating the word in the same way that a parrot might. He shot Ben a sideways look. "Do I approve?"

"Don't look at me. Buggered if I know."

"Right. I'm going to assume it's fine, then," said Logan, turning back to Hamza. "Good thinking. Just keep an eye on it. I don't know what it is, but I don't like the sound of it."

Tyler opened his mouth.

"I don't care what it is, either," Logan said, cutting him off. "DC Khaled is responsible for it. If it blows up in some way, you're the one with his balls in the vice, Hamza, and I'll be the bastard cranking the handle. Got that?"

"You might want to write that down," Tyler told the other DC, gesturing to his notebook. "Balls... in... vice."

"Got it, sir," Hamza said, ignoring Tyler completely. "I'll keep a close eye on it."

Logan nodded, then turned his attention back to the Big Board.

The map took up a third of it, and around another third was currently empty. The space between these was mostly filled with photographs of Mairi Sinclair. There were four in total, only one of which showed her alive. A few Post-It notes had been stuck around the photographs with various comments and questions on them, and there was a list of addresses stuck with a magnet to the board's shiny white surface.

Hamza's drawings of the symbols that had been carved into the victim's skin were stuck down near the bottom of the board, and there were two other photographs to the left of the pictures of Mairi, both joined to her by lines of red marker pen.

"Who are these two?" Logan asked.

"That's the son, Stuart," Caitlyn said, indicating a school photograph of a boy aged around twelve or thirteen. "And that's his father, Robbie Steadwood. He and Mairi were never married, and have been separated since just before Stuart was born."

"What's the relationship like?" Logan asked.

"Dire. History of domestic call-outs when they were together. She's made a couple of complaints against him over the years since then. Harassment stuff, mostly. No charges ever pressed," Caitlyn said. "CID have tried to get hold of him all week, but they haven't had any joy. They're keen to talk to him about some potential drugs charges, too, unconnected to this case."

"Got a home address?"

"Aye, but he's not there. He's not working, as far as we know, and the few known associates we've been able to identify have all denied seeing him."

"Surprise, surprise," Ben muttered.

Based on his photo, Robbie Steadwood wasn't much of a family man. His head was shaved down to the bone, and his neck and face were like a gallery of bad tattoos. The picture they'd been able to source of him was a police mugshot. This didn't exactly come as any surprise.

"What's his previous?"

"Did a stretch in Peterhead. GBH and attempted sexual assault," Caitlyn said. "Neither on Mairi Sinclair."

"Charming lad. Chief suspect, then," Logan said.

"We've got the feelers out for him," Ben said.

"Fine tooth comb. And get me a report on the progress," Logan said. He rapped his knuckles off the man in the photograph's forehead. "I want this arsehole found and brought in today."

"I'll get on that, boss," Tyler said.

Logan turned away from the board. "Right, then. Caitlyn, I want you with me. We're going to go talk to the son, see if there's anything else he can tell us. Ben, I'm saddling you with DC Neish. Get those building sites locked down and checked out. Hamza, you're Office Manager. Get someone from CID brought in for Exhibits."

Hamza blinked in surprise. "What? I'd rather be out and about, sir."

"I get that. I do," said Logan. "But you're just back. You need to take some time and get back in the swing of things."

"That's bollocks, sir," Hamza said. His eyes widened, like he was surprised by his own outburst. "I mean... with all due respect."

"He's right, Jack," said Ben. "He needs to get back on the horse. I can run the office."

Logan rubbed a hand across his unshaven chin, then turned away from the others and motioned for Ben to do the same. "You sure about this?" he asked, dropping his voice to a low murmur.

"Sitting on my arse with a nice cup of tea? What's not to be sure of?" Ben asked. "Right up my street, that."

"You know what I mean."

Ben nodded and smiled. "He's grand. It'll be good for him."

Logan sighed, then both men turned back to the rest of the team. "Fine. Hamza, you're out and about."

"Thank you, sir. I appreciate it."

"But you're doing all the boring shite. I'm not having you

overdoing things," Logan warned. "DS McQuarrie, you'll take Hamza on a drive-by of those building sites. Take a look, see if you get a feeling from any of them. Don't go poking around too much at this stage, though, we don't want to draw attention."

"Got it, sir," Caitlyn replied.

Logan exhaled slowly through his nose. "Which means..."

Tyler's face split into a grin. He jumped up from where he'd been half-sitting on the edge of a desk. "Which means I'm with you, boss."

"God help me. But aye. You're with me."

"You'll no' thank yourself for that, Jack," Ben warned.

"Probably not, no," Logan agreed. He took another look at the Big Board, then nodded. "Everyone know what they're doing?"

"We're on it, sir," said Caitlyn, after a quick glance at Hamza.

Tyler rubbed his hands together, playing up his excitement. "Ready when you are, boss!"

"As for me, I'm already working on prioritising next steps," said Ben. He picked up his mug. "I'm thinking tea *then* biscuits, but it's early days and that's still liable to change."

Before anyone could reply, there was a knock at the Incident Room door, then a *squeak* as it was opened. A uniformed sergeant put his head around the door, looked across the faces of the team, then settled on Logan.

"Sorry to interrupt. There's a woman here says she has information about the murder. Wants to talk to the SIO."

Logan felt a little rush of hope, but quickly squashed it back down.

"Is there an interview room free?" he asked.

"They're all free, sir. But someone chucked their guts up in

Room One last night, and it's still a bit ripe. I'd suggest Two," the sergeant told him.

"Right. Stick her in there, then," Logan said. "I'll be through in a minute."

The door swung closed as the sergeant retreated.

"DS McQuarrie, I want you in there with me. Tyler, get me that update."

Tyler's face went momentarily blank, before he remembered. "Oh! The ex. Right. I'll check up."

"Hamza, you do the... thing. Whatever that thing was you said."

"Subreddits, sir."

"Aye. That. You check that. See if anything's come in," Logan said.

He turned to the door, made a vague attempt at making himself presentable, which essentially just involved smoothing down his hair, then nodded.

"Right, then. Let's go see what's fallen into our lap."

CHAPTER TEN

MARION WHITEHEAD SAT ACROSS THE TABLE FROM LOGAN and Caitlyn, looking borderline beside herself with excitement.

Before they'd entered the Interview Room, the uniformed sergeant had remarked that the woman looked like 'Doctor Who after a night on the lash,' and Logan couldn't fault the man on his observation skills.

She was in her late sixties, with a shock of silver-white hair that stood out from her head, no two strands of it going in the same direction. The contrast of the hair colour highlighted her skelping red cheeks, and there was a sense about her of someone who had recently come in from a bitingly cold winter's day.

This impression was backed up by her clothes. She wore a long camel hair coat and a longer scarf that looped around her neck and chin, then hung down below the top of the table at both ends. On her hands were a pair of fingerless gloves, with a little mitten-covering buttoned back so her fingertips remained exposed.

She was thick-set and sturdy, but there was a lightness to her movements that didn't quite fit with her appearance.

Marion nursed a cup of tea close to her chest, her eyes swinging between the two detectives like she couldn't quite decide which one she should be looking at.

Logan made the introductions while Caitlyn took out her notebook and sat back a little, focusing the spotlight on the DCI and helping the older woman make up her mind.

"The front desk tells me you have some information for us, Miss Whitehead."

"*Ms*," Marion corrected. Her accent was from south of the border. Quite a bit south, in fact. "I prefer *Ms* Whitehead. But Marion's fine. Should you have a tape?"

Logan raised his eyebrows. "Sorry?"

"A tape. You know. 'State your name for the benefit of the tape.' That's what they do, isn't it? On the telly."

"That won't be necessary at this stage," Logan told her. "DS McQuarrie will just take a few notes as we're talking."

"Oh." Marion looked disappointed. Her eyes went to the spot where she presumably assumed a tape recorder should be, then she gave herself a shake. "Right. Yes. I suppose you know best."

"So, what was it—"

"I have a phone," Marion said. She leaned back in the chair and began fishing in the pockets of her coat. "We could record it on that, if you like?"

"Honestly, Marion. Not necessary. We only tend to do that if you're a suspect, and we have no reason to believe you are," Logan said. "So, please. What was it you wanted to tell us?"

Marion continued rifling through her pockets. "Not *tell* you, Sergeant," she said, reaching inside her coat. "Show you."

Caitlyn smirked and met Logan's eye.

"Sergeant," she mouthed, then they both turned their attention back to Marion as she let out a little cheer of triumph.

"Aha! Here we are."

She slapped a small bundle of six-by-eight photographs down on the desk then sat back, arms folded like she'd just won a game of chess and wasn't about to be particularly gracious in victory.

"What do you think of *that*?" she asked.

Logan looked from the photographs to the old woman, then back again. He leaned over and studied the top picture. It was blurry and slightly pixelated, like it was a blown-up section of a wider digital photograph that had been printed out.

From what he could tell, it showed a stretch of water, with a dark shape sticking out near the centre of the image.

Sliding the top photograph aside, Logan glanced at the one below. It was almost identical, but zoomed out a fraction so the shape in the middle was even more impossible to clearly make out.

"What am I looking at?" he asked.

"Exhibit A for the prosecution," said Marion, looking pleased with herself. "Do you know when I took these photographs, Sergeant?"

Logan gave a shake of his head to indicate that he did not.

"Tuesday!" Marion cried, then she banged the flat of her hand on the table for emphasis. "Tuesday morning. Six-twenty-seven, to be exact. I always write the date and time on the back."

Logan turned the photograph over. Sure enough, the details were written there in studious, but slightly shaky, handwriting.

"Up at the Drum end of the loch," Marion continued. "Not my usual spot. I'm usually down at the other end, but you know what they say. A change is as good as a rest. And how right they are!"

She gestured to the photographs with both hands, then sat back again triumphantly.

When it became clear that neither Logan nor DS McQuarrie were appreciating the significance of the images, she gave a wry little chuckle. "Well, it's the monster, isn't it? It's Nessie. I got her."

Logan flicked his eyes down at the pictures again, then brought them back up to meet the beaming smile of the woman opposite.

Beside him, Caitlyn quietly closed her notebook.

"Nessie?"

"A real beaut, isn't she?" said Marion, her eyes blazing with excitement. "Beautiful, yet deadly, it seems."

Logan wasn't bothering to look at the photographs now. Caitlyn picked up the top one and regarded it for a moment as Marion watched on eagerly.

"There's a whole pile there from all around the loch, although those are the most interesting," Marion said. "I managed to get a glimpse of her earlier in the week, too. Not far from where the body was found. Although, the photograph is nowhere near as good as this one."

"It's a stick, isn't it?"

"A *stick*?!" Marion's tone was scornful. Mocking, even. "Of course it's not a stick, you silly girl. Look at it! It's curved at the end."

Logan felt DS McQuarrie bristle beside him. To her credit, she didn't bite.

"It's a bendy stick, then," she said, putting the photo back on the pile.

"It's a head. It's clearly a head," Marion insisted. She leaned forward and tapped the bundle of pictures. "I've been living out there by the loch for twelve years and have never caught a whiff of her. And now this, right before that poor woman's body washes up? That can't be coincidence."

"You're right. When you put it like that it does sound pretty conclusive," said Caitlyn, making no effort to hide the sarcasm. The old woman didn't seem to pick up on it.

"Precisely."

Marion leaned in closer, clasping her hands in front of her. She lowered her voice, as if letting them in on a secret. "My theory is that she went in swimming."

"The monster?" said Logan.

Marion rolled her eyes. "Come on, man, keep up. The woman. She went swimming. Or possibly fell in. Was she found clothed?"

"I'm afraid I'm not at liberty to disclose that information," Logan told her.

Marion twitched in irritation. "I can't very well help you if you don't give me the details, Sergeant," she scolded. "No matter. I think she went in the water, disturbed Nessie in some way, and then... *Snap*. Dead. Just like that. She's lucky she wasn't eaten, really."

Logan met DS McQuarrie's eye. The expression on her face mirrored the one he could feel he was wearing on his own.

"It's tragic, of course, and I almost feel guilty for saying it, but this is all *very exciting*," Marion continued in a slightly breathless whisper. "I posted the photographs in some online groups I'm a member of and there's a real buzz about it all. People are *thrilled*."

This time, Logan felt himself bristle.

"A woman died."

"Of course. And, like I say, it's utterly tragic. *Utterly* tragic," Marion conceded. "But think of the bigger picture. We've got evidence! We've finally got proof that the Loch Ness Monster exists!"

She indicated her photographs again and settled back, arms

folded once more. "I bet you wish you'd recorded this now, don't you, Sergeant? History in the making."

Logan blinked a couple of times, then puffed out his cheeks. "Well."

He put both hands on the table and pushed his chair back, standing up.

"Thank you for the information, Ms Whitehead. You've given us an interesting new line of enquiry."

Marion looked a little confused. "Oh. Is that it? Don't you need me to sign anything, or...?"

"It's fine. We have all we need," Logan told her.

"You can keep the photographs. They're copies, I have the originals," Marion said. "Safely under lock and key," she added, eyeing both detectives with a degree of suspicion.

"It's fine. We have all we need," Logan reiterated. "You keep them."

"Won't you need them? You know, as evidence, or what have you?" Marion asked.

Logan shook his head. "We can hardly prosecute the Loch Ness Monster, can we?"

"Wouldn't fit in the court for a start," Caitlyn pointed out.

Marion picked up the photographs and flicked through a few of them. "No. No, I suppose not," she said, missing the sarcasm once again.

She held the bundle out to Logan. "I really think you should hang onto them. I had copies made special."

Logan relented with a barely contained sigh. "Fine. We'll hang onto them. Thanks," he said.

He took the photographs without looking at them.

"Hang on there for a few minutes, Ms Whitehead," he instructed. "I'll have someone take your details, then see you out."

"Have I been helpful, Sergeant?" Marion asked, and there was an earnestness there that stopped Logan stating the obvious.

"Aye. It's been... eye-opening," he told her, and her face lit-up. "Thank you for your assistance."

Marion was still beaming when Logan and Caitlyn left the room and pulled the door behind them with a *click*.

"Nicely handled, *Sergeant*," Caitlyn said, smirking. "We'll make a DI of you yet."

"Fingers crossed," Logan said. He looked down at the photos, shaking his head. It was a stick. It was *clearly* a stick. "What a nutter."

"Oh, God, aye," Caitlyn agreed. "Still, harmless enough, I suppose."

"Aye," Logan agreed. He set off along the corridor, but stole a glance back at the door to the Interview Room. "We'll see."

CHAPTER ELEVEN

"USEFUL CHAT, WAS IT?"

Ben had a hopeful expression on his face, like he was envisioning a quick wrap-up to the case, followed by a slap-up lunch at the Chinese Buffet over by *Johnny Foxes*.

"We've cracked it. Case closed," Logan told him, briefly waving the photos before tossing them onto the desk that had been set aside for the Exhibits Officer. "The monster did it."

"The bastard. Had to happen sooner or later," Ben said, almost, but not quite, managing to hide his disappointment.

"Anything back for me, yet?" Logan asked, raising his voice to the rest of the room.

"No sign of Robbie Steadwood yet, boss," Tyler reported, visibly steeling himself for a bollocking. Instead, Logan just grunted and turned his attention to the team's other Detective Constable.

"Couple of replies on Reddit, sir, but nothing overly useful," Hamza said.

"What have we got?" Logan pressed, hoping for *something* they could use.

"Spoiler for the new Marvel movie, and some guy called me a paedo," Hamza said. He raised his eyes above his monitor and smiled apologetically. "The internet, sir."

Logan sighed. "No' exactly the most auspicious start."

He grabbed his coat, then beckoned to Tyler with a crooked finger. "Right. Let's crack on. Everyone knows what they're doing."

"We'll do the drive-by of those sites, sir," Caitlyn said. "Hamza, grab a photo of the map before we go, will you?"

"No bother."

Logan nodded. "Good. And be careful. No unnecessary risks," he reminded them. "We'll meet back here when we're done and see where we are."

"Best of luck," said Ben, dipping into a pack of chocolate digestives. He raised one in salute, then dunked it in his tea. "Oh, and Jack?"

Logan pulled on his coat, then looked back at the DI. Ben smiled. It wasn't his usual smile, exactly. There was something deliberately coy and mysterious about it, Logan thought. It made him vaguely uneasy.

"When you go meet the family, say hello to the liaison officer for me."

LOGAN AND TYLER sat in Logan's Ford Focus just down from the house where the victim's sister, Michelle Sinclair, lived. With a name like Druid Road, Logan had been half-expecting some quaint old witch's cottages, but instead the street was lined with rows of boxy terraced houses with postage stamp gardens.

The houses had all been clad in that exterior insulation

material that made them all look even more uniform than they previously might have. Wooden pallets and blue plastic ties in some of the gardens suggested it had all been done fairly recently.

"So, what's our plan?" Tyler asked.

"The plan," Logan began, unclipping his belt, "is for me to do the talking and you to keep your trap shut."

"Right," said Tyler, a little flatly. "I could just stay here, if it's easier? Or, there's a pub around the corner. I could wait for you there. I mean, if you don't need me in there, boss."

"Did I say I didn't need you in there?" Logan asked. "Keep your mouth shut, but your eyes open. Watch how they respond. Listen for inconsistencies. Get a feel for them while I'm talking."

Tyler nodded, suitably chastised. "Right. Aye. Will do, boss."

Logan reached for the door handle, then stopped. "And stop humming that tune."

DC Neish blinked. "What tune?"

"The tune you've been humming all the way here."

Tyler continued to look blankly back at him.

"The tune. The bloody... the tune. You've been humming a tune."

"Have I?"

"Yes!"

Tyler thought for a moment. "Was it that Marshmello one?"

"Was it *what*?"

"Marshmello. You know? The DJ," said Tyler. "Huge on YouTube. Head's a big marshmallow."

It was Logan's turn to just sit and stare.

"No' an actual marshmallow, like."

Logan tutted. "Aye, funnily enough I guessed he didn't have

an *actual marshmallow for a head*," he scowled. "Just stop it, whoever it is. It's getting on my nerves."

"Will do, boss," Tyler said.

"Good. Right, then. Game face on," Logan said. He checked the wing mirror, then opened the car door. "And remember—eyes peeled, ears open."

IT WAS the Family Liaison Officer who opened the door. Logan took half a step back, not quite believing what he was seeing.

"Hello, sir."

"Sinead?" the DCI said, looking the uniformed constable up and down. "What are you doing up here?"

"Transferred up, sir," said PC Bell. "DI Forde convinced me. Too many bad memories down the road, so it made sense."

Logan knew exactly what she meant.

PC Bell had handled herself well during the child abduction case in Fort William. Exceptionally well, in fact. She was young, but she had a tough few years behind her, and probably more to come, and Logan had been impressed by the way she was handling things. He'd mentioned to DI Forde that she was going to go far, but he hadn't expected the crafty old bugger to take it literally.

"What about your wee brother? Harris, wasn't it?"

"Aye. He's loving it," Sinead said. "Already made some pals, and there's a breakfast club and loads of after-school stuff, so it works out well for work."

"Good. That's... I'm really pleased for you," Logan said. He jabbed a thumb back over his shoulder. "If I'd known you were here I wouldn't have bothered bringing this one along."

"Hiya," said Tyler, flashing Sinead a smile that Logan didn't see, but still somehow disapproved of. She nodded and smiled back at him.

"DC Neish."

"Call me Tyler."

"Call him DC Neish," Logan suggested. He looked past her into the hallway. "Family in?"

"They are, aye. Just in the living room. I was making them a cup of tea." She gave a backwards tilt of her head. "Want one?"

"Aye, go on then," said Logan. He moved to step inside, but Sincad blocked him.

"Shoes."

"Eh?"

Sinead pointed to the rough mat the DCI was standing on. "She's quite... particular. You have to wipe your feet out there, and then again in here."

She indicated a second, thinner mat just inside the front door.

"Trust me. Someone trudged in some dirt yesterday and she spent the next twenty minutes hoovering the same three foot section of the living room."

She glanced back over her shoulder, then leaned out of the doorway and dropped her voice further. "I wouldn't mind, but it's laminate flooring."

"Christ, one of those," Logan muttered. He wiped his feet. "Happy?"

"Ecstatic, sir," Sinead smirked. She stepped back. "Now this one, then I'll introduce you and go get the kettle on. You don't take milk, do you?"

"No, just black," Logan confirmed, stepping inside.

Sinead leaned around his tall, broad frame until she could see Tyler.

"DC Neish?"

"Is there any Earl Grey?" he asked.

Logan replied before Sinead could open her mouth. "No, there is not," he said. "You're on duty. You'll have proper tea. You can drink your bloody potpourri on your own time."

He was too busy wiping his feet on the second mat to notice the little nod that passed from Sinead to Tyler, or the wink and the thumbs up he gave her in reply.

"They're just through in the living room," Sinead said. She gestured ahead to a door at the end of the hall, through which Logan could hear the sound of gunfire coming from a TV. "I explained you were coming."

"How do they seem?"

"Are you asking how they're holding up, or what I think of them?" Sinead asked, keeping her voice low.

"Bit of both," Logan replied.

"They're holding up as well as can be expected, I suppose," Sinead said. She narrowed her eyes and ran her tongue across her teeth, thinking. "And can I get back to you on the other bit? Maybe best that you see what you think yourself first."

"Good idea," Logan said. "And it's Michelle, isn't it?"

"Aye. Not *Chelle* though. She hates that," Sinead said.

"OK. Good to know."

"*Mish* is fine, apparently, but don't call her *Chelle*," Sinead explained. She smiled and did the tiniest of eye rolls. "Like I said, she's a wee bit..."

"Of an arsehole?" Tyler whispered.

"*Particular*," Sinead corrected. She took a moment to compose herself, stifling a laugh, then closed the door behind the detectives and gestured along the hallway. "In you go. I'll come and introduce you all."

CHAPTER TWELVE

MICHELLE SINCLAIR WAS HOVERING BY THE WINDOW when Sinead brought Logan and Tyler into the living room. Even from behind, Logan recognised her as the woman he'd seen with Malcolm Sinclair back at the campsite.

At the sound of them entering, she quickly turned, and Logan noticed that her eyes went right to their feet before flitting up to check out the rest of them.

She was the type of woman who might normally be 'bubbly,' were it not for the fact her sister had recently been brutally murdered and dumped in a loch. She was in her mid-twenties, with hair so blonde it could only have come from a bottle. Her nails were long red talons that she picked at while Sinead made the introductions. She was in pretty decent shape, but probably a stone or so heavier than she'd like to be.

Michelle wore jeans and a dark blue shirt that she hadn't tucked in. Logan got the impression that it wasn't her usual style, although he had nothing to really base that on at the moment besides the hair and nails.

Her eyes were ringed with red, and there were some telltale

mascara streaks that she hadn't quite managed to dab away. She offered up a smile to the detectives as they entered, but it was a hollow and lifeless one. An automatic rearrangement of her facial features. Nothing more.

"Michelle. Stuart," said Sinead, addressing the woman and the back of an armchair positioned to face a big telly that was mounted on the wall. A fifty-incher, Logan reckoned. Maybe more. "This is DCI Logan and DC Neish, who I told you about. They're just here to ask a few questions."

"Hello," said Michelle. "Although, we met, didn't we? With my dad?"

"We did," Logan confirmed. "How is he doing?"

"You know."

Michelle's voice was thin and flat. Absent, almost. She looked over to the armchair and forced her face into a more convincing smile. "Stuart. The police are here. Can you pause that, sweetheart?"

"No, I can't pause it," a voice grunted. "It's online. I can't very well pause everyone else in the world, can I?"

Michelle turned her smile towards the detectives, but her eyes told a very different story. Logan gave her an almost imperceptible shake of his head, dismissing her non-verbal apology as unnecessary.

"Well, can you come out of it?" Michelle pressed. "These detectives would like to talk to us."

The video game that had been playing on the TV screen froze. There was a heavy sigh, then a teenage boy stood up, an Xbox controller clutched in one hand.

Logan knew from the report that he was fourteen, but he looked a couple of years older. His face was a dot-to-dot puzzle of plooks, with some coarse hairs sprouting here and there from his jaw. He wore a t-shirt with a print of some sort of green blob with eyes on the front, and while he looked in Logan's direction, he didn't look *at* him, exactly.

Logan was almost relieved about that. There was a deadness to the boy's eyes—a haunted, faraway look that Logan had seen on too many people in too many living rooms over the years.

"This is Stuart," Sinead said again. The boy did manage to bring himself to look at her, and his eyes spluttered back into life a little. "He's Mairi's son."

"*Was* Mairi's son," Stuart grunted. His voice was tight. Hoarse. Like he was keeping the words on a firm leash.

"You still are," Logan told him. "Always will be."

Something in the boy's expression softened then hardened again, but he said nothing. After a moment, he gave the tiniest of shrugs, before his shoulders sagged back to their original position.

"Sorry, where are my manners?" fretted Michelle. She lifted a big sequined cushion from the couch, plumped it up, then set it back down. The couch was a small two-seater with high arm rests and a straight back. It looked just about the most uncomfortable bastard of a thing Logan had ever seen. "Take a seat, please."

Stuart wasted no time in doing just that. He slumped back into the armchair, and the room was filled with the sound of gunfire as he rejoined the game.

"Stuart, can you not?" Michelle said through a smile that was all teeth. "Just for five minutes, can you... Can you not?"

He didn't bother to sigh this time, and Logan got the impression he knew he'd been pushing his luck. As the detectives took a seat on the couch, the boy turned the armchair around with his feet so he was facing them. The couch was exactly as uncomfortable as Logan had been expecting, and the size of it meant he and DC Neish were practically pressed against each other.

"Cool. A spinny one," Tyler remarked, watching Stuart turn in the chair. He nodded to the telly. "Was that Blackout mode on Black Ops Four?"

Stuart looked at his Xbox controller, then up at his auntie, as if one or the other might answer on his behalf.

"Well, I don't know, do I?" said Michelle, rubbing his hair as she walked behind him. "It's all just shooting to me."

Stuart looked vaguely in Tyler's direction, then nodded. "Yeah."

"Nice. You played Fortnite?" the DC asked.

"Don't really like it."

"Nah, nor me. It's all eight-year-olds. Blackout's better."

While they'd been speaking, Michelle had perched herself on the wide arm of Stuart's armchair. It tilted ever so slightly, but she draped her right arm across the chair's back, better distributing her weight and keeping it all balanced.

"I'll go get that tea," Sinead said, slipping out of the room and leaving them to it.

In estate agent speak, the living room could be described as 'cosy'. Which, in the real world, meant there was barely room to swing a cat. There was just enough room to fit the armchair and two-seater couch, a small coffee table, and a three-shelf bookcase. The bookcase was filled with a row of *Dan Brown*s and assorted *Fifty Shades*, a row of DVDs, and a larger section at the bottom with four cookbooks and a lot of empty space.

A six-inch wooden cross with a little ceramic Jesus on it was fixed to the wall above the bookcase, and now that Logan looked more closely he could see a Bible rammed in between the thrillers and the soft porn, like Moses pushing apart the Red Sea.

The walls were a very pale blue, aside from the one the TV was mounted to, which was patterned with a print of looping silver flowers. Logan had heard such things referred to as 'feature walls,' although this one was nothing but a bloody eyesore.

"They flooded the map recently," Stuart volunteered.

Logan was momentarily confused by this revelation, before realising the boy was still talking to Tyler.

"No! Did they? I'll have to check that out. Thanks for the tip," said the DC with what sounded like genuine enthusiasm.

Stuart gave a little nod and the slightest upturning of the corners of his mouth that suggested there was a smile still in him somewhere.

"No problem."

On the arm of the chair, Michelle rolled her eyes, then kissed the boy on the top of his head. Considering how greasy his hair was, Logan hoped she was up to date with her jags.

"We appreciate you both seeing us," Logan began. "I understand what a difficult time this must be for you."

"Very difficult," Michelle agreed. She sniffed, and took one of Stuart's hands—the one not currently clutching the game controller—and clasped it in her own. "But we're both determined to do whatever we can. Aren't we, sweetheart?"

Stuart gave a nod of what could, Logan supposed, be generously described as 'broad agreement.' His eyes had glazed over into a thousand-yard-stare again, and he was looking between the detectives rather than at them.

"I was brought in to lead the case yesterday," Logan explained. "So I wasn't involved in the original search for..."

He stopped himself saying 'the victim' just in the nick of time.

"Mairi. As such, I'd like to just go over a few things to make sure I have the clearest possible picture."

"Of course. We understand," said Michelle. She rubbed the back of Stuart's hand with a thumb. "You were the one who found the boy down in Fort William, Sinead tells us."

Logan glanced to the door. Luckily for Sinead, she was still through in the kitchen and so managed to avoid the dirty look he would otherwise have thrown at her.

"Aye. That's right," he confirmed, then swiftly brought the conversation back on track. He leaned forward a little and offered Stuart a well-rehearsed smile of sympathy. "I know this is difficult, Stuart, but I'd like to talk about the weekend. About the last time you saw your mum. Is that alright?"

Michelle kneaded his fingers between her own. "Go on, sweetheart," she whispered, giving his shoulder a squeeze with her other hand. "Just tell them what you know."

Stuart shrugged. "Just... Like I already said."

"It's a pain in the arse to keep going over it, isn't it?" said Tyler. He gestured to his notepad. "Imagine how I feel. I've got to write it all down."

"Can't you just record it?" Stuart asked.

Tyler straightened, his eyes widening. "Shite. Aye! That makes much more sense. Great idea." He took his phone from his pocket. "Is that alright with you?"

Stuart glanced at his controller again, like he might scc the answer written there, then looked up and nodded. "Yeah. It's fine."

"Nice one. That makes things much easier," Tyler said, hitting the big red button on his audio recording app. The briefest of glances passed between the detectives, then Tyler gave Stuart the nod. "Right. Up and running. In your own time, mate."

The boy shuffled around in the chair, getting comfortable. Michelle continued to hold his hand.

"What do you want to know?" Stuart asked.

"You said you last spoke to her on Sunday morning. Around... when, would you say?" Logan asked.

"About eleven."

"You're sure?"

Stuart nodded. "She woke me up. I remember checking the time on my phone. It was three minutes past eleven."

"Did she say where she was going?"

A shake of the head.

"Would she normally go out on a Sunday morning?"

Another shake.

"I've tried to get her to come to church for years," said Michelle. "But she's not interested."

Her use of the incorrect tense struck her. She didn't mention it, but Logan saw the moment it dawned on her.

"So, it was unusual for her to be heading out on a Sunday morning, you'd say?" Logan pressed.

A nod, this time. "Yeah," Stuart said. His throat was tight, and the word took a couple of attempts before it came out.

"You're doing really well, mate," Tyler encouraged.

"Did she take the car, do you know?" Logan asked.

"Think so, yeah," said Stuart.

"But you didn't see?"

"No."

"Didn't hear the engine, or anything?"

"No, but it's gone, isn't it? So she must've," said Stuart, his tone becoming a little impatient.

Logan nodded. "Did you see it outside the night before?"

"What?"

"The night before. Saturday. Did you see the car then?"

Stuart's unibrow knotted above his nose. "I don't... I'm not sure."

He looked up at his auntie. She smiled and gave his hand another squeeze. "You're doing really well."

"She sometimes couldn't get parked outside the house," Stuart explained. "So she had to park down the road a bit. I didn't see. But why wouldn't it have been there?"

"No reason, son. Just trying to get as full a picture as possible."

He became aware of Sinead hovering outside the living room door, and sat back a little. "In you come, constable."

Sinead entered carrying a tray laden with three mugs, a milk jug, sugar bowl, and a can of Irn Bru. She sat them down on the coffee table, and passed one of the mugs to Michelle.

"There we are," she said.

"Thanks, Sinead," Michelle said. She looked past the constable to where Logan was reaching for one of the other mugs.

"I don't know what we'd have done without her. Isn't that right, Stuart?"

Stuart gave a non-committal shrug. "Yeah."

"It's nothing. Don't be silly," said Sinead. She turned back to the tray, spent a second or two just staring at it, then raised her eyes to Logan just as he took a sip of his tea.

His mouth twisted into a grimace of disgust and he looked down into the mug.

"That's DC Neish's, sir," Sinead told him.

Logan drew the constable a foul look, then set the mug of Earl Grey back down on the tray. His tongue moved inside his mouth, like it was trying to scrub the taste away, then he washed what was left of it down with a mouthful of proper tea from the other mug.

The questioning continued. Gentle. Probing. Michelle held

Stuart's hand through most of it, but as he relaxed, the boy became more forthcoming with his answers.

It was only at that point that Logan began with the questions he'd come there to ask. He finished his tea and set the cup down on the tray and cleared his throat. He shot a glance at Tyler's phone to make sure it was still recording before leaning forward just a fraction.

"One more thing, son," he began.

His gaze flitted from Stuart to Michelle, then back again.

"What can you tell me about your father?"

CHAPTER THIRTEEN

HAMZA SAT IN THE PASSENGER SEAT OF CAITLYN'S CAR, the engine humming its impatience for them to move on.

He knew how it felt. This was the fifth site they'd checked out, and it was already shaping up to be as much of a bust as the previous four.

"This is the other extension job," Caitlyn said.

"Aye," Hamza agreed, looking across the front of the house. The main building was a traditional stone cottage, but the extension was much more modern. Offensively so, in fact. "Someone's got *Grand Designs* on Series Link."

There was an open bag of mints sitting in a dookit in front of the gearstick, and he'd been gradually working his way through them since they'd left Inverness over an hour ago. He reached for another, then yelped when his hand was slapped away. "Hey!"

"Hey nothing. You've had nearly the whole bloody packet," Caitlyn retorted.

"I've had about three!" Hamza protested.

"My arse you've had three," said Caitlyn. She relented with a tut. "Go on, then. But you're buying me another bag."

Hamza took one of the mints and unwrapped it. He popped it in his mouth and they both sat for a while watching a couple of workmen clambering about on the roof of the house extension. It was a B&B located just back from a single track road. The front looked out over the loch, and judging by the size of the windows in the new part, they were taking full advantage of it.

"Cracking view, right enough," Hamza said.

Caitlyn turned and looked out across Loch Ness. The edge of the road was lined with trees, but the house was raised up on a hillside enough that it peeped over the top of them.

"Not far to carry a body," the DS remarked.

"Have to cross the road, though," Hamza pointed out.

"Hardly a road, though, is it? It's barely a wide path."

"Risky, though." The mint *clacked* off Hamza's teeth as he moved it around in his mouth. "And then there's the trees. Probably a drop down into the water." He shook his head. "Last site was better. If I was going to kill someone, I'd have killed them there."

Caitlyn couldn't dispute that. The last site had been a new-build and stood right down by the water's edge. One of the balconies even hung out over the banking. It would've been easy for someone to wrap a body and just dump it straight into the loch without even setting foot outside the house.

Unfortunately, Caitlyn's information had been a little out of date. Construction had finished on the house six weeks previously, and the place was now a family home, complete with three kids and at least a couple of dogs. Hardly the place for a ritualistic murder.

"Nice place that one," Hamza remarked, not for the first time. "Wonder how much a gaff like that costs."

"More than we'll ever make," Caitlyn said.

"Heh. Aye. Fair point," Hamza agreed.

He reached for another mint, ignoring the glare it drew from DS McQuarrie, then snapped off a couple of photos of the site on his phone.

"Should we go talk to them?" he wondered.

Caitlyn checked her mirrors, then indicated to pull out from where they were stopped across the entrance to the house's driveway. "No, it's just a drive past," she said. "What's left?"

Hamza consulted the notepad on his lap. "Path repair."

"That's it?"

"That's it. Unless... Hang on."

He consulted his phone's map, then nodded ahead. "Boleskine House is straight along this road. We'll pass it in five minutes. We should swing in there and check it out." He sat up a little straighter in his seat. "They say you get a really weird vibe off it. You know, because of all the demon stuff."

After checking both directions for oncoming traffic, Caitlyn pulled out onto the narrow road.

"Do you believe all that stuff?" she asked.

Hamza side-eyed her. "Why, do you?"

"Obviously not."

"Nah. Nor me," Hamza said, just a little too quickly. "Still, interesting though, isn't it?"

"In what way?"

"Just, you know..."

He helped himself to another mint.

"Interesting."

Caitlyn waited for Hamza to unwrap the sweet, then plucked it from his fingers before he could do anything with it.

"Aye, suppose," she said, quickly shoving the mint in her mouth. "But if your head starts spinning and you projectile vomit pea soup on me, I will *not* be bloody happy."

CHAPTER FOURTEEN

AT THE MENTION OF HIS FATHER, EVERYTHING ABOUT Stuart's demeanour changed. His face hardened. His body language became stiff. His eyes shone with something that might have been contempt, but might equally have been fear.

"What can he tell you about his father? Not a bloody lot," said Michelle, answering on the boy's behalf. She shot an apologetic look to the porcelain Jesus on the wall, and slowly traced the back of her nephew's hand with her thumb. "Stuart hasn't had much to do with Robbie over the years."

"I understand. And I'm sorry to have to ask these questions. I wouldn't be asking if it wasn't important," Logan said, his attention still firmly on the boy. "When did you last see him?"

Stuart looked to Michelle for reassurance. She gave him an encouraging nod. "Go on."

"Like... six months ago. He turned up the day after my birthday."

"He had the wrong date, can you believe?" said Michelle. Her expression suggested she not only *could* believe it, but expected nothing less from the man. She shook her head. "His own son, and he had the wrong date."

"What did he say?" Logan pressed.

Stuart shrugged. "The usual. Sorry, he'd make it up to me, whatever. Same stuff he always says when he shows up. Wanted to take me to the pub to celebrate."

"His *fourteenth birthday*," Michelle stressed. "I mean..."

"He gave me a card with five hundred quid in it," Stuart said. His cheeks reddened a little. "Mum wanted me to give it back, but..."

"Five hundred quid's five hundred quid," said Tyler. "Least he could do."

"That's what I said," Stuart replied, and the reassurance from the detective constable seemed to encourage him. "Exactly."

"What about your mum? Do you know when she last saw him?" Logan asked.

Stuart shook his head. "No. Why?"

Beside him, Michelle sat up a little straighter. "Oh," she said. She looked and sounded a little surprised but not, Logan noted, particularly shocked. She recovered quickly and smiled around at everyone. "We should have some biscuits! You'll have a biscuit, won't you, Mr Logan?"

"Aye. Aye, I wouldn't say no," Logan said.

"You know where they are, sweetheart," Michelle said, smiling down at Stuart from her perch on the arm of his chair. "Get the nice ones, will you?"

Sinead, who had been standing quietly by the door, beckoned Stuart over. "You can show me where they are so I know for next time."

Stuart grunted, then stood up. "I know what you're doing,"

he said, but he trudged out anyway. Sinead bustled out after him, then closed the door behind them.

"You think Robbie did it, don't you?" said Michelle, taking Stuart's place in the armchair.

"We're keeping an open mind at this stage," Logan replied. "But we're keen to speak to him."

Michelle looked to the door, then lowered her voice. "She met him recently, I think. Or, she was going to. I don't know if she did."

"When was this?" Logan asked.

"About... Three weeks ago, maybe?"

"Did she say why?"

Michelle shook her head. "No. She seemed annoyed at him, but then there was nothing unusual there."

She dropped her voice further until it was scarcely a whisper. "He ruined her life. I mean, she wouldn't be... She wouldn't *have been* without Stuart, but... Robbie ruined her life."

"In what way?" Logan pressed.

"Sent her right off the rails. Messed with her head. Turned her against us all for a long time," Michelle explained. "She was sixteen when he got her pregnant. Sixteen! Had his way on her birthday, she eventually told me. Years later, I mean."

Michelle looked up at the ceiling, as if it were a screen replaying all the murky details of the past.

"She saw sense eventually, but only after she caught him having his way with some other poor unsuspecting lassie."

"Any reason to think he might do something like this?" Logan asked.

Michelle puffed out her cheeks. "Oh, I don't know. There's no predicting that man. Maybe, yes. I mean, if I had to pick someone?" She made a head gesture that was neither one thing nor the other. "Maybe."

Logan glanced at DC Neish, then back to Michelle. "Thanks. Very useful. We've got people looking for him now, so hopefully we'll find him soon."

"He not at work, then?"

Logan felt a flutter in the pit of his stomach. "Work? I didn't realise he had a job."

"He probably doesn't officially. It'll be cash in hand, I'm sure," she said, with a venom that suggested she considered this to be almost as bad as the other crime he was implicated in. "It's that building company. Bunch of cowboys. What are they called?"

"Not Bosco Building, is it?" asked Tyler.

"Yes! That's them," said Michelle. "You've heard of them?"

"Aye. You could say that," said Tyler.

Logan turned to him, an eyebrow raised.

"Explain later, boss. Long story."

There was a knock at the door, then Sinead's head appeared around the doorframe. Logan noticed, for the first time, another cross fixed above the doorframe.

"Just checking if you're ready for the biscuits?"

Logan nodded, beckoned for her to come in, then got to his feet.

"You've been very helpful, Miss Sinclair," Logan told Michelle. "And you too, son," he added, as Stuart trudged into the room behind Sinead, carrying a plate on which an array of biscuits had been half-heartedly arranged.

"Ooh, I'd like a little *Drifter*," Tyler said, helping himself to one of the brightly-wrapped chocolate fingers. He gave Stuart a beaming smile, then tucked the *Drifter* into the top pocket of his shirt. "Thanks."

"As soon as we have anything to pass on, we'll be in touch," Logan said.

Michelle jumped up from the armchair, took a moment to smooth the seat, then took the plate from Stuart and motioned for him to sit down.

Stuart hovered by the armchair, not yet sitting.

"You alright, mate?" Tyler asked.

"I forgot something," he said.

Michelle gave a little laugh. "Don't worry. It's just biscuits."

"No. About mum. I just remembered."

A hush fell.

"What was it you remembered, son?" Logan asked.

"She was arguing with someone. On the phone. Thursday night, I think it was."

Michelle frowned. "You never mentioned."

"I just remembered. I was in the kitchen. On Thursday, I mean. Her bedroom's right above it, and I could hear her arguing."

"Do you know who it was with, or what she said?" Logan asked.

Stuart shook his head. "No. Sorry. It was muffled. She didn't come downstairs for a while after it, and I forgot to ask her." He blinked several times, each one faster than the last. "I should've asked her."

"It's not your fault, mate," said Tyler, putting a hand on the boy's shoulder. "Alright? You weren't to know."

"Do you know what time you heard her arguing?" Logan pressed.

Stuart's eyes narrowed in concentration. "Not really. Between six and eight, maybe. I think."

"That's really helpful, son. Well done," Logan said. He looked from the boy to his aunt. "If either of you remember anything else, please let Sinead know."

"We will. And thank you. We're grateful for everything you're doing," Michelle replied. "Both of you. Sinead, too. It's..."

Her voice took on a note of hoarseness, her throat constricting. "We appreciate it. We... It's..."

Logan gave her a nod that told her he understood. Whatever it was she was trying to say, he understood.

"We'll be in touch," he told her. "And if there's anything you need, Sinead will take care of you."

He caught the constable's eye. "Call into the station later. We'll catch up."

"Will do, sir," Sinead said, as Logan brushed past her out of the room.

Tyler hung back with Sinead for a moment. "So, yeah," he began, shuffling on the spot and clicking his fingers down by his sides. "Thanks for the tea. Don't forget, if there's ever anything—"

"Get a move on, Detective Constable," came a gruff voice from the hallway. "We don't have all day."

LOGAN WAS ALREADY SITTING behind the wheel of the Focus when Tyler climbed into the front passenger seat. He waited until the DC had closed the door before voicing what was on his mind.

"Bosco Building?"

"Hmm? Oh, aye. They've been on the radar for a while," Tyler said. "CID reckons it's—"

"A front for a drugs operation. Russian led. Bosco Maximuke."

Tyler blinked. "Aye. That's right. You read the report?"

Logan shook his head. "He used to be based in Glasgow. He upped sticks and relocated his whole operation up to this neck of the woods."

"Oh. Right," Tyler said. "What made him do that?"

Logan slid the key into the ignition and fired up the engine.

"Me," he said.

DC Neish whistled through his teeth. "Oh. OK. So... we going to pay him a visit?"

"I am. You're not," Logan told him.

"What? Why not?"

"Because I said so. You can go back to the station and check in with Ben."

Tyler chewed on his bottom lip for a moment. "You don't think I should come, boss? Strength in numbers, and all that."

"I'm sure I'll cope," Logan said. He looked very deliberately to DC Neish's door handle. It took the younger detective a moment to figure out the meaning.

"Oh. You want me to get...?"

Logan nodded. "Aye."

"Right. Aye."

Tyler hesitated, then opened his door and got out. Logan pressed the button to wind down the window as the DC closed the door behind him.

"How am I supposed to get back?" Tyler asked, leaning down.

"Call an Uber," Logan told him.

"Uber doesn't do Inverness."

"Oh. Don't they?" said Logan. He mulled this over, filed it away, then clicked the button to wind up the window again.

Tyler watched from the kerb as the Focus pulled away and drove off down the road.

"Nice one, boss," he muttered. He kept watching until the car had turned the corner at the end of the street. "Cheers for that."

CHAPTER FIFTEEN

"You alright?"

Hamza stood halfway up a grassy hill, massaging his lower back with both hands and labouring for breath. The sun had found a route through the clouds just as they'd arrived at Boleskine House, and the direct heat coupled with the steep hike up the hillside wasn't doing him a lot of favours.

"Be fine in a minute," he puffed, looking up to where DS McQuarrie had been powering ahead.

She headed back down to join him, but he waved her back. "Seriously. It's fine."

"I told you you should've waited in the car."

"What, and miss the devil house?" Hamza said. He gulped down a couple of big breaths. "No chance."

Boleskine House was too far back and too well-hidden by trees to be seen from the road. The driveway leading up to the house had been blocked off with boulders, and a sign warned that trespassers would be prosecuted. The same sign also claimed that the site was protected by CCTV, but Caitlyn was sceptical. It was much cheaper to buy a sign claiming there was a CCTV system than it was to actually fit one, especially in a ruin this remote.

It wasn't impossible, of course, and she'd be delighted if she was wrong, but she'd also be very surprised.

Fortunately, there was a well-trodden path and a big hole in the fence close to where she'd stopped the car. The parking space probably belonged to the little graveyard across the road from the house, but none of the residents were in any real position to voice their objections, and there was nobody else around.

Hamza gave his back another rub, and felt the lines of scarring through his shirt. They stung when he got hot. Or cold. Or sometimes when he got tired. In fact, there was rarely a day went by when they didn't make their presence felt at some point or another.

He winced down another couple of breaths, then nodded to Caitlyn. "Right."

They resumed the climb, DS McQuarrie setting a slower pace this time. She tried to disguise it by making a show of looking out across the loch behind them, and to the open field over on the right, but Hamza saw through it and was only spurred on to walk faster.

As they approached, they were able to see more of the house. Or what was left of it, anyway. Fire had ravaged the place a few years back, consuming the roof and gutting the inside, but leaving most of the old stone walls standing.

A couple of chimney stacks stood steadfast and upright, the brickwork scorched but otherwise unaffected by the flames that had done a number on the rest of the place.

It was when Hamza saw the boarded windows that he felt the first fluttering of panic in his chest, and the scars on his back nipped at him in protest. He stopped, his legs turning to lead, memories of another ruined house not far away or long ago spinning around in his head.

"You OK?" he heard Caitlyn ask, and he forced his feet to move, to carry him on up the rest of the hill, ignoring the way his breathing was becoming erratic and his head was going light.

"Fine."

He felt her looking at him, saw her concerned expression from the corner of his eye. He ignored that too, and powered on past her up the hill, then through the gap in the fence that marked the boundary of Boleskine House.

Hamza stopped then, chest heaving, dark sparkles colouring the corners of his vision. Was it exertion, or panic? He couldn't tell. Both? Neither?

Or something else entirely?

The route had led them to the front of the house, where...

No. Not the front. This wasn't the front. He'd seen the plans. He knew this.

He thought about the floorplan he'd found online. Focused on it until he could see it in his mind's eye. He tried connecting it with the ruin in front of him now.

Beside them on the right was the library. The boarded windows made it impossible to see inside, but a big room full of books was unlikely to have fared well in a fire, Hamza thought.

To the left of that, a curved wall belonged to the... What was it? What was it?

He closed his eyes and tried to conjure up a clearer picture of the map.

"Drawing room!" he said aloud.

Caitlyn, who had been watching him with concern, switched to staring at him in confusion. "Huh?"

Hamza pointed to three different parts of the building ahead of them. "Drawing room, dining room, lounge."

DS McQuarrie regarded the house. "How do you know that?"

"It was on the plans," Hamza said. The icy fingers that had been squeezing the air from his chest were slackening their grip now, and colour was gradually returning to the edges of the world.

The wing of the house where the library was situated had fared better than the rest of the place. It still had some of its roof, and was the only section where anyone had bothered to barricade the windows. Presumably, it was to keep out squatters, although a few pieces of chipboard were unlikely to deter the buggers in Hamza's experience.

The rest of the place was so utterly destroyed that blocking the windows up was pointless. Through the holes in the walls, Hamza could see the blackened detritus of a family home. Most of the furniture had been entombed by the collapsing roof, but the skeleton of an armchair was visible amongst the wreckage. Something that might once have been a TV was now warped and buckled into some sort of modern art reimagining of its original form.

"Small rooms," Caitlyn observed.

Hamza gave himself a shake. Pulled himself together.

"What?"

"The rooms. They're smaller than I'd have expected."

Hamza managed a smile. "It's the home of the guy they called 'the wickedest man in the world.' He's supposed to have unleashed demons who still inhabit the grounds," the DC said. "And the thing you're worried about is that the rooms are a wee bit pokey?"

"Well, they are," Caitlyn said, raising herself up on her tiptoes to see in through one of the gaps where a window used to be. "The living room in my flat's bigger than this one."

"Aye, but your flat doesn't have a drawing room or a library, does it?"

"How do you know?" Caitlyn asked him. "It might have."

She stepped back from the house, looked it over, then they both started walking around to the other side of the building.

"What's a drawing room for, anyway?" Hamza asked, as they ducked under a solitary piece of 'Keep Out' tape strung across a pathway. "It's not for, like, *drawing* drawing. I know that."

"Well, it's for... You know."

"What?"

"Like... receiving guests."

They stopped at what would once have been a side door, but which was now just another hole in the wall. The floor beyond had fallen into the foundations, exposing some ancient-looking plumbing.

"Kitchen," Hamza said. "And what do you mean 'receiving guests?'"

Caitlyn shrugged. "Just, like, when you have guests, you put them in there."

"For how long?"

"What do you mean? There's not a set time. You're not roasting them in the oven."

"*He* might've," said Hamza, gesturing to the house beside them with a thumb. "Crowley. That was probably right up his street."

Hamza swore below his breath as he tripped on something. A *Sanyo* DVD player went skidding along the path, its once shiny-silver casing now marbled with black and grey. Down on the path by Hamza's feet, next to where the device had been, was a plastic DVD slip-case. The face of actor, Adam Sandler, had been partially melted, giving him an Elephant Man-like appearance.

"Ha. The Wedding Singer," said Hamza, recognising what was left of the DVD's cover. "Good film."

Caitlyn snorted. "What are you talking about? It's shite."

"It's not shite. It's decent. Drew Barrymore's in it."

"Drew Barrymore's been in a lot of shite."

"She was in a lot of good stuff, too!" Hamza protested.

"Alright, Adam Sandler, then," Caitlyn said.

Hamza stopped at the corner of the house and considered this.

"Aye, OK. He's shite, right enough," he conceded, then they stepped off the path and found themselves at the front of Bole-skine House.

The first thing they saw was a stack of building materials. Concrete blocks. Wooden beams. That sort of thing.

The very next thing they noticed was the tarpaulin. It was tucked in close to the house's double front doors, which had partially survived the blaze. It was green. Bright green.

The same bright green that had been wrapped around Mairi Sinclair like a shroud.

"Oh-ho," Hamza remarked. "That looks familiar."

Caitlyn took a look around them. Her gaze followed the front of the house, tracked across to the moss-covered steps that led up to an overgrown garden, then returned to the bundle of plastic sheeting.

"Sure does."

She approached the tarp slowly, raising a hand for silence when Hamza started to remind her of the 'look, don't touch' order she'd been only too quick to remind him of back at the last couple of places.

There was a faint *snap* as Caitlyn pulled on a thin vinyl glove she'd produced from one of the pockets of her coat. Glass *crunched* beneath her feet as she closed in on the tarpaulin.

There were no birds, Hamza realised. No cheeping or twittering from the trees. Had they been silent since they'd arrived? Or had they just fallen quiet now, holding their breath just like he was as DS McQuarrie crept closer to the tarpaulin.

It was probably just the angle, but there was a bulge in the middle of the plastic. A lump. Big, too. Big enough to be a person.

There was no reason anyone would be hiding under a sheet of tarpaulin out here, of course. Hamza knew that. And yet, his gut twisted and his scars burned as Caitlyn took hold of the tarpaulin sheet.

Besides, if there was someone under there, there was no saying they were hiding. There was no saying they were alive.

The plastic crinkled as Caitlyn lifted a corner. She exhaled, suggesting her thoughts had been roughly along the same lines as Hamza's.

"Cement," she said, giving one of the heavy-looking bags a prod with her foot. "It's just cement."

"Well, *obviously*," said Hamza, the words coming out as a throaty giggle of relief. "What else would it be?"

He was still grinning when a shape exploded through the remains of the doorway beside him. Still smiling when a shoulder clipped him, sending him into a spin.

And then, a moment later, the impact with the ground finally wiped the smirk off Hamza's face.

CHAPTER SIXTEEN

LOGAN SAW THEM WATCHING HIM AS HE TRUDGED ACROSS the yard towards a Portakabin marked 'Office' tucked away at the back. There were three men, although they could easily have been mistaken for three clones of the same guy. Same bald head, same piggy eyes, same bulky frame. Same accent, too, Logan guessed, although they were currently still too far away for him to hear what they were muttering to each other.

One of the men broke ranks and moved to intercept. Logan didn't slow. Instead, he eyeballed the bastard, daring him to challenge him. One of the other two duplicates started walking in the direction of the office, while another took out a phone and pecked away at the screen with a sausage-like finger.

"Yes?"

The voice of the man approaching was pretty much exactly what Logan had been expecting. Eastern European. Russian, possibly. It was curt and gruff, the word coming out as more of a demand than a simple question.

He stepped fully into Logan's path. The detective sighed impatiently, but stopped walking.

"I'm here to see Bosco."

The guard—because he was a guard, no matter what his contract of employment might state—looked Logan directly in the eye, like he could make him turn around and leave through sheer willpower alone. It had probably worked on plenty of people in the past, too.

Not today.

"Aye, very good, son," Logan told him. "You been rehearsing that with your pals, have you?"

The guard's smooth brow furrowed.

"All squinting at each other, an' that. Giving it the big I am."

He produced his warrant card while the guard was still running the translation in his head. Judging by the rate at which recognition spread across the brute's face, it wasn't the first time he'd had one flashed at him.

"Just go tell your boss there's an old friend here to see him, alright?" Logan instructed. "And save the Clint Eastwood act for the tourists."

The clone who'd been texting on the phone during the conversation hollered something in a language Logan didn't understand. He understood the hand gesture well enough, though, indicating that Logan should be allowed past.

Smiling, Logan raised both eyebrows and waited. The man in front of him grunted, then reluctantly shambled aside, giving the detective room to pass.

"Good effort, though," Logan said, patting the man's broad chest. "Keep it up."

And with that, he thrust his hands in the pockets of his coat, and swept on past the man towards the office.

The door opened at his approach, revealing the third guard. He was bigger than the last one, with a scar that ran from one side of his mouth almost all the way up to his ear. Now that

Logan was seeing him up close, he reckoned there was a good chance that he was actually related to the last guy. Not twins— they weren't that similar—but brothers, almost certainly.

Bosco always did like to keep things in the family.

"Through back," the guard instructed, gesturing to a door marked 'Manager.' He blocked Logan's path before he could move. "Are you alone?"

Logan looked the other man up and down. "That depends. Are we counting you?"

There was a moment of confused silence.

"What?"

"Aye. I'm alone," Logan said. He indicated the door with a nod of his head. "Now, d'you mind?"

"Let him through, Valdis."

Logan recognised the voice, even muffled by the door. He felt his fingers automatically ball into fists at the sound of it, but shook them loose again.

"You heard him, Valdis," Logan said, holding the brute's gaze. "Best do as he says."

Valdis' lips pulled back, revealing a row of yellow-brown teeth. He made a sound at the back of his throat that could've been a grunt or could've been a growl, but then the flooring of the cabin creaked as he stepped aside.

"I'll be waiting right here."

"Aye. Well." Logan looked the man up and down. "Have fun with that."

Bosco Maximuke was on his feet when Logan entered the office, arms held out in a gesture of welcome. "Jack! Look at you! Here!"

The Russian was half a head shorter than Logan, and a full third wider. He was dressed in a red nylon tracksuit he must've somehow had transported through time from the late 8os, and someone had attempted to perm what little hair he had left, with predictably awful results.

"Bosco. Almost didn't recognise you."

"Ha! Yes! The moustache? You like?" Bosco asked, smoothing down the clump of dark hair that crouched above his top lip.

"No, really," Logan told him.

"No? My wife, she agrees. She not like. Me? I like. My daughter? Oy. She *hate*."

Logan followed the Russian's gaze as he looked to the corner of the cabin. A girl of maybe seven or eight sat at a desk, headphones on, her attention focused on an iPad on a stand in front of her.

"She off school. *Sick*," Bosco explained. "To me, I not think she is sick. I think she is..."

He concentrated, trying to summon the word from somewhere.

"*Chancer*. Yes? I think she is *bloody chancer*."

He looked very deliberately from Logan to the girl and back again.

Logan nodded his understanding.

"So, as you see, now is not good time for me," Bosco said. "Although, it is good to see you. You must come by again when you are next in town. Yes?"

"Oh, I wouldn't worry about that. I've moved up here," Logan told him.

He enjoyed the subtle change to Bosco's face. The way the crow's feet around his eyes deepened. The way a shadow seemed to pass across him. The way he tried so very hard to keep his smile in place.

"What, did you miss me?" the Russian eventually managed to ask.

"Something like that, aye," Logan confirmed.

"And here, I thought I had seen last of you. 'No way he finds me up here,' I thought. 'No way he track me down.'"

"It wasn't exactly difficult. You called the company *Bosco Building*," Logan pointed out. "I mean, what's your logo? A big arrow with 'We Are Here' written on it?"

Bosco made a sound that was a bit like a laugh, but very clearly wasn't one.

"Anyway, I won't keep you long this time, but I'll make sure I pop back in soon," Logan told him. "Have a good look around the place. Be like old times."

He let the thought of that sink in.

"For now, I'm hoping you can help me out."

Bosco lowered himself into his chair and shot the briefest of looks in the direction of his daughter.

"What do you want?" he asked. He was still making an effort to sound amicable, but it was so paper-thin as to almost be see-through.

"Robbie Steadwood. He works for you."

Bosco shook his head. "No."

"What do you mean, 'no?'"

"I mean no. He does not work for me. He *did*," Bosco said. "But now, he does not."

"And why's that?"

"Because I no fucking see him, that's why not," Bosco snapped.

He shot a sideways look to his daughter, but she was still focused on a YouTube video playing on her iPad, and hadn't heard a thing.

"He vanish. Poof," the Russian explained, adding a little hand gesture for emphasis. "I no hear from him, I no see him. Not since his bitch-whore go missing."

The floor *groaned* beneath Logan as he shifted his weight on his feet. Bosco picked up on the impending danger and raised both hands.

"His words, not mine. 'She is bitch-whore,' he always say. Bitch-whore this, bitch-whore that. 'Bitch-whore won't let me see my kid!' You know? He says this about her, not me," Bosco explained. "And then she go missing, and he go missing, and now here you are. Looking."

He gave a dismissive wave, the movement curt and angry. "Well, they not here. Neither one."

"Aye. I know she's not here," Logan said. "She's dead."

Bosco's reaction was one of surprise. Logan couldn't quite figure out if it was real or not. He could usually get a pretty good bead on the Russian, but that stupid bloody moustache was throwing him off.

"Bitch-whore is dead?"

"Robbie Steadwood's ex-partner is dead," Logan corrected.

"You think Robbie did this?" Bosco asked.

"I don't know yet. Do you?"

The Russian leaned his chair back, then rocked it a little. His bottom lip came up and sucked on his moustache as he thought. "Could be. Maybe. They did not get on, I think. When she came round here one time, they had argument. Big argument."

Logan's eyes narrowed. "What did she want?"

"I do not know. I do not pry into things that are not my business."

Logan knew that was far from the case, but knew there was no point in pushing.

"When was she here?"

Bosco shrugged. "I do not remember."

Logan moved a little closer to the desk. The light from the window cast his shadow across the man in the chair.

"Try."

Bosco tutted. "Olivia, sweetie-heart?" he said, turning to the girl in the corner. When she didn't respond, he slapped his hand on the desk a few times and tried again. "Olivia!"

The girl tapped the screen a couple of times, tutted, and then turned to her father. The look on her face made her thoughts on being interrupted very clear.

"What?"

A conversation followed in Russian. It started off quite measured, but both parties grew increasingly agitated as it went on.

Eventually, Bosco seemed to get what he was after, and the girl turned back to her device.

"She thinks two weeks ago. Maybe fifteen, sixteen days."

"She off school then, too, was she?"

"Like I say. She is chancer," Bosco said. "Oh! Bitch-whore also phone me. Around same time, maybe. Day after."

"Phoned you? Why?"

"Asking where Robbie was working. Asking where she could find him."

"Did you tell her?"

"Not on first call. Third call? Yes. Third call, I have enough. I tell her. Get her out of my hair."

He stood up and gave an apologetic sort of shrug. "I wish I could help better, yes? But I know nothing. Where Robbie is now? It is mystery."

"Aye. Well. We'll find him," Logan said.

Bosco smiled, showing a little too many teeth. "Or, we might find him first," he said.

A silence hung between them for a moment. An unspoken understanding that this would not be in Robbie's best interests.

Then, the Russian laughed and thrust a hand out for Logan to shake. "Good to see you again, my friend. But, you will give me warning before you come around next time, yes? You will call on the telephone."

Logan regarded the offered hand for a moment, then grasped it with his own much larger one.

"No," he said, squeezing good and hard. "I won't."

CHAPTER SEVENTEEN

As he hit the ground out front of Boleskine House, Hamza instinctively curled himself into a tight ball, wrapping his arms over his head for protection. He shut his eyes, bracing himself for the pain that had screamed through him when the blade had been buried in his back all those weeks before, and every night again since, when he'd eventually given in to sleep.

Instead of the pain, he heard crunching footsteps. Panicked breathing. A shout from Caitlyn, ejected mid-run.

"Police! Stay where you are!"

The voice that replied was frantic. Desperate-sounding.

"Don't shoot! Don't shoot!"

Hamza opened his eyes. A small, slight figure dressed all in black stood with his back to DS McQuarrie, both hands raised to the sky. A boy. Even from this distance, Hamza could see he was visibly trembling.

"Put your hands down," Caitlyn instructed.

The boy did as he was told, dropping his arms to his sides but not yet daring to turn.

"You alright?" Caitlyn asked, shooting a look back over her shoulder at Hamza as he clambered to his feet.

"Fine. Aye. Wee bastard just caught me off guard."

She nodded, then turned her attention back to the kid. "Turn around."

The boy shuffled anxiously, like this might be some kind of test he didn't dare fail.

Caitlyn sighed. "We can do this the hard way or the easy way. And, just so we're clear, the hard way involves you being face down on the ground with my knee between your shoulder blades. The easy way doesn't. Up to you."

The boy turned around. Hamza groaned.

"He looks about twelve. I got knocked on my arse by a twelve-year-old."

"I'm thirteen," the boy squeaked.

Caitlyn looked back at Hamza, smirking. "Hear that? He's thirteen. Nothing to be ashamed of."

Hamza flashed a sarcastic smile back at her, then they both approached the kid.

"What's your name?" Caitlyn demanded.

The boy straightened, as if standing to attention. "Lucas."

"Lucas *what*?"

A pause. A furrowing of the brow. "Lucas, *Miss*."

Hamza bit his lip to stop himself laughing. Caitlyn rolled her eyes.

"I'm not your teacher. I meant what's your surname?"

"Oh. Sorry. Lucas Findlay."

Caitlyn gestured to the house. "What were you up to in there, Lucas Findlay? It's off-limits."

"And what did you knock me over for?" Hamza asked. He turned the sleeve of his jacket to reveal a big dirty mark. "Look at this."

Lucas shifted awkwardly. "Sorry."

"*Sorry* doesn't answer my question. What were you up to in there?" Caitlyn demanded. She drew herself up to her full height. "Or would you rather answer down at the station?"

Lucas shook his head so frantically Hamza worried it might come off.

"No, I was just... It was just..."

The boy swallowed, composing himself, then spat the rest out in one big breath.

"Barry Madsen dared me."

Caitlyn put her hands on her hips. "What?"

"Barry Madsen. He's in my school. He said I was too much of a chicken. And... and..."

He looked down at his feet. "Everyone laughed."

"Too much of a chicken to do what? Crouch in a house?" asked Caitlyn, growing visibly impatient.

Lucas shook his head. "Ouija board. I was meant to take a selfie," he said. "They say the place is full of—"

"Aye, I'm familiar with what they say," said Caitlyn, and Hamza got the distinct impression that was aimed at him.

"There was a girl who did it years ago," Lucas said. "She went mental. They think she got possessed."

Caitlyn sighed. "Do they really? So, you thought you'd do the same, did you?"

Lucas' eyes widened, like the implications of what he was doing had finally occurred to him.

"Where's your Ouija board, then?" Hamza asked.

"That's a point. If that's why you're here, where is it?"

Hesitantly, and without a word, Lucas reached into the back pocket of his trousers. He unfolded a piece of paper, on which he'd drawn something that might, with a bit of imagination, be a Ouija board.

"Did it work?" asked Hamza.

"Shut up. Of course it didn't work," Caitlyn interjected. "It's not real, and he shouldn't be messing around with the bloody thing up here."

"If you're so sure it's not real, then what's the problem?" Hamza asked. He looked pleased with himself, as if he'd just ensnared the DS in a cunningly set trap.

"Well, maybe because the roof's caved in, the place is full of broken glass, and the whole site's off-limits?"

Hamza's face fell a little. He considered the wreckage of the house. "Oh. Aye. Fair enough."

Caitlyn crossed her arms and looked the kid up and down. He was short and skinny, with fair hair poking out from beneath the hoodie he wore. If he really was thirteen, then he didn't look it. She'd have put him a year or so in the other direction.

He was doing his very best to stand still, but nerves were making him shift from foot to foot, his hands fidgeting down by his sides. When he wasn't talking, his mouth was a thin line, lips clamped together through the effort of not crying.

"Right. Cuff him," Caitlyn decided.

Hamza frowned. "What, seriously?"

"Sorry! Sorry! Please!" Lucas begged, his eyes filling.

Caitlyn held a hand up, calling for calm.

"Look, do you want your bloody photo or not?"

Hamza and the boy both blinked in surprise.

"What?" Lucas croaked.

She jabbed a thumb back over her shoulder in Hamza's direction. "Give him your phone," she instructed. "You can show Barry what's his name that not only did you do the Ouija board, thank you very much, but you got lifted for it, too."

The already panicky expression on Lucas's face ramped up a notch.

"We're not actually arresting you. Relax." Caitlyn raised an index finger and held it close to the boy's face. "But don't say I'm not bloody good to you."

Lucas didn't argue. He handed over the phone, the cuffs were applied, and Hamza then took a full three minutes to get 'the perfect picture' set up. This involved the careful positioning of the Ouija board—or Ouija *sheet*—if you wanted to get technical about it, plus some clever framing to get enough of the house in to make the place recognisable.

They'd cuffed the boy's hands in front of him so they could be seen in the picture. Caitlyn stood behind him with a hand on his shoulder and a scowl on her face, like she was about to huckle him to the ground.

"Right, are we ready now?" she asked.

"One sec," said Hamza, pinching the phone screen.

Lucas gently cleared his throat. "Can... can you swap?" he asked.

"What?"

"It's just... Barry Madsen will be more impressed if it's a man who's arrested me."

Caitlyn tutted. "Aye, well Barry Madsen's a sexist wee bastard," she said, clamping her hand on the back of Lucas's neck and grimacing at the camera. "Now, shut up and say cheese."

CHAPTER EIGHTEEN

"The wanderer returns," said Ben, as Logan entered the Incident Room.

The DI motioned with his mug to where Tyler sat behind a desk, combing through a few pages of printouts.

"The boy tells me you went to meet an old pal of yours."

"Aye. Could say that," said Logan shrugging off his coat.

"How is the mad Russian bastard?" Ben enquired.

"Same as ever. Except he's got a moustache now," Logan said.

"That's nice for him. Did he give you anything useful?"

Logan shook his head. "No. Just the usual spike in blood pressure. He hasn't seen Robbie Steadwood in weeks."

"And you believe him?" Ben asked.

"As much as you ever really can. I got the distinct impression he wants to find him for reasons of his own. I think it'll be very much in Mr Steadwood's best interests if we find him first."

Logan recounted what little Bosco had told him about Robbie, about Mairi Sinclair turning up at the yard, and about the argument that had followed.

"Things are no' looking good for young Robert, are they?" Ben remarked. "Still no sign of the bastard. I've asked for some extra resources to find him, and the call's going out on MFR within the hour. They're going to repeat it after every news bulletin."

"Good. He'll know we're looking for him, anyway. It's not going to hurt."

Tyler looked up from the sheets of paper spread out in front of him. "I made it back alright, Boss. You know, in case you were worried."

Logan shook his head. "I wasn't. It's a small city, and you're a grown man."

"Almost a grown man," Ben corrected.

"You're almost a grown man. I was confident that even you could find your way back, eventually."

Tyler smiled. "Wow. Is that a compliment, Boss?"

Logan briefly considered this. "I mean... no. Not really."

"You could argue it's the opposite, really," Ben added.

Logan approached the younger detective's desk. "What I will say..." he began. "Remember how I said that you should take notes and let me do the talking back at Michelle Sinclair's house? You remember us having that conversation?"

Tyler winced a little.

"I do."

Logan gave a nod. The lines of his face tightened, like it pained him to say this next part.

"Aye. Well. Good work in there with the boy. With the..." He made a vague gesture with a hand. "...whatever shite it was you were talking about. It was a big help."

Tyler's face widened into a grin. "OK, *that* was a compliment!"

"More or less," Logan conceded. He picked up a stapler

from the DC's desk. "But, just so we're clear—the next time you disregard one of my direct instructions, I am going to shove this stapler right up your arse."

He held it horizontally.

"That way. Is that clear?"

Tyler eyed the stapler for a moment and squirmed in his seat, then he touched a finger to his forehead in salute. "Aye-aye, cap'n."

Logan set the stapler back down and indicated the documents spread out on the desktop around it. "What have you got?"

"It's phone records, Boss. Mairi Sinclair's. Waiting for more, but this covers the last couple of weeks."

"Got them already? That was quick."

"CID put a request in when she went missing. They just arrived."

"Ah, right, that sounds more like it," said Logan. "Anything coming up?"

"Possibly. There are three numbers that stood out. I've been able to identify two of them," Tyler said, consulting the notes he'd been making in a pad. His writing was impeccably neat, Logan noticed. He half-expected to see little bubbles above the lower case letter i's.

"Christopher Boyd's the one you'll be most interested in," the DC continued. "I counted six-hundred-and-twenty-seven texts, plus sixteen phone calls."

"Over what period?"

"About a fortnight, Boss. Just under."

Logan whistled. "Right. Aye, that's interesting."

"And get this," Tyler said. "I checked him out. Guess what his job is."

"No."

Tyler looked a little crestfallen. "Oh. Right. Well, he's a climbing instructor."

Ben strolled over to join them, coffee cup still in hand. "And what's that got to do with the price of cheese?" he asked.

"Climbing rope," Logan said. "Mairi Sinclair's body was tied with climbing rope."

"Last message was on Saturday morning," Tyler said. "It was pretty constant until then, then nothing after that. He texted her back and tried to call a couple of times, but no response."

Logan twisted his neck to get a better look at the phone records. "Was that message to him the last one she sent?"

"No, boss. That would be the other number that might be of interest. Shayne Turner. Female," Tyler said. "I looked her up. Pretty fit, actually."

He caught the look of disapproval from both senior officers, then quickly moved on. "Colleague of the victim. They worked together at the primary school. Shayne's a teacher, too."

"Friends, then," Logan said.

"Not exactly. Mairi sent four texts to her over the same nearly-two-week period. No calls."

"Why's she of interest, then?" Logan asked.

"Two reasons. First, Shayne was the last person she messaged. Sunday morning. Just before ten."

"Not long before she left the house," Logan remarked.

"Exactly. Secondly... I've compared incoming and outgoing records. With Christopher Boyd, they're pretty balanced. Back and forth, sort of thing. With Shayne Turner, that's not the case."

He consulted his notes again. "Like I said, Mairi sent four texts over the twelve days. Shayne Turner sent two-hundred-and-seventy-two. She also made three phone calls. None of them were answered."

"Have we got the contents of the messages?" Logan asked.

"Working on it, but it'll take time. The phone company's being a bit of a dick about it. We're having to go through the..." He made quote marks in the air. "...proper channels."

"No surprise there, then. They can be pernickety bastards," Logan remarked. "What about the other number you mentioned?"

"We haven't been able to identify it yet. Unregistered Pay as You Go. She called it twice in the week before she went missing. It's the only number we haven't been able to identify as friends or family," Tyler explained. "We're working on trying to trace its location, but haven't had a hit yet."

"OK. Well, keep doing what you're doing," Logan said. He tapped a finger on the paperwork. "And good work on this."

Tyler winked. "Two compliments in one day, Boss? I am on a roll."

Ben leaned over the desk, a hand extended, palm down. "Speaking of rolls."

Tyler took the offered item and unrolled it. It was a five pound note.

"One bacon and one black pudding," Ben said. He turned to Logan. "You having anything?"

Logan opened his mouth to decline, but his stomach chose that moment to loudly voice its objections.

"Aye, I should probably eat something, right enough," he conceded. "Flat sausage. Brown sauce."

"From the place across the road," Ben said. "No' the canteen here. They don't do black pudding."

For a moment, it seemed like Tyler might refuse, but then his shoulders slumped and his chair trundled back away from the desk as he got to his feet.

"Right. Fine," he said. "But someone else is getting it next time."

Ben watched him pick up his jacket and start trudging towards the door.

"Tyler, hold on, son. Wait up," he called after him.

DC Neish turned to find Ben smiling at him in his usual good-natured sort of way. Ben put a hand on the younger man's shoulder and squeezed.

"Get yourself a wee sweetie with the change, alright?"

Despite his irritation, Tyler couldn't help but smirk. "Too bloody right I will," he said.

Logan and Ben both watched as he left the Incident Room, and waited until the door had swung closed again.

"There's no' going to be any change, is there?" Logan said.

Ben shook his head. "No."

The door swung open again. Logan expected DC Neish to come storming back in again, but a woman entered, instead. He didn't recognise her at first, probably because she looked markedly less dishevelled than she had the first time they'd met.

Dr Shona Maguire's hair pulled back into a loose ponytail, and she'd swapped the crumpled lab coat and *Batman* t-shirt for a satiny blue shirt and a pair of jeans. The fact that she wasn't currently slurping down a *Bombay Bad Boy* Pot Noodle also helped smarten her up a bit.

"Aha. There you are," she remarked, sidling through the door and into the room. She carried a *Smyths Toys* bag that looked reasonably full, if not very heavy. "Sorry, was going to just email you the latest, but I was passing anyway so I thought I'd come in and tell you in person."

She smiled at both men in turn.

"Hello, by the way." She held a hand out to Ben. "Shona Maguire. Pathologist."

"Aye, we've met," said Ben, but he shook the hand anyway.

"Aha! So we have," said Shona. "It's..."

She made various shapes with her mouth, like her brain was running through all the possible syllables his name might start with.

"DI Forde. Ben," he said, putting her out of her misery.

"Ben! Yes! Ben Forde!" Shona said, pumping his hand with almost demented enthusiasm. "That's you."

"It is," Ben confirmed, taking his arm back.

"What have you got for us?" Logan asked.

"Cannabis," said Shona.

Logan raised his eyebrows and whistled quietly through his teeth. "That's a bold move," he said.

"Go on then, we'll take half an ounce," Ben whispered, furtively glancing around.

"Huh?" Shona looked momentarily confused, then it clicked. "Oh. Funny. Good one," she said. Her expression rapidly cooled. "No. I'm talking about the victim. About the young woman who was brutally murdered not far from here. Tragically cut down in the prime of her life."

She looked from one detective to the other.

"Hardly seems like a joking matter, does it?"

Ben shifted uncomfortably. "Well... No. I mean, obviously—"

"Ha. Got you back," said Shona. Her smile returned and she fired a finger-gun at DI Forde while simultaneously winking and making a *click-click* noise out of the corner of her mouth.

She quickly became more serious again.

"But yes. Toxicology reports show the victim had used cannabis in the days leading up to her death. Probably quite regularly, in fact, judging by the build-up in her system."

Ben looked up at Logan. "She's a teacher, isn't she? I thought they did checks?"

Logan shrugged, but said nothing.

"Anything else?" he asked the pathologist.

"I think that's about your lot," she said. She looked apologetic, like she'd let them both down in some way. "Couldn't retrieve any useful DNA. Water took care of that, like I thought it would."

She shook a fist and pulled an angry face. "Bloody water."

Shona lowered her fist again. "Anyway, thought you should know about the drugs. I've stuck it all in an email."

"I thought you said you hadn't emailed," Ben remarked.

Shona hesitated. "Hm?"

"You said you decided not to email and just swing by," Ben reminded her.

The pathologist briefly met Logan's eye, then looked away again. It was hard to tell with the harsh glow of the overhead strip lights, but Logan thought he detected a slight reddening of her cheeks.

"I decided to stop by *and* email," she explained. "You should always try to double-up on important messages. You know who said that?"

Ben shook his head. Shona gave him a bump on the shoulder with the side of a fist.

"Well, there's something for you to find out," she said, then she flashed them another smile and backed towards the door. "Good luck with it all. Anything else you need. You know, corpse-wise, you know where to find me."

She waved at them both as she reached the exit. "Until next time, gentlemen," she said, and then she nudged the door open and slipped out into the corridor.

It was Ben who eventually voiced what was on both their minds.

"She's a strange one."

"Aye," Logan agreed, still watching the door. "She's that, alright."

CHAPTER NINETEEN

THE NEXT COUPLE OF HOURS WERE FILLED WITH THE MEAT and potatoes of polis work. Or, as Ben insisted on calling it, the mince and tatties.

He had a knack for co-ordinating that sort of thing. Possible car sightings were chased up. The additional resources the investigation had been allocated were put to work hunting for Robbie Steadwood. Phone calls were made to everyone who'd been staying at the campsite in Foyers around the time Mairi had gone missing, and a team was set up to handle the influx of phone calls they were expecting after the MFR broadcasts started going out. Plenty of them would be nutters, but there might be something useful in amongst it all.

Caitlyn and Hamza came back, and filled the others in on the green tarpaulin they'd found at Boleskine House. They'd already arranged for uniform to cordon the place off, and a forensics team was dispatched to give the place a going over.

They mentioned the boy with the Ouija Board but not, to Hamza's relief, the fact that he'd been unceremoniously knocked on his arse when the kid had tried to flee the scene.

Caitlyn updated the Big Board with all the new information they'd gathered, while Hamza and Tyler ran some cursory background checks on Shayne Turner and Christopher Boyd.

"I want to talk to the victim's parents, too," Logan announced, midway through reading over the typed-up version of the recording DC Neish had made at the victim's sister's house. "Can someone get me their details?"

"It'll be on HOLMES, sir," Caitlyn said.

"Can you print it off for me?" Logan asked. "Bloody thing always crashes as soon as I go near it. I don't think it likes me."

"God, and you such an affable fella, too," Ben remarked.

A bit more digging later, Hamza and Tyler gave a rundown on Shayne Turner and Christopher Boyd. Hamza took the floor first, and was almost blinded when Tyler clicked the projector on. He hissed for a moment like a vampire caught in sunlight, blinking and shielding his eyes until he found a route out of the projector's beam.

"Sorry," Tyler said, although it was immediately apparent to everyone in the room that he wasn't really.

Hamza scowled at him, then indicated the slightly fuzzy image of a young woman with jet-black hair and deep brown eyes that was projected onto a blank area of wall.

"Shayne Turner. Age twenty-three. Moved with her family from Australia eight years ago, now teaches Primary Four at the same school Mairi Sinclair taught at."

"My teachers never looked anything like that," Tyler remarked, his tongue practically hanging out. "Pretty sure they were all in their eighties."

"She started at the school in September last year," Hamza continued, ignoring him. "The head runs a sort of staff mentorship programme, where new members of staff are paired up with someone who's been there a while."

Hamza gestured to the soft-focus image. "Guess who she was paired up with."

"Mairi Sinclair," said DS McQuarrie.

"Right."

"What else do we have on her?" Logan asked.

Hamza consulted his notes. "Not a lot. No previous. Looking at her social media, she lives alone, has a couple of dogs that look like big rats, and buys a *lot* of stuff off Etsy."

He looked very deliberately at DC Neish.

"She's also gay."

"Gay?" A battle raged on Tyler's face as he tried to work out how he felt about this new piece of information. "I don't know if that's better or worse."

Hamza didn't have much more to add about Shayne, so he sat down and gave the floor to Tyler.

Christopher Boyd's photo was taken from the website of his climbing instruction business. It showed him hanging off an icy wall by a length of rope that looked not dissimilar to the type used to tie up Mairi Sinclair's body. The shadow of his climbing helmet obscured the top part of his face a little, but he was smiling broadly and offering a thumbs-up to the camera with his free hand.

Tyler rattled through his basic stats—age forty-two, divorced, father of two. He'd set up a family-friendly climbing wall in the Eastgate Centre a few years back and won a local business award for it. There were a couple of call-outs for alleged domestics at the house he'd shared with his ex-wife, but no charges were ever pressed, and they divorced a year and a bit later.

"Anyone spoken to him since Mairi went missing?" Logan asked.

"No. No one CID spoke to mentioned him," Tyler said. "If they were having a relationship, I reckon it was on the sly."

"And he hasn't come forward himself?"

Tyler shook his head. "Doesn't look like it, Boss."

Logan's chair creaked as he sat forward and regarded the man's grinning image. "Interesting."

He ran his tongue across the front of his teeth, then looked between both DCs. "Any suggestion that either of them are into that supernatural guff?"

"Nothing on Shayne Turner, no."

Tyler shrugged. "Looks like he went as Harry Potter to a fancy dress party in October. Does that count?"

"No. That doesn't count," Logan said.

"Maybe if he went as Voldemork," Ben remarked.

When the others turned to look at him, he rocked back on his heels, looking pleased with himself.

"Ha. You think I don't know about this stuff," he said. "Finger on the pulse, me."

"It's 'Voldemort,' sir," Caitlyn told him.

Ben's eyebrows twitched.

"Hm?"

"It's *Voldemort*. Not Voldemork."

"Is it?" Ben cleared his throat. "Aye. Well. You know which one I meant."

"Finger on the pulse? Head up your arse, more like," Logan muttered. "Right, I want to talk to both of them."

"Want me to have them brought in, sir?" Caitlyn asked.

Logan drummed his fingers on the desk in front of him, considering the options. "Bring the teacher in. But after school finishes, don't go making a scene."

Ben checked his watch. "Should be done now. It's twenty to five."

"Already? Jesus," Logan muttered. "But aye. Fine. Get her in."

"And Boyd, sir?" Caitlyn asked.

Did you say his place is at the Eastgate? Does he work out of there?"

"Yeah, Boss," Tyler confirmed. "Based there through the week. Part-time staff run the place at weekends."

"Right. Good. We'll go to him, in that case. See how he likes having me traipsing through his place of business. Might give us more of an insight into him."

He cast his eye across to the Big Board, running through a quick mental recap.

"Symbols," he said, his gaze falling on the sketches Hamza had made. "Where are we with that?"

"Hang on, I'll check, sir," Hamza replied, turning his attention to his computer. A couple of mouse-clicks later, he sat up straighter. "Got something. The symbols are..."

He hesitated, as if taking a run-up to the word.

"Apotropaic, apparently."

Based on the complete lack of expression on the faces of the others, Hamza decided to read on.

"It says that Apotropaic magic is a branch of magic designed to ward off evil influences. Misfortune, demonic possession, the evil eye. That sort of thing. This guy reckons the symbols are a real mish-mash of cultures. Egyptian, Greek, Roman, Serbian."

"A big old mixed bag of bullshit," Tyler commented.

"Anything connected to Crowley or Boleskine House?" Caitlyn asked.

Hamza used his mouse wheel to scroll down the page a little. "Nothing I can see, no," he said. "I'll have a proper read and see what else it says."

"Good. The rest of you, find me Mairi's car, and find me

Robbie bloody Steadwood," Logan said, getting to his feet. "Ben, once Forensics have any news from Boleskine—"

"You'll be the first to know," DI Forde confirmed.

"DS McQuarrie, you're with me," Logan told Caitlyn. "We're going to go pay Mr Boyd a visit."

He turned to Ben, a thought striking him. "Any word on the rope used to tie up the vic?"

"Aye. I think I saw they've got a match. I'll text it to you," Ben said.

He checked his watch again, then shot Logan a warning look. "Just don't take too long," he said. "Alice tells me she's doing something nice for dinner."

"What, is she getting someone else to make it?"

"Chance'd be a fine thing," Ben replied. He called after the DCI as he and Caitlyn headed for the door. "Just don't be bloody late!"

CHAPTER TWENTY

BOSCO SAT BEHIND HIS DESK, SMILING AND NODDING AS HIS daughter explained every intricate detail of the latest round of YouTube videos she'd just been watching.

He wanted to be interested. Sort of. He wanted to support her in what she chose to do, but it wasn't easy when all she chose to do was watch groomed twenty-somethings of indeterminate genders applying make-up, or making slime, or opening little bags with toys inside, or whatever else they had moved onto these days.

Where was the conversation to be had there? Where was the common ground?

God, he wished she was back at school.

"Uh-huh. Uh-huh," he said. His eyes were pointed in her direction, but he wasn't looking at her. Not really. Nor was he listening. He was hearing, yes—just enough to be able to nod and smile at the right time—but not actively listening.

His thumb rubbed along the length of a badly-chewed pencil he'd picked up off his desk, and which he now held clutched in a white-knuckled grip. He could feel the wood bending under the pressure, hear the little groans it made, even over the *quack-quack-quack* of whatever inane bullshit his daughter was blabbering about now.

It would've been easier for him if she was talking in Russian, but she felt more comfortable using English, and it was important that she kept practising. He was pleased at how well she spoke the language. He just wished she'd stop with that upward inflection at the end of each and every fucking sentence.

Another gift from YouTube.

A knock at the door offered some momentary respite.

"Come," Bosco said.

Olivia appeared mortally offended by this, and glared daggers at her father.

"What? I have work, yes?" Bosco told her. "I not get to be sick."

The door opened, and Valdis, the guard with the scar on his face, ducked through.

"What you want now?" Bosco asked.

Valdis looked very deliberately at the girl. She managed to hold his gaze for almost a full three seconds, before blinking and looking away.

"Sweetie-heart. Daddy has business to talk. You go..." He mimed putting on headphones. "Yes? Yes."

The girl wheeled her rolling chair back over to her iPad, pushing herself along on her feet. Once there, she chanced another quick look up at the towering Valdis, before pulling on her headphones. She tapped the play button on the tablet's screen, and her eyes glazed over at once, like a junkie getting a long-overdue fix.

"What is problem?" Bosco asked, once Olivia was fully engrossed in the screen.

Valdis still looked a little uncertain, but Bosco dismissed his concerns with a twitch of irritation. "She is fine. She not hear nothing. What is problem?"

"There was a message on the radio. About Robbie," Valdis said. While different, his accent was just as thick as Bosco's, although his grasp of the language was better.

Bosco's face darkened. "They found him?"

"No. It was asking people to help look for him."

The Russian relaxed a little. "Good. I mean, not good they are looking. Good they not yet found him."

He jabbed at the desktop with a finger. *Thunk-thunk-thunk.* "We find him first. We find piece of shit Robbie before police."

"We're trying."

"*Try fucking harder!*" Bosco roared, leaping to his feet.

Over in the corner, Olivia jumped in her seat, but didn't turn. She quickly turned up the volume and pressed her head-phones tighter to her ears as her father continued to shout.

"Don't come here and give me excuse! 'We can't find him. We try our best!'" He brought his clenched fists to his eyes and mimed crying. "*Waah. Waah. Waah.*"

Not just Olivia, but everything on Bosco's desk jumped this time as he slammed both hands down on it. "I don't want excuse. I want piece of shit Robbie before he talk to police. I want to..." He mimed gripping something between both hands. "...what is word?"

"Strangle," Valdis said.

"I want to strangle him with my two hands until his piece of shit eyes come out of his head!"

Valdis's eyes darted to Olivia again. Bosco's body language remained furious, but he lowered his voice by a few dozen decibels.

"She not hear. Her brain is fucking rotted by that shit," he scowled.

He took a breath, composing himself, then dropped back down into his chair.

"You find Robbie. Tear city apart if have to. Put tail on Logan."

He scowled at the thought of him.

"Fucking Logan," he muttered. "Put tail on him. Someone good. Follow and report. I want to know everything he does. If he goes for shit, I want to know what it smells like. Yes?"

Valdis nodded. "Understood."

"Good. Because, if piece of shit Robbie talks to police," Bosco said. His eyes fell on his daughter and stayed there for a moment, before flicking back to the towering skinhead standing before him. "Then we all are fucked."

CHAPTER TWENTY-ONE

"GREAT, CARRIE. WELL DONE. YOU'RE DOING BRILLIANT. Now, left foot over. No, left foot. That one, not... There. See, that was easy, wasn't it?"

"Christopher Boyd?"

The climbing instructor turned away from the artificial rock face at the sound of his name, a big welcoming smile plastered across his mug. It wilted a little when he saw DCI Logan and DS McQuarrie standing there, all-business.

"Yes?"

The detectives flashed their warrant cards and Logan quickly ran through the introductions. Around them, half a dozen children and a couple of adults traversed the wall, manoeuvring themselves across a series of brightly coloured rubber hand and footholds.

Two other staff members were on hand to offer advice to those climbing. Logan reckoned Boyd could spare himself for a few minutes.

"We'd like to talk to you, Mr Boyd," Logan said. "Somewhere private would be best."

"Chris?" came a voice from the wall behind him.

"One second, Carrie," Christopher said. He pulled a perplexed sort of smile for the benefit of the detectives. "Why? What's this about?"

"We should probably talk in private," Logan reiterated.

"Chris!"

"One *second*, Carrie," Christopher said. The words snapped out of him, but he quickly brought the smile back. "I'm in the middle of a lesson. Can you come back at another—"

"It's about the murder of Mairi Sinclair," Logan told him. He watched the expression on the instructor's face go from fake smile to genuine terror, then leaned in a little closer. "Would you like me to say that again, but louder?"

Christopher shook his head. "No."

"Chris, I'm going to fall!"

"You're three feet off the ground, Carrie!" the instructor hissed. "Just jump. That's what the mats are for."

He turned back to the detectives. Behind him, there was a "Waah!" and a *thwack* as an eight-year-old girl dropped onto the crash mat.

"We can talk in my office," Christopher said. He gestured in the direction of a *Staff Only* door nestled in an artificial rocky crag. "This way."

ALTHOUGH THE CLIMBING wall area of the business was impressive, the manager's office was less so, and looked like it had been added as something of an afterthought. The only thing that identified it as an office was a desk, a chair, and an In Tray that had overflowed to the point where much of the paper had cascaded out and onto the floor.

If Christopher hadn't specifically referred to it as his office, it could've been almost any kind of room, with *Random Junk Storage* being the most likely candidate. Boxes of flyers, membership forms, and other assorted paperwork were stacked haphazardly around the room, a brief description of their contents scribbled on the partially collapsed cardboard walls in black marker.

One of the boxes had caught Logan's eye almost immediately, thanks to the end of a purple and black rope that hung over the top and down the side of it. The branding on the box said 'Edelweiss.' Logan had received the same word via a text from Ben during the drive over.

The desk was positioned up against one of the few patches of wall not stacked high with cardboard containers. A year planner was tacked in place above it, hundreds of sticky coloured dots making it look like some sort of collage.

There were two seats in the room—a threadbare office chair by the desk, and something that would've looked more at home in a 1970s kitchen. Logan chose to sit on neither. As standing in the cramped space forced all three of them awkwardly close together, Christopher sat on the one by the desk.

He then realised that he had to crane his neck to look up at the towering detective, and so perched himself on the desk, instead.

"Murdered?" was the first thing the instructor said, once he'd got himself into a position he felt comfortable with. "I knew she was missing, but... murdered?"

Logan nodded. Behind him, Caitlyn had her notebook out, pen nib poised above a blank page.

"Body was discovered in the early hours of yesterday morning," Logan confirmed. "It was in the papers."

"I don't read the papers," Christopher said. He stared at the floor by Logan's feet for a while, then muttered, "Shit," and raised his head again. "Do you know who did it?"

"Not yet. We're still trying to ascertain what happened."

Christopher's eyes widened. "Wait. Wait. Hold on. Why are you here, exactly?" he asked. "You don't think I had something to do with it?"

"Like I say, we're still trying to ascertain what happened," Logan said. "We're hoping you can help us paint a better picture of Mairi's final days."

"I didn't see her," Christopher said. The words rushed out a little too quickly, and he spent the next few seconds trying to make himself appear more relaxed than he was. His shoulders lost some of their tension, and he managed to arrange his expression into something suitably sad.

And yet, his hands gripped the edge of the desk so hard that Logan could see his knuckles turning white.

"But you spoke to her," said Caitlyn. Her voice was softer than Logan's. Encouraging. Comforting, almost.

Logan didn't know the DS very well, but he suspected this was a voice she saved especially for just this sort of occasion. He couldn't imagine her speaking like that in many other circumstances.

"Right?" she said, egging Boyd on with a nod of her head.

"Yes. I mean... Yes. But not in person. Just a few texts and a couple of calls."

"A few texts?" said Logan, seizing on the phrase. "How many texts would you say you'd exchanged? Roughly?"

Christopher puffed out his cheeks, buying himself some time. "I don't know. Quite a lot."

"Aye. Well, you're not wrong there," Logan agreed. "In fact, I'd go so far as to say it wasn't *quite* a lot. It was a lot."

He turned to Caitlyn. "DS McQuarrie, would you agree with that description?"

"Aye, sir," Caitlyn said. "It was a lot."

"It was a whole lot," Logan said, turning his attention back to the instructor. "Seems like you were close."

"No. I mean, not really. I mean... it was early days, you know?" Christopher said. "We weren't, like, what you might call... exclusive."

Another turn of the head in Caitlyn's direction. "What does he mean by that?"

"He was shagging other women, sir," said Caitlyn. Her softly-softly tone had hardened already. Logan was surprised it had lasted as long as it had.

"Aye. Thought that's what he was saying," Logan agreed. He looked back at Christopher and gave a disapproving shake of his head. "Did Mairi know?"

"Yes! We weren't... It wasn't like... It was just a thing, you know? Just, like, I don't know. Flirting, I suppose."

"Six hundred plus texts in a fortnight? That's a lot of chat-up lines," Logan said. "What were you doing, sending them one letter at a time?"

"No, I—"

"She texted you on Saturday morning," Logan said.

Christopher hesitated, expecting a question to follow.

"Yes," he said, when one didn't arrive. "We were supposed to be meeting up."

"Why?" Logan asked.

"Just, like, lunch. I was going to give her a lesson, then we were going for lunch."

Christopher looked suddenly flustered, like he might've just incriminated himself. "But she cancelled. That was the text. She said she had a headache, and couldn't come."

He fumbled for his phone. "Here, look. I kept it."

With a few taps and swipes, he brought the thread of messages up and passed the phone to Logan. The DCI kept drilling into the instructor with his stare, and passed the phone over to Caitlyn.

"He's right, sir," the DS said, skimming through the last few messages. "They arranged it on Friday morning, but she cancelled on Saturday. He sent a few follow-up messages, but no reply."

"And through the following week!" Christopher said, directing her attention further down the thread. "Look, I tried messaging and calling her half a dozen times to ask where she was! If I'd killed her, I wouldn't do that, would I?"

Logan continued to hold the man's gaze. Christopher seemed to shrivel before his eyes.

"Well, I mean, I suppose I might," he muttered. "But I didn't! I didn't see her since her lesson the week before."

"Too busy with your other lady friends?" Logan asked.

"Too busy with work. We both were," Christopher protested. "She wanted to keep it low key. Said she didn't want her son getting confused. She was worried about her ex, too."

Logan's ears pricked up. Caitlyn stopped scrolling through the phone.

"In what way?"

Christopher shrugged. "I don't know. I think she was scared of him. I got the impression he was a nasty piece of work. They hadn't been together for years, but he still seemed to want to control her. I mean, that was the impression she gave me, anyway. I never met the guy myself. Don't think I really want to."

"So, you made arrangements on Friday morning, then the next message was... when?"

"Saturday," Christopher and Caitlyn both said at the same time.

"There's dozens of messages on Thursday, Wednesday..." Caitlyn said, scrolling back through the texts while Christopher squirmed on the desk.

"Should you be...? I'm not sure you—"

Caitlyn held up the phone. On screen was a close-up of a fully erect penis. From the expression on the DS's face, she was unimpressed on a number of levels.

"Seriously?" she said.

"It was just... She asked for it."

Logan raised an eyebrow. "Interesting choice of words, Mr Boyd."

"What? *No!* I mean... look at the messages. She egged me on. I don't just send... Just send..."

"Dick pics," said Caitlyn, finishing the sentence for him.

"Yes. Exactly. I don't just do that without... You know? Being asked."

"You're saying you don't just send pictures of your penis willy-nilly?" asked Logan. "I should hope not."

He motioned to Caitlyn. "Put that thing away, DS McQuarrie, before you have someone's eye out."

He returned his attention to Christopher. "So, dozens of messages every evening, but nothing on Friday?"

Christopher took his phone back from Caitlyn and hurriedly stuffed it in his pocket, his cheeks burning red. "No. She didn't send anything."

"And nor did you?"

"I was... out. On a... I was meeting someone."

"You were on a date," Logan said. He glanced back over his shoulder. "Is that still a thing young people do?" he asked.

"I believe so, sir."

"Although, you're nearly as old as I am, Mr Boyd," Logan said. "You'd think a man of your age would know better than to go sending photos of his boaby to women. Especially ones ten years younger."

"And a primary school teacher, sir," Caitlyn added.

"Aye. And a *primary school teacher*, at that," Logan said. He inhaled deeply through his nose, making his displeasure obvious. "Can you confirm your whereabouts over the weekend, Mr Boyd?"

Christopher's eyes blazed with panic. His hands gripped the desk again, knuckles quickly turning the colour of snow. "Uh, yes. I was here most of Saturday. One of the part-timers is off, so I'm doing Saturdays to cover."

"And Sunday?" Logan pressed.

"Sunday? Sunday. *Sunday*," Christopher said, his voice becoming lower. "What did...? Oh! Yes. Aviemore. I went across to Aviemore. There was a talk on at one of the hotels, organised by Waterstones. You know, the bookshop?"

"I'm aware of Waterstones."

"Well, I was there. I left at about ten and didn't get back until about eight."

The expression of utter relief on his face told Logan what the answer to the next question would be.

He asked it, anyway.

"Can anyone confirm that?"

"Yes! Loads of people. A few of us went over from the climbing club. We went in John's car. Maitland. John Maitland. Mountain Rescue. You might know him?"

Logan's demeanour gave nothing away.

"Well, anyway. Him. I can get you his details."

Reaching into his coat pocket, Logan produced a card.

"Please do that, Mr Boyd. And, if anything else occurs to you that you think might be useful to us, be sure to pass it on."

Christopher took the card and turned it over in his hand a couple of times, looking at it, but not really seeing. "Is... is that it?"

"For now. But I wouldn't leave the country," Logan told him. He reached over to the box with the Edelweiss branding, and tapped the cardboard. "Do you mind if I take one of these?"

Christopher's eyes went to the box, then back to the detective. "A rope?"

"Aye. Would you mind?"

The request had clearly caught the instructor off guard. After a few moments spent alternating between different confused looks, he shrugged and nodded. "Sure. If you like."

Logan nodded to Caitlyn, and Christopher watched as she pulled on a pair of rubber gloves and fished out a clear plastic evidence bag.

"Much appreciated," Logan told him, as Caitlyn carefully placed the rope in the bag. "I've always wanted one of these."

Christopher watched, silent and impassive, as Caitlyn ziplocked and tagged the bag.

That done, Logan nodded his approval. "Nice to meet you, Mr Boyd," he said. He regarded the man and his office for a moment. "We'll be in touch."

CHAPTER TWENTY-TWO

MAIRI SINCLAIR'S PARENTS LIVED IN ONE OF THE NEW houses out near ASDA. With a bit of imagination, you could almost convince yourself it was on the way back to Ben Forde's house. And, after dropping Caitlyn back at the station car park and telling her to knock off for the night, Logan did exactly that.

"Is that Mairi?" Logan asked, motioning with his cup and saucer to a framed photo on the wall. It showed a young woman in her late teens or early twenties. She looked unimpressed at having her picture taken. Possibly embarrassed by the inch-thick black eyeliner and brows that could've been drawn on with a Sharpie, Logan reckoned.

"Her *Goth phase*," sighed Mr Sinclair. Clearly, he hadn't approved at the time, and Mairi's death had done nothing to change his opinion. "The less said about that, the better."

Malcolm looked better than he had when Logan had met him at the campsite earlier. Logan had been braced to find him sitting rocking back and forth in the corner, but he'd clearly had a talk with himself and now looked more angry than upset. He hadn't mentioned their previous meeting, and Logan had made a point of not bringing it up, either.

Elaine Sinclair, Malcolm's wife, was sitting on the couch beside him, a few-feet-wide gulf of couch between them. She crossed it just long enough to slap him on the thigh and tut her disapproval.

"Oh, shut up, Malcolm," she snapped. Her face was thin and gaunt. Not a recent development, Logan thought, but he doubted the past few days had done much to help. "She was only into it for a year or so," Mrs Sinclair explained to the detective. "Snapped out of it shortly after Stuart was born."

"When she got shot of that arsehole, you mean," Malcolm Sinclair grunted.

Logan cocked his head back a little.

"Steadwood," Malcolm said. He spat the word out, like he couldn't bear the taste of it. "Ruined her bloody life, he did."

"Oh, behave. You're being dramatic."

"Dramatic? What are you talking about, Elaine?" Malcolm blustered. "He turned her against us. Against all of us."

"She was a teenager. They all turn against their parents sooner or later!"

"Michelle didn't!"

"Yes, she did. Just in a different way," Elaine insisted. "She went all... churchy."

"What's wrong with that?"

"I didn't say there was anything *wrong* with it."

"Better a Christian than a bloody ghoul!"

"Goth, Malcolm. *Goth!*"

Malcolm scowled across the desert of couch that lay between them. "You know what I meant!"

Logan watched the argument unfolding over the rim of his cup. Malcolm Sinclair wasn't coming across particularly well at this point, but there was no denying that the man made a fine cup of tea.

Elaine Sinclair took a cushion that was wedged between her and the arm of the couch, plumped it up on her lap, then set it back down, this time between her and her husband so there was no longer just a gulf between them, but a wall.

They'd been like this since Logan had arrived. Picking away at the scabs of a relationship he suspected should have been over years ago. The death of a loved one—particularly under such horrific circumstances—was often a 'make or break' point in a relationship. Sometimes, it brought families closer, strengthening bonds that were already there, and helping to heal any cracks that may have started to appear.

Often, though—more often—it went the other way. Grief took those hairline cracks and made them fractures. Over the course of longer investigations, Logan had seen even the strongest relationships fall apart. Given that the Sinclairs didn't seem to be on a particularly solid footing at this stage, he didn't fancy their chances.

"Do you mind me asking what happened?" said Logan, sitting his cup back in the saucer, then setting them both down on the side table Mrs Sinclair had dragged out of the corner for his benefit. "With Robbie Steadwood, I mean?"

"Ugh. He got her pregnant for a bloody start," Malcolm said. "She was sixteen. He was, what? Twenty?"

Malcolm breathed deeply, forcing himself to relax. His head was shaking from side to side, as if denying everything he was saying.

"He'd got her into drugs before that, of course. Oh, yes. *Cannabis*. She used to reek of it."

"She said it was only once," Mrs Sinclair told Logan. "And I believed her."

"Because you're a gullible bloody idiot," her husband muttered.

"Oh, *shut up*, Malcolm."

Logan decided not to tell them about the toxicology report on Mairi's body, if only to stop Malcolm Sinclair lording it over his wife as some sort of victory.

"They were only together about a year," Elaine said. "They broke up while Mairi was pregnant with Stuart."

A fond expression played briefly across her face as she thought of her grandson. It was the closest Logan thought he'd get to seeing her smile. It was probably the closest she'd come to smiling in a very long time.

"*He* dumped *her*, would you believe?" Malcolm said. "Him a bloody... I don't know... child-molesting junkie, and her from a good family. And she *was* a child, Elaine," he stressed, anticipating an interjection from his wife. "She might've been sixteen when she got pregnant, but do you think he hadn't had his way with her before then? Honestly? You ask me, he should've been bloody jailed."

Mr Sinclair leaned forward, locking eyes with Logan. "He was, eventually, you know? Locked up, I mean. Not for what he did to Mairi, but he was thrown in jail."

"I was aware of that, Mr Sinclair, yes," Logan confirmed.

"You should've kept him in. You should've thrown away the bloody key. Maybe if you had, then Mairi wouldn't—"

A sob caught in his throat. No, not a sob. A *sound*. It was something primal. Something broken. The kind of sound a wounded animal might make when it realised that all hope was lost.

His movements, which had been driven by anger, suddenly lost all their energy. His hands fell onto the cushions beside him, and everything about him just sort of sagged into the couch, like whatever strings had been holding him up had all been cut at once.

He coughed and cleared his throat several times. It reminded Logan of someone desperately trying to turn over an engine that was refusing to kick in.

Elaine's hand slid across the cushion and rested on top of her husband's. Her fingers interlocked with his and squeezed. They didn't look at each other. They didn't have to. That touch had said it all.

Maybe those cracks didn't run too deep, after all.

Logan's phone buzzed in his coat pocket. He checked it quickly, saw a message from Ben asking him where the bloody hell he was with a lot of question marks on the end, and slipped the phone away again.

"News?" asked Elaine.

"No. Sorry. Another matter," Logan told her. His eyes went back to the wall again. There were dozens of photos in all, each one individually framed in mismatching styles and colours. Younger incarnations of Mr and Mrs Sinclair appeared in a few of them, but mostly they showed Mairi and Michelle, with a couple of Stuart's school photos in amongst them.

"The girls were inseparable when they were younger," Elaine said, following the DCI's gaze. "So alike, too. When I look back at some of the pictures I have to stop and think which one I'm looking at. They've always stayed similar. Even on the phone, you can never tell who's who, they sound so much alike."

She glanced down for a moment.

"Sounded."

"Of course, Robbie Steadwood put paid to that, too," Malcolm grunted.

Elaine sighed. Her hand returned to her side of the barricade. "God, what are you talking about now? How on Earth did Robbie Steadwood stop them looking and sounding alike?"

"Not that! Being close, I mean. Ruined their relationship, he did. After he came along, Mairi had no interest in Michelle. None."

"Because she was sixteen, and Michelle was ten, Malcolm," Elaine explained. To her credit, she was trying to be patient. She just wasn't being particularly successful. "She was becoming an adult, and Michelle was still just a child. Of course, they were going to drift apart."

"It wasn't a drift, it was a bloody schism!"

"Oh, shut up."

Malcolm muttered under his breath and shifted around in his seat, but chose not to argue any further.

"Michelle was always so good with Stuart, though," Elaine said, smiling fondly. "They've always been very close. More like brother and sister than nephew and auntie."

"We told him he could come stay here, of course," said Malcolm, sounding maybe a touch put out. "When Mairi went missing. We've got a spare bedroom. But he opted for Michelle's, in the end."

"She's closer to his age. And, like I say, they've always got on. More like brother and sister, than anything," she reiterated.

The rest of the conversation played out pretty much as Logan had been expecting. Mr Sinclair had some very strong thoughts when Logan asked if they could think of anyone who might have wanted to hurt their daughter. They concerned Robbie Steadwood and involved what was, to Logan's ears, some fairly light swearing, but which seemed to shock Mrs Sinclair no end.

"Malcolm!"

"Well, he *is* a wee arsehole, Elaine. There's no two ways about it!"

Logan had quickly steered the conversation back on track, while ignoring the insistent buzzing of his phone in his pocket.

"When did you last see Mairi?"

"A few weeks ago," Elaine said. "She usually popped around a few times a month, but she hadn't been around in a while."

"Any reason for that you can think of?" Logan asked.

"No."

"No fallings out?"

"No. What are you saying? Nothing like that!" Elaine said, visibly offended.

"I'm not saying anything, Mrs Sinclair. Just trying to get a full picture," Logan said.

After a couple of further questions, he decided that enough was enough. The Sinclairs were flagging now, their grief wilting them before his eyes. There was more to be had from them, he was sure, but he'd heard all he needed to for the moment.

"I'll see myself out, you're fine," he said, waving Elaine back into her seat when she made a move to stand and show him the door. "If you think of anything else, or there's anything you need, just give us a call. Either I or one of my team will be right out with you."

"Thank you, Mr Logan," Elaine said, clutching the card he'd given her right before he'd stood up. "We will."

"Please," Logan said, smiling grimly. "Call me Jack."

THE DOOR to the Focus shut with a comforting *thunk* as Logan pulled it closed behind him. A quick glance at his phone showed two missed calls from Ben and four texts, each one less amused than the one before. Logan's dinner was now 'in the dog,' apparently. Considering the Fordes didn't have any pets, Logan wasn't quite sure whose dog it was in, but it was in someone's.

Chippy on the way back, then. He dimly recalled there being a *Harry Ramsden's* nearby somewhere, although he couldn't quite place where.

He was about to type out a quick apology when the screen lit up with an incoming call from a local 01463 number he didn't recognise.

"Logan," he said, pressing the phone to his ear.

The voice on the other end hesitated, caught off-guard by the speed of the response. "Uh, hello, sir. It's Sinead. PC Bell, I mean."

"Sinead. Hello."

"I swung by the station, sir. You weren't there, so I thought... I hope you don't mind me calling? It just seemed like you wanted to ask me something."

She was good.

"Aye. Thanks. It was just a general thing, really. Just..."

He glanced up at the Sinclairs' house, then checked his rear-view mirror, like he might find someone there listening in. There was only one other car parked on the street—a black Audi—sitting a good forty feet behind him. Someone was in the driver's seat, but short of maybe the Six-Million Dollar Man, nobody could be listening in from that distance.

"I feel bad even asking it, but did you think—"

"That Michelle is a bit touchy-feely with Stuart?"

Logan exhaled, like all his nasty little suspicions had somehow just been vindicated.

"Aye! Exactly. There was a lot of patting and stroking going on there, wasn't there?"

"It's pretty constant, sir, yeah," Sinead agreed. "Caught me off guard a bit to start with, but I think it's maybe just how she is with him. But probably amplified, given the circumstances."

Logan ran his tongue across his teeth. She was probably right, of course. The Sinclairs had told him that Michelle and Stuart had always been close. 'Like brother and sister,' Elaine had said. Emphasised it twice, in fact.

She was comforting the boy, that was all.

Almost certainly.

"The sister's got an alibi for the Sunday, aye?"

"Church in the morning, then Aerial Hoop in the afternoon."

Logan's silence spoke volumes.

"It's a fitness thing, sir. They do it at the leisure centre. And Stuart was streaming online on Twitch from around twelve through until five."

Another silence.

"It's like TV for gamers. He was broadcasting live most of the day."

"Right. Aye. Fair enough," Logan said, briefly wondering when he became so completely out of touch with... well, everything, it seemed. "And you're probably right about all the physical contact stuff. It's probably nothing. But keep an eye on it, will you?"

"I'm not back in until Sunday, but I've already passed it on," Sinead said. "I'm going with them to Mairi's birthday thing in the afternoon."

Logan wracked his brain for information on a birthday thing, but drew a blank.

"Some of the teachers at the school arranged it. It's at four o'clock. The kids from Mairi's class are all going to release paper boats they made into the loch. They've invited her family along."

"Right. Sounds... nice, I suppose."

"Maybe if they weren't doing it from the spot the body was found."

"No!"

Sinead gave a chuckle. "Aye. Someone at the school thought it was a good idea."

"And nobody thought to dissuade them?" Logan asked. "I mean, Jesus Christ. 'Say goodbye to your teacher, kids. Oh, and by the way, this was where her eyeless mutilated corpse was first dragged ashore.'"

"I doubt that's the wording they'll use, sir," Sinead said. "They'll probably paraphrase it a bit."

"Aye. Maybe for the best," he agreed.

"I'll let you know how it goes. And, like I say, I've passed on the touchy-feely thing. Whoever's on tomorrow should take note."

"Good. You're doing well," Logan told her, and he could practically hear her shoulders straighten all the way down the line. "Keep it up," he added, then immediately felt like a patronising old bastard and wished he could take it back.

"Will do, sir."

"Right. Good. Well, enjoy your day off, constable."

"Harris has friends coming over. I'd rather be on traffic duty, to be honest," Sinead said.

"I'm sure that could be arranged," Logan told her. "Have fun."

"Definitely won't."

Logan gave a dry little chuckle. "No. I wouldn't imagine so. Bye, Sinead."

"Bye, sir," she said. Then: "Oh, sir?"

"Aye?"

"Did you...? You know? Your daughter? You said you were going to get in touch."

When Logan didn't answer immediately, she jumped back in.

"Sorry. Shouldn't have asked. None of my business. Sorry."

"I did get in touch, yes," the DCI told her, although he wasn't entirely sure why. "We... made arrangements to have lunch."

"That's great!"

"She didn't turn up."

It was Sinead's turn to miss a beat.

"Oh," she eventually said. "I... Oh."

"Goodnight, constable."

"Goodnight, sir."

And with that, Logan jabbed the button to disconnect the call. He rattled off a quick 'on my way,' text to Ben, then tossed the phone onto the passenger seat.

"Right," he breathed, firing up the engine. "Where's that bloody chippy?"

Logan pulled away from the kerb and drove off down the street, leaving the Sinclair's house behind.

A few seconds later, the only other car on the street hummed into life and came creeping after him.

CHAPTER TWENTY-THREE

THERE WAS A SOLEMN AIR ABOUT THE INCIDENT ROOM THE next morning that immediately made Logan uneasy.

He'd had another sleepless night spent in the Fordes' spare room. The first few hours had been spent running over the details of the case, then the deepening darkness and increasing tiredness had conspired to drag his mind back to past failures, both personal and professional.

He thought of the Sinclairs' house, with all those family photos on the walls. He had a couple of photos of Madison when she was younger, he thought, but they were in a box somewhere, and she hadn't looked particularly happy.

But then, none of them had. Not then.

And, in his case, not since.

Jumping back into things at the station was going to sort him out, he'd thought, but the long faces of the rest of the team, and the way none of them were meeting his eye told him that things were not about to start well.

"What?" he demanded. "What now?"

DS McQuarrie looked to Tyler and Hamza to see if either

of them were going to volunteer the information, but neither of them showed any signs that they might be about to open their mouths.

"Guessing you haven't seen the papers, sir?" she said.

"What papers?"

Caitlyn winced. "All of them."

Tyler held up a copy of *The Sun*. The sight of that rag got on Logan's tits at the best of times, but the headline splashed across the front now almost brought his blood to an immediate rolling boil.

"Monster attack?" he spat. "Fucking *monster attack*? What's this shite?"

"You're joking," Ben groaned, taking the paper from Caitlyn. He held it at arm's length, either because of his eyesight, or because he didn't want to get too close to the bloody thing.

"Your woman that was in yesterday, sir," said Tyler. "The Nessie hunter. With the photos. She went to the press."

"Big time," added Hamza.

He held up copies of *The Daily Record* and the Scottish edition of *The Daily Mail*. Both sported similar headlines and scenic images of Loch Ness, although neither had gone as far as *The Sun*, which had an artist's impression of the monster leering out from the water right below the headline.

"Bastards!" Logan barked.

"Is that... Is that blood around its mouth?" Ben asked, studying the image more closely.

"Utter *bastards*!"

Caitlyn quietly cleared her throat. "Would now be a bad time to tell you it's all over the internet, too, sir?" she ventured. "They're running with the story in the foreign press, too."

A vein on Logan's temple pulsed a troubling shade of

purple. He clenched and unclenched his fists, his nostrils flaring as he fought to compose himself.

"Still, at least—" Tyler began brightly.

Logan stabbed a finger at him.

"Don't!" he warned. "I want you to think very carefully about what you were going to say. *Very* carefully."

Tyler hesitated. He gave a little cough.

"Nothing, boss," he said.

"That woman and her fucking photos!" Logan spat. He looked around. "What did we do with them, anyway?"

Ben folded up the newspaper he was holding, then filed it in the bin.

"Exhibits Officer we borrowed from CID has bagged them and checked them in," he said, motioning to a cluttered desk in the corner of the room. There were assorted sizes of plastic bags laid across it, each containing something pertinent to the case.

Even in a case like this one, where they had almost bugger all in the way of clues, let alone actual evidence, the amount of clutter in wee plastic bags soon started to pile up. Logan was in no mood to sift through that lot just to find some photos which he was essentially just planning to glare angrily at, so he just shot a vague look of contempt in the direction of all the wee bags, instead.

"Right. It is what it is," he said, after a bit more deep breathing. "That's the bad news, what's the good news? Because I'm *really* hoping you have some good news to give me."

A few wary looks were exchanged. Logan's deep-breathing became a groan.

"What now?"

"Tests on the tarp taken from Boleskine House came back," said Ben, offering himself up as sacrifice. "No match to the one used to wrap Mairi Sinclair."

Logan buried his face in his hands, and the Incident Room was filled with the sound of muffled swearing.

The others waited for him to emerge from behind his hands again. He raised and lowered his shoulders and cricked his neck around, trying to ward off the tension that was building there.

"It is what it is," he said again. It hadn't sounded particularly convincing the first time, but that performance had seemed Oscar-worthy compared to the second attempt. He turned to Caitlyn and Hamza. "And there was nothing at any of the other sites?"

"No, sir," Hamza confirmed.

"You checked them all?"

"Yes, sir."

Beside Hamza, Caitlyn's face fell. "Shit."

"DS McQuarrie?" asked Logan. His voice was flat and level, but carried a distinct promise that this could change quite quickly. "What's the problem?"

Caitlyn shot Hamza a sideways look. "The path, sir. The path repairs. We didn't check there."

Logan consumed half the air in the room in one big sniff. DC Neish sidestepped away from Caitlyn and Hamza as quietly and casually as possible.

"What?" Logan asked.

He didn't need to ask the question. He already knew the answer. He was asking for their sake, not his. He was giving them a chance to change their mind. To correct their statement. To tell him that they were 'just joking, sir,' and reveal that they weren't actually the pair of useless bastards they were currently claiming to be.

"My fault, sir," said Caitlyn. "Once we had the tarp at Bole-skine, I thought—"

"Bollocks. It was my fault," Hamza said. "I was struggling,

and it's a steep walk down to the site. I'd been moaning about it the whole way there."

"He hadn't, sir," Caitlyn insisted. "I was the senior officer, I should've—"

"Aye, too fucking right you should've!" Logan barked, throwing his arms up. "I mean, Jesus Christ, what were you thinking? You had one job. *One*. 'Check out all those building sites.' Remember me saying that to you? Remember that? Key word, 'all.'"

"Jack," said Ben. "Mistakes happen. You know that."

Logan spun, eyes practically bulging. "*What?*" he asked, for much the same reason as he had the last time.

Ben, however, wasn't having it.

"You heard me. And you know I'm right," the DI said. He rocked back on his heels and crossed his arms across his barrel-like chest. "Now, do you want to keep storming about and ranting, or will we crack on with being the polis and try to solve this case?"

They faced each other down. Logan was much taller than Ben, but the sight of him there all red-faced and with steam practically billowing from his nostrils didn't seem to faze the older detective in the slightest.

"Your wife's cooking is shite, by the way," Logan told him, but the bluster had already started to fade.

"Aye. You're not wrong," Ben agreed.

He gave the DCI a clap on the arm, then walked past him and addressed the others.

"Right. Obviously, there was an issue on this occasion. All those sites should've been checked."

Caitlyn and Hamza both nodded.

"Of course, sir," the DS said, folding her hands behind her back. "Won't happen again."

"Oh, it probably will," Ben said. "Not this, specifically, but mistakes happen. Wasn't the first time, certainly won't be the last. There's no avoiding that. What matters is how we deal with those mistakes afterwards."

He gestured to the two officers responsible for this particular balls-up. "DS McQuarrie, DC Khaled, you two will go back to Foyers and check out that site. Snoop around, see what's there to be seen, but don't get too involved."

"Yes, sir," Caitlyn said.

Hamza didn't look overly excited by the prospect, but nodded his agreement. "Sir."

Ben turned his attention to Logan. "Jack, we've got the teacher coming in this morning. Shayne Turner."

"The fit one," Tyler added. He rubbed his hands together, then stopped when he saw the vein on Logan's temple double in size again.

"I thought she was coming in yesterday?" Logan said.

"Aye, well, maybe if you hadn't been out gallivanting until the wee small hours, you'd have known she couldn't make it in yesterday. Parents evening. We told her this morning would be fine."

"I was back at yours by quarter to nine," Logan protested, but it fell on deaf ears.

Alice Forde had given him the cold shoulder when he'd arrived at the house with a *McDonald's* brown paper bag. He hadn't been able to find a chip shop, and while he knew there was one across the road from the station, he also knew that if he went there he'd only end up heading back to work.

Her husband hadn't been overly impressed by Logan's later-than-expected arrival, either, and Logan's peace offering of a Creme Egg McFlurry had done nothing to ease the tension.

Ben had eaten it, mind. Wolfed it down, in fact. It just

hadn't stopped him being a miserable bugger for the rest of the evening.

Logan shook his head. "Change of plan. Ben, you and DS McQuarrie handle the interview. I'll take the boy and check out the site."

Tyler snorted and shot Hamza a patronising look. "Ha! 'The boy.'"

He felt Logan's eyes on him. His smirk fell away as the penny dropped. "Wait. Who's the boy? I'm not the boy, am I?"

"Aye, son," said Ben. "You're the boy."

"Why am I the boy?!" Tyler yelped.

"We were all boys once," Ben said. He looked Tyler up and down. "Some of us just grew out of it quicker than others."

"I'm not having you mooching around the place when the teacher's in, oozing hormones behind you like a slug," Logan told him. "So, you're with me."

It looked like it was taking all Tyler's effort not to throw up his hands and stamp his feet, but he managed to keep a lid on it. "Right, boss," he said, the words coming out as a sort of hollow sigh. "Fair enough."

"Hamza, follow up on those symbols. See if anything else has come in. And get me an update on Robbie Steadwood. The more I hear about that wee scrote, the keener I am to meet him."

"Right, sir. And I found something already," Hamza said. "The holes in the skull? More occult stuff. It's meant to be a way of letting demons out."

"Sounds scientific," said Tyler.

"Aye, I'm not saying it actually works, like," Hamza replied. "Just that's what people used to believe, and some civilisations still use it to cure cases of demonic possession." He looked slightly embarrassed by the explanation. "Note, there should've been quotation marks around a lot of the words in that last sentence."

Logan's frown, which was never far away, took up residency on his face. "So, what are we looking at? Some sort of Exorcism?"

"Very possibly, sir. Might even be possible to tie in the missing eye thing. I mean, if you're a believer in that sort of thing, what do you do if someone's giving you the literal evil eye?"

"Pop 'em out," said Tyler.

Hamza nodded. "Pop them out."

Logan took a few moments to consider all this, but remained non-committal.

"Right. All interesting stuff," he said. He clicked his fingers at DC Neish. "Tyler, with me. Let's go."

"You'll need to be back by one," Ben told Logan. "Hoon wants to see you."

"Hoon? Bob Hoon? Is he up here now?"

Ben nodded. "Aye. He made Detective Superintendent."

Logan tapped himself on the side of the head. "Shite. Aye. Of course he did. I knew that."

"He's suggesting a press conference to try to nip the monster business in the bud. Emailed me about it in the early hours of the morning. Wants to see us both."

"Right. Fair enough," said Logan, nodding. "Wait a minute. So, you knew about all the monster shite in the papers before we got here?"

"Hm? Oh, aye," said Ben. He glanced across to the others and smiled. "But there was no bloody way I was going to be the one to break it to you."

CHAPTER TWENTY-FOUR

DC NEISH HAD NEVER HEARD A HUMAN BEING GROWL before. Not really.

Sure, he'd heard people say things in a way that *implied* growling. He'd heard people pretend to growl. *Attempt* to growl. He'd even once had a girlfriend who used to make all manner of animal noises in the right sort of situation.

But he'd never *actually* heard another human being growl before.

Until now.

It started when Logan saw the press photographers, then rose in his throat when he realised what they were taking pictures of.

A group of twenty or so men and women stood posing in the campsite car park, their arms filled with cuddly Nessie toys, fishing nets, and various other props. The loch formed a backdrop, framed on either side by the conifers that marked the edge of the campsite.

It had barely been forty-eight hours since Mairi Sinclair's

body had been found, and now this... this *pantomime* was taking place just metres from where she'd washed ashore.

Logan roared the Focus up behind the photographers, then slammed on the brakes, spraying gravel behind the car as he skidded it to a stop.

He was out of the car before Tyler had unclipped his belt, and didn't have time to warn the photographer who'd come closest to being hit before the man could open his mouth.

"What's your fucking game, mate?" the photographer demanded. "Driving like a bloody maniac."

Tyler unfastened his belt, but decided it was probably safest to stay in the car for now.

"Who are you?" Logan demanded, pointing at the man who had spoken to him.

"What?"

"You heard me. Who are you? What's your name?"

"None of your business, that's who."

A female photographer turned to Logan, camera raised. His head snapped in her direction, anger blazing behind his eyes. "Press that button. I dare you."

The woman's finger hovered over the camera's shutter release, but then she sensibly lowered it without taking a picture.

"Aye, thought so," Logan said, scowling.

Tyler got out of the car and stood behind his boss as Logan produced his warrant card and held it up for everyone to see. "Detective Chief Inspector Logan. Senior Investigating Officer in the murder of Mairi Sinclair," he announced.

Once he was sure they'd all had a good look at the card and knew he was telling the truth, he closed it over and put it back in the pocket of his coat.

"I'm going to say this once and once only," he said. "So, it's in all your best interests if you listen, and listen carefully."

He cleared his throat, glanced across their faces to make sure they were all paying attention, then jabbed a thumb back over his shoulder. "Fuck off."

There was some silence from the press, some anxious murmuring from the people with the props.

"Did I stutter?" Logan asked Tyler. The younger detective shook his head.

"No, boss."

"No, I didn't think so. And yet, they haven't fucked off like I told them to," Logan said, turning his glare back on both groups.

It was then that he spotted her. The instigator of this whole bloody thing. The madwoman with the monster photos, Marion Whitehead.

"You. You caused all this... this... Whatever this shite is," Logan snapped, eyes boring into the woman while his hands gestured vaguely at the gathering of people and press.

Logan didn't consider the press themselves to be 'people'. They were cockroaches. Lower than that, even. If cockroaches got parasites, that's what the press were.

"Good morning, sergeant!" Marion chirped, elbowing her way through her gaggle of cronies. "I am indeed responsible for all this excitement. See? I told you those photographs were dynamite!"

She stood in front of Logan, barely two-thirds his height but all peacocked up with pride.

"It's my pleasure, though, sergeant. You don't have to thank me."

One of Logan's eyes twitched.

"*Thank you?*"

"Like I say, no thanks necessary," beamed Marion.

Tyler jumped in before Logan exploded.

"Hi. Detective Constable Neish," he said, smiling at both groups in turn.

None of the press pack had started firing out questions, suggesting they were all photographers and not reporters. This was a staged photo-opp at the moment, and nothing more.

The crowd with the props were a mixed-bag. Weirdos mostly, but a couple of oddballs in there, too. You could see it a mile away.

"And you are... monster hunters, is that right?" Tyler asked.

There was some excited chattering from the group, but none of them actually confirmed or denied this until Marion piped up.

"Bang on, sonny! We're all members of the same Facebook group. We are the Paranormal Investigation Society Scotland."

"Right. Very cool," Tyler said. "It's just—"

"Piss," said Logan.

Tyler hesitated. "Boss?"

"Paranormal Investigation Society Scotland. *PISS*."

The younger detective snorted, but Logan wasn't amused. Tyler's interjection had bought him a few seconds to bring his temper under control, but it was still bubbling away below the surface, ready to erupt at one wrong word.

"A woman died here. A mother," Logan said. "She was murdered by a human being, no' a monster."

"How can you be so sure?" asked a man from the Nessie-hunting group. His accent was North of England, but he wore a tartan bunnet with a ginger wig attached, and carried a cuddly Loch Ness Monster under one arm.

"Because there's no such fucking thing," Logan barked, feeling the fury surging through his veins again.

"Obviously, you didn't look at those photos," sniffed Marion.

"I knew you wouldn't. None are so blind as those who will not see."

"Well, unless you lot want to see the inside of a jail cell, I suggest you pack up all your shite and go back to where you came from," Logan said. He glowered at the photographers. "And that goes for you, too."

"You can't do that," the female photographer who'd briefly considered taking Logan's picture said. "You can't arrest us."

"Can't I? You think? Will we find out?" Logan asked her.

His head tick-tocked between both groups. Marion was still standing at the front of the PISS Squad, or whatever the hell they were calling themselves, but she was less puffed-up now than she had been a moment ago.

"No, thought not," Logan said. "If you want to go play dress-up, do it somewhere else. A woman died."

He yanked the *See-You-Jimmy* hat off the Northerner's head and threw it to the ground. "Have some damn respect."

He marched through the group, shouldering them aside and forcing them to stumble out of his path. Tyler scurried along behind him, and almost collided with the DCI's back when he stopped and turned.

"And if any of you get in the way of my murder investigation," he spat, "I'll drown you in your own fucking acronym."

———

TYLER HURRIED along the uneven path, struggling to keep up with Logan's much longer strides. The DCI had spent the first twenty seconds of the walk ranting about 'those sad bastards,' but had then fallen into a sort of seething silence that had lasted for the past several minutes.

At first, Tyler had tried making conversation, but Logan

hadn't risen to any of it, and now the pace and the uneven terrain were taking their toll, and Tyler was more focused on breathing than making small talk.

Most of the path had been hewn out of the side of a hill that ran alongside the loch. They'd been climbing for a while, picking their way across rocky stretches, and striding across channels made for little streams that ran down the hillside to the water below.

Occasionally, they'd come to a bridge, or a stretch of the path that had clearly been worked on in recent months, and would enjoy a few moments of strolling on flat ground, before the surface fractured into another few hundred yards of wobbly rocks and gravel.

But the views, though. God, the views.

Now they were that bit higher, they could see a good couple of miles along Loch Ness in both directions. The sky was overcast, and the water was more grey than blue, but it still would've been breathtaking, had either of them any breath left to give.

"You sure... this is... the right way?" Tyler wheezed, each little clump of words punctuated by a heave of his chest.

"So Hamza tells me, aye," Logan said, his own breathing almost as laboured as Tyler's.

He stopped at a bend and leaned on the railing that had been erected along the side of the path that overlooked the water. It was a nasty drop from here. A couple of hundred feet, with a few bounces on the way to the water. If you were lucky, you'd hit the grass, but more likely you'd be smashed against one of the big boulders that dotted the hillside below.

"There must be an easier way than this," Tyler complained. "We must've walked miles."

"Yer arse. Less than a mile," Logan said. "And, aye, there is an easier way."

Tyler blinked. "What?"

"There's a path from up top. By the cafe. Leads you right down."

"What?" Tyler said again. "Then why did we come this way?"

"Wanted to see how far it was from the camp to the building site," Logan said. He was bringing his breathing back under control now, and Tyler groaned when the DCI set off marching again. "This is the most direct route."

"Why does that matter?" the younger detective asked.

"Because we're assuming the body was dumped elsewhere," Logan said. "For all we know at the moment, she was killed on-site or nearby, then dumped right where she was found. You said yourself, it's not tidal, so there's not a huge amount of movement in the water."

"So, what...?" Tyler panted. "You think someone could've killed her up here, then carried her down?"

"No, I don't think that. I'm ruling out possibilities," Logan corrected.

"Aye, well, I think we can safely rule this one out, boss," Tyler said. "No way anyone's lugging a corpse all this way."

Logan didn't like to agree with DC Neish if it could be helped, but there wasn't much else for it on this occasion. "No. Can't see it," he agreed. "Now, keep up. We should be almost there."

CHAPTER TWENTY-FIVE

"Thanks for coming in," said Ben, smiling warmly at the woman in the chair on the other side of the table. "Tea? Coffee?"

"Uh, no," said Shayne Turner. "Thanks."

Her accent was Australian, with that implied question-mark on the end of everything that came out of her mouth. Her hair was dark, cut short and choppy, and perfectly compli-mented the golden-brown of her skin tone. Everything about her was small and slight, except her eyes, which seemed cartoonishly wide.

Not for the first time since Shayne had arrived in the build-ing, Ben was thankful that DC Neish wasn't here.

Shayne's cartoon eyes went from DI Forde to DS McQuar-rie, who stood just behind and off to the side of the seated senior officer. Caitlyn's arms were crossed, and her expression carried none of the warmth that Ben's did.

"Should I... Should I have a lawyer?" Shayne asked.

"You can do, if you like. We may use some of what you tell us in court," Ben said. "But you're not under arrest or any of that stuff, Miss Turner. You're not suspected of anything. This is just a chat. We're just hoping you can help us clarify a few things about Mairi Sinclair. Square away a few details, sort of thing."

At the mention of the victim's name, Shayne stiffened. At the same time, her face seemed to crumple.

"I still can't believe what happened," the teacher said.

"What *did* happen?" asked Ben. The question took her by surprise, and he cranked up his smile a little. "From your point of view, I mean. When was the last time you saw Mairi?"

"Friday," Shayne said. "Not... I don't... Last Friday, I mean. Not yesterday."

"We understand," said Ben. "Last Friday...?"

"After school. Well, at the end of the day. We were just, you know, like chatting? Just catching up, or whatever. Then, she left, and... Well. I guess she died."

"How did she seem?" Ben asked. "And are you sure I can't get you something? Water, maybe?"

Shayne shook her head. "I'm fine, thanks. She seemed fine. A little stressed, maybe, but it had been a long week. We've got OFSTED coming in in a couple of weeks, so it's all a bit hectic."

"Gotcha. I don't envy you that. Good luck with it."

Shayne allowed herself a brief smile. "Thanks," she said, then she flicked her gaze to Caitlyn, and the smile fell away again.

"Was she more stressed than usual, would you say?" Ben pressed.

Shayne considered this, then shrugged. "Dunno. Hard to say. Maybe a little. She said something about her ex. I think he was back on the scene in some way. Think she'd had a fight with her dad about it."

"Her dad?"

"Yeah. Reckon that's what she said. I think there's some history there. Don't think her dad likes her ex much."

She gave a sort of half-shrug and a little wave of a hand. "But, I don't know. Just how it seemed. I might be wrong."

There was a scratching of pen on paper. Caitlyn had unfolded her arms now, and was jotting down notes as the conversation unfolded.

"I don't mean a *fight* fight," Shayne clarified. "Just, like, an argument. And maybe not even that. It was just the impression I got, you know?"

"We understand," Ben said again. He sighed, good-naturedly. "Families, eh?"

"Yeah. Families."

"Would you say that you and Mairi were friends?" asked Caitlyn. Her tone was more abrupt than Ben's, like she was in more of a hurry to get down to business.

Shayne hesitated. She looked from Ben to Caitlyn and back again. Ben nodded encouragingly.

"Go on."

"Uh, yes. We were friends," Shayne said.

"Close friends?" Caitlyn pressed.

"Yeah. I think so. Pretty close. She really helped me when I started at the school. Totally took me under her wing. She was pretty cool."

"More than friends?"

A frown troubled Shayne's carefully sculpted eyebrows. "What? What's that supposed to mean?"

"Were you in a sexual relationship with Mairi Sinclair?" Caitlyn asked bluntly.

"No! What? No. Nothing like that."

"But you wanted to be?"

Shayne looked to Ben for support, her already large eyes

widening further. He said nothing, just waited patiently for her to answer.

"I'm not... I don't..."

She rallied, pulling herself together, and looked Caitlyn right in the eye. "No. She was my friend. That was all. I didn't think of her in that way."

Ben took up the reins again. "Right. No. You were just friends. Close friends, like you say."

"Yeah. Exactly," said Shayne, but the way she shifted in her seat suggested she knew something more was coming. Her eyes followed a sheet of paper that Caitlyn slipped onto the desk in front of Ben.

"You kept in contact regularly?" Ben said. "Texts. Phone calls. That sort of thing?"

"Sure. Yeah. I mean, I guess so."

"You did," Ben said. He gave the paper a little wave in front of her. "We've got the records. You kept in near-constant contact, in fact."

He peered down his nose at the paper, regarding it as if for the first time. "Her? Not so much. In fact, in the twelve days prior to her disappearance, you sent her a total of two-hundred-and-seventy-two text messages."

Ben sucked air in through his teeth and looked up at Caitlyn. "Is this right, DS McQuarrie?"

"It's correct, sir, yes," Caitlyn confirmed, not taking her eyes off Shayne.

"Two-hundred-and-seventy-two. Wow. That's a lot. Isn't it? That seems like a lot."

Shayne shrugged. It came off nowhere near as nonchalantly as she was evidently aiming for.

"I text a lot."

"You do."

"I used WhatsApp back before I moved up here, but the data connection's not great out where I am," Shayne said, as if this somehow explained everything.

"Oh, aye. It can be a nightmare up here," Ben confirmed. "Government's working on it, but they've been saying that for a while. You're fine in the city centre, but once you go outside, forget it."

Ben peered over the top of the paper at the woman across the table. "Where was it you lived again?"

"Out by Dores," Shayne said. "Private rent."

"Oh, lovely. Lovely spot, that," Ben said. He sucked in his bottom lip, giving this some thought. "That's out on the Foyers road, isn't it?"

"It is, sir," Caitlyn was quick to confirm.

DI Forde sighed sadly. "Not far away from where poor Mairi was found, then."

He let that hang there for a few moments, then went back to the printout he was holding.

"So. Two-hundred-and-seventy-two text messages over twelve days. Can you remember how many times Mairi replied?"

Shayne shrugged again. This time, there was no mistaking the tension in it. "Not sure."

"Rough guess?"

"Like, I don't know, a hundred?" Shayne ventured.

"Four," said Ben.

He gave that one a few seconds to sink in, too.

"She texted you four times."

Silence.

"During that same twelve day period. Four."

"That can't be right. I'm sure it was more than that," Shayne said.

She was leaning back from the table a little now, her hands crossed in front of her, the lines of her body all straight and stiff.

"Nah, it was more than that."

"Not according to her phone records," Ben said. "Four. See?"

He turned the page around for Shayne to see. The same number had been picked out four times in yellow highlighter. "That's your number, isn't it? The last message she sent you was Sunday morning. An hour before she was last seen alive."

Shayne barely glanced at the page. "I think I should have a lawyer."

"Why? You haven't done anything, have you?" Caitlyn demanded. "What are you worried about?"

"No, but—"

"It must've been frustrating," Ben said.

Shayne's brow furrowed. "What?"

"Four replies. To all those messages. And three phone calls that she never picked up." Ben clasped his hands in front of him and offered up a sympathetic smile. "How did that make you feel?"

"Fine. She was busy. I got it."

"Did you?" asked Caitlyn. "Because you sent two-hundred-and-seventy-two messages. At what point did you *get it*, exactly?"

"It was just silly stuff. Jokes, mainly. Me bitching about the job. Most of it wasn't even looking for a reply," Shayne said. "The jokes I sent to loads of people at the same time."

"I love a good joke," said Ben, rubbing his hands together. "What sort of thing was it?"

Shayne shrugged again. "Can't remember."

"What, none of them?" asked Ben. "You can't remember a single joke you sent?"

"I don't know. Only a few were, like, jokes or whatever."

"You said 'mainly,'" Ben told her. "You said you sent, 'jokes, mainly.'"

"Are you changing your story?" Caitlyn asked.

"What? No. I mean... I just mean... They weren't *joke* jokes. Just, you know, messages about funny stuff that had happened at school. Things the kids had said. That kind of thing."

"And her message to you on Sunday?" Ben asked.

That seemed to catch the teacher off-guard a bit. "Yeah, I don't know. She replied to a joke. Just said, like, 'good one,' or whatever."

"And that was unusual?" Ben asked.

"Yeah. I guess so."

"Would you mind showing us your phone?" Caitlyn asked.

"Yes, I fucking would mind, actually," Shayne snapped. Her cheeks reddened as she focused her attention on Ben. "You said this was just a chat about Mairi, so why do I feel like I'm being interrogated by Good Cop and Bitch Cop all of a sudden? I should have a lawyer for this. You're not allowed to just keep me here without a lawyer."

"I can assure you, no one is keeping you anywhere, Miss Turner," Ben said. "We're just—"

"Oh, so I can go, then?"

Ben's hesitation lasted only a half-second, but it was enough.

"Sweet. Then see ya. I'm going," Shayne said, pushing back her chair and standing up. "If you want to speak to me again, you can go through my lawyer."

"Who would that be?" Ben asked.

This took the wind from Shayne's sails a little. "Well, I don't have one yet. But I'll get one."

She motioned to the door and shot daggers at Caitlyn. "Can you let me out?"

Caitlyn waited for the nod from DI Forde, then knocked on the door. She stepped aside as it was opened from the other side, and Shayne went thundering past her.

"See Miss Turner out, would you?" Caitlyn said to the uniformed officer in the corridor.

She turned back to Ben to find him laughing quietly.

"*Bitch Cop,*" he chuckled. "Aye, she got the measure of you, alright."

CHAPTER TWENTY-SIX

THE SIGN ON THE DOOR OF THE HUT DID NOTHING FOR Logan's mood. Tyler had seen it first, and had a full second to groan inwardly before the DCI spotted it.

"Bosco Building," he spat. "*Bosco fucking Building*! Did we know this was them? If not, why not?"

"Not sure, boss. I'll check," Tyler said.

"I mean... Jesus Christ! That's been sat here this whole time!"

"I guess so, boss."

Logan looked straight up at the sky overhead, chewed over a few angry insults, then swallowed them back down.

"Right. Well. It is what it is," he said. "Gloves and shoe coverings on."

The works hut was a small Portakabin style construction, with a flat roof, no windows, and a single door that had been secured by a sturdy-looking padlock. It was at the very end of the path, situated right on the Falls of Foyers viewpoint. Had the hut been built with windows, it would've had a cracking view of the falls as they cascaded down the steep stone wall directly across from the viewpoint.

"Where does this go?" Logan asked, as he and Tyler both pulled on gloves. "The waterfall?"

Tyler leaned over the metal barrier and peered down into the water fifty or sixty feet below. A spray of white mist rose up from where the tumbling water pummelled against the rocks. "Dunno. Into the loch, I suppose."

"Aye. That's what I was thinking," Logan said. He produced a pair of shoe coverings from his pocket and slipped them over his feet.

"I haven't got any shoe ones, boss," Tyler said.

"For f—" Logan sighed. "Fine. You'll have to stay outside. Be careful where you step."

The DCI picked his way over to the hut, gave it a quick once-over, then checked the padlock. Up close, it was even sturdier than he'd thought. Someone was keen to keep people out.

Still, way out here, unguarded like this? There was no saying what might happen. Opportunistic thieves. Teenage vandals. Anyone could come along and put a door like this in.

Logan stepped back, took aim at the lock, then drew back a foot.

"Boss!"

Logan stopped. "Look away if it bothers you, son," Logan told him.

"What? No, it's not that," Tyler said. "I was just going to say..."

Logan looked back at him over his shoulder. Tyler held up a little leather pouch that was open at the top. Several curved pieces of metal stuck up from the opening.

"...there are alternatives."

"MY WAY WOULD'VE BEEN QUICKER," said Logan.

He was watching Tyler kneeling in front of the door, digging around inside the padlock with his tools. His brow was furrowed, and his tongue was sticking out in concentration.

"You have done this before, yes?"

"Yeah, boss. I do it all the time," Tyler said. He glanced up at the DCI. "For fun, I mean. I'm not a cat burglar."

"Evidently," Logan said. "I mean, you'd struggle to make it as a sloth burglar at this rate."

He looked around, glanced at his watch, then sighed. "Watch out. I'm going to kick it in."

"Hold on... I think..."

There was a *clunk* as the top part of the lock sprung open. "Bloody hell, it worked!" Tyler exclaimed.

"What do you mean, 'it worked'? I thought you'd done it before?"

"Well, yeah, but I've got this see-through lock that lets you see what you're doing," Tyler explained, standing. "I've never tried a proper metal one before."

Logan tutted. "Now you tell me."

"Worked, didn't it?" Tyler said, slipping the tools back into the pouch.

"Aye," Logan begrudgingly conceded. "It did. Good job." He indicated the lock-picking set with a nod. "How long you been carrying that about for?"

"About two years," Tyler admitted. He slipped the set back into the pocket of his jacket and gave it a pat. "Eight quid off eBay. Worth every penny."

"Bargain," said Logan. He took hold of the door handle and

motioned for the DC to keep back. "Right. Let's see what we see."

The door opened with a long theatrical *creeeeak*. Weak sunlight spilled in through the widening gap, barely making a dent in the darkness painting the walls.

There were three cords hanging from the ceiling like old-style bathroom light switches. Logan pulled one, and a fan roared into life. He pulled it again, then tried the next one. A blast of heat rolled down on him from above the door.

Muttering, he tried the third cord. With a *ka-klack*, an overhead light came on, and the hut's secrets were revealed.

Even before his brain had processed the details of what he was seeing, Logan knew this was it. This was the place.

This was where Mairi Sinclair had died.

The inside of the hut was a clutter of tools and equipment with space left over for two people, maybe three if they all knew each other well enough.

There was a chair by the back wall—a metal number with a torn padded seat and sturdy-looking arm rests. Logan's eyes were drawn instinctively down. They spotted the cable-ties almost immediately, a split in each one where they'd been cut off.

The floor itself was a square of uncovered plywood. Stains marked it below and around the chair. A variety of fluids, all now dried into the fibres of the wood. Logan could identify one of them immediately, and could hazard a good guess at the nature of the others based on what he knew of Mairi Sinclair's final hours.

Logan had been braced for this. Of course he had. After everything he'd seen, he was *always* braced for this.

And yet, his throat tightened, his stomach twisted into a

knot, and the skin on his face prickled at the thought of the suffering that had been inflicted here.

"Boss," said Tyler. His voice was low and measured, and came from right behind Logan.

The DC pointed past Logan and up at the hut's ceiling. There was a shelf fixed to the wall just below it. A roll of green tarpaulin sat there, one uneven end hanging down.

"Aye," was all Logan said.

He clenched his teeth, forced himself to take another look around the hut, then pulled the door closed.

"Call it in, son," he instructed.

He inhaled deeply, hurrying along the departure of the hut's air from his lungs. "Tell them we found it."

CHAPTER TWENTY-SEVEN

"WHERE THE SUFFERING FUCK HAVE YOU BEEN?"

Logan closed the door to Hoon's office and joined Ben in front of the Superintendent's desk. Hoon sat on the other side of it, perched on a wooden chair that creaked and groaned whenever he shifted his not-inconsiderable weight. The office was windowless, with the only light coming from the overhead strips. They cast a clinical white glow directly down on the Superintendent, picking out all the old acne scars that pitted his face like craters.

Big Boaby Hoon, wi' a face like the moon.

Logan had always got on well with Hoon. Or, as well as anyone could get on with the venomous old bastard, at any rate. They had never been friends, exactly, but they had shared a mutual respect. Hoon had accepted promotion grudgingly, and Logan suspected he'd like nothing more than to be back out on the streets, taking names and—if the rumours were to be believed—cracking heads.

They were alike in a lot of ways. Hoon had played on some of the meaner streets of Glasgow as a child, then policed them as an adult. He was an East End lad, grew up somewhere off Duke Street, Logan dimly recalled.

Hoon'd had some high profile collars in his time, but his share of balls-ups, too. After Logan's failure to save yet another of Owen Petrie's child victims a few years back, he'd been considering jacking everything in, until Hoon had cornered him and talked some sense into him.

Or maybe some sense out of him. The jury was still out on that one.

Either way, the man had shown a softer side to the gruff, foul-mouthed persona he'd become famous for as he'd moved up through the ranks.

"One o'clock, I said," Hoon barked. He pointed to a clock on the wall. "Does that look like one o'fucking clock to you?"

"No, sir," Logan said.

"What time does that look like to you?"

"Twenty past one, sir."

"Does it? Really? Look closer."

Logan tried not to show his irritation. "Twenty-two minutes past one, sir."

"Bingo. Fucking *well done*. Twenty-*two* minutes past one," Hoon said. He smiled broadly, showing off his yellow teeth. It was, perhaps, the most unauthentic smile Logan had ever seen. "Well, thanks for eventually gracing me with your presence. So nice of you to squeeze me into your busy schedule."

He splayed his hands out in Logan's direction, palms upwards, in an abrupt gesture. "Well?"

Logan knew this game. He'd played it before. Hoon was looking for an excuse. Ideally, a feeble one he could rip apart.

Fortunately, Logan had an absolute belter.

"We found the murder scene, sir," he said. "That's why I was held up."

"You found it?" Ben asked.

"Did he no' just fucking say that, Benjamin? Did you no' just hear those words come out of his fucking mouth?" Hoon spat.

He glowered at DI Forde to make his feelings on any further interruptions very clear, then turned his attention back to Logan.

"Where?"

"It's a works hut. Down by the Falls of Foyers. I've got a team there now going over it."

"The Falls of Foyers? Then why in fuck's name has it only been found now?" Hoon demanded. "That's, what? Half a mile from where the body washed up? For fuck's sake, Jack."

"It was... overlooked, sir," Logan said.

Hoon's chair groaned as he leaned forward, like it knew what was coming next.

"*Overlooked?*"

Out of the corner of his eye, Ben saw Logan nod.

"Bad call on my part, sir," the DCI said. "Won't happen again."

"See that it fucking doesn't," Hoon warned. "You're just in the door here, Jack, you can go straight back out it just as fucking quick."

He gave that a moment to sink in, then leaned back. "We have any idea who was working out of the hut?"

"We do," Logan confirmed. "According to Bosco's secretary's records..."

He braced himself.

"Robbie Stead—"

"Don't fucking finish that sentence," Hoon warned, slamming a hand on the desk. "Seriously, Jack? The victim's abusive ex-partner working half a mile from where the body was found and nobody fucking noticed?"

"Like I said, sir. An oversight on my part."

"I'll fucking 'oversight' you," Hoon muttered.

His face contorted and his nostrils flared, like he'd just caught wind of a daud of dogshite on his top lip.

"Well, what's done is done, I suppose. But these monster-hunter pricks. What do we make of them?" he asked. "Because I know what I'd like to make of them. A big pot of fucking soup."

"DC Neish and I met some of them at the campsite on our way to investigate the hut. They were doing some sort of photo call."

Logan saw the colour of Hoon's face change. There was always a vague sort of reddish tinge to the man, but he was literally going purple before their eyes as his temper rose.

So, that's what that looked like from the outside.

"*A fucking photo call?!* A woman was murdered!"

"Aye. That's what I said before I chased them off," Logan said.

"Next time you see them, arrest them. Fucking arrest the fucking lot of them," Hoon instructed. He anticipated Ben's question before he could open his mouth to ask it. "I don't care how. Think of something. Shove a kilo of coke up their collective arses, if you have to. I don't want those pricks parading around for the tabloids, got it?"

"Got it, sir," said Logan.

Hoon exhaled through his gritted teeth. "Right. Good," he said. He looked Logan up and down. "How you settling in?"

"Hitting the ground running," Logan said.

"Good. Well..." He gestured vaguely. "You know where I am."

He turned his attention to the computer beside him and started to peck at the keys with his fingertips.

"You can fuck off now," he said. "Ben already gave me everything I need for the press conference. He bothered his arse to get here on time."

Logan glanced at Ben. The DI rocked back on his heels, looking pleased with himself.

"Right, sir. Let us know if you need more."

Hoon gave the detectives the briefest of looks which successfully managed to convey the phrase, "Aye, you're fucking right I will," without him saying a word, then went back to typing.

Logan and Ben were at the door when the Superintendent spoke again.

"Jack?"

"Sir?"

Hoon tore his eyes away from his screen. "Nail this bastard quickly for us, eh?"

Logan nodded. "Aye," he said. "That's the plan."

CHAPTER TWENTY-EIGHT

LOGAN AND THE OTHERS STOOD AND SAT BY THE BIG Board, each of them chipping in their own findings from the past few hours.

DS Joyce, the Exhibits Officer they'd temporarily nicked from CID, sat by her desk, alternating between typing on her computer terminal and peering over the top of her glasses at one of the sealed evidence bags piled up in front of her.

"So, while you two were living the high life doon by the water, some of us were doing some proper polis work," Ben told Logan and Tyler. "First up, me and Bitch Cop over there spoke to Shayne Turner."

Tyler's ears practically pricked up. "What was she like?"

"A bit cagey. Got riled in the end and stormed off."

"That's not really what I meant," Tyler said.

Ben sighed. "No, I know. But that's all I'm telling you."

"You ask her about all the messages she sent?" Logan asked.

"Well, since that was the whole point of getting her in here, aye," said Ben. "Been a bit of a wasted opportunity if not, eh?"

"And?"

"She says they were mostly 'jokes.'"

"Jokes?"

"That's what she said," Ben confirmed. "Jokes."

"Did you buy it?"

Ben and Caitlyn exchanged glances. Both shook their head at the same time.

"Not really, no," Ben said. "But she said something else interesting."

Logan crossed his arms and half-sat on the edge of a desk. "Go on."

"She says Mairi had been a bit on edge lately. She'd been fighting with her dad because, and I quote, 'Her ex was back on the scene in some way.'"

"In what way?"

"That was all she seemed to know," Ben said. "We can haul her in and press her properly, if you like."

"We'll see," Logan said.

He looked over at the Big Board, and was heartened a little by it. He'd felt like they hadn't been making much progress on the case so far, but the board was barely recognisable from what it had been yesterday. Caitlyn had pinned up printouts of the pictures Tyler had taken of the murder site, and she and Hamza had put together a timeline of everything they knew so far. At last, some kind of picture of Mairi Sinclair's last few days seemed to be emerging.

"There's been a fair bit of new information," said Ben, reading Logan's expression, if not his mind. "I think it'd be good for everyone if we did a quick recap."

"Aye," Logan agreed. "Good call."

"But first, the big news," Ben said.

"You're pregnant, sir?" Tyler guessed, placing a hand on his chest and gasping with delight.

Logan flinched, all too aware of Ben and Alice's painful history with pregnancy. Ben, for his part, glossed right over the comment and carried on.

"The rope taken from Christopher Boyd's office? Exact match for the one used to tie up Mairi Sinclair's body. Same make, same model, same colour. Same rope."

Logan's eyes widened just a fraction at this new information, but he said nothing.

"So... it was him, then?" said Tyler. He looked around at the others for confirmation. "It must've been him, then. Right?"

"Not necessarily," said Hamza. He was sitting behind his desk, the glow from his computer monitor casting half his face into shadow. "Could be coincidence."

"Hell of a coincidence," said Caitlyn.

"Want me to have him brought in?" Ben asked Logan.

The DCI gave this some thought, then clicked his tongue against the roof of his mouth. "Not yet. Get eyes on him. Find out where he is and what he's up to. But subtle. Let's not spook him if we can help it."

He gestured to the board. "Where are we otherwise?"

"Caitlyn," said Ben, perching himself on the desk beside Logan. "Would you do the honours?"

Over the next few minutes, DS McQuarrie went over the timeline they'd been able to put together covering Mairi Sinclair's final days. Logan knew all of it. He'd gone over the timeline a dozen times the night before while lying awake in Ben's spare room, and had been able to slot in the new pieces of information as they'd come up.

He listened, anyway. It was sometimes useful to hear someone else talking it through. Occasionally, it would trigger some new thought or idea that could help crack a case wide open.

Mairi Sinclair had been agitated in the days leading up to her death, and was possibly seeing her ex-partner, Robbie Steadwood, which had led to conflict with her father, although Malcolm Sinclair hadn't mentioned this to Logan or any of the other officers he'd spoken to.

Phone records for Thursday evening, when Mairi had been overheard arguing, showed three calls, two incoming, one outgoing.

The outgoing call was to the Pay As You Go number they hadn't yet been able to identify, and had lasted just shy of seven minutes.

The incoming calls were from Mairi's sister, Michelle—a short call of under five minutes—and her parents' landline number. That call had gone on for almost twenty minutes. Any one of the three of them could've fit with Stuart's vague estimate of the timing, and he hadn't heard enough about the argument to help them pinpoint who she'd been speaking to.

Caitlyn's money was on Malcolm Sinclair, though, and the rest of the team were leaning towards being in agreement. Based on the length of the call, and Shayne Turner's information regarding the friction between father and daughter, it was by far the most likely possibility. Not a dead cert, but as close as they were likely to get to one.

She'd gone to school on Friday, as normal, but hadn't returned texts or calls until Saturday, when she'd cancelled her lunch appointment with Christopher Boyd. The text messages they'd seen on his phone confirmed this, and corroborated the lack of response seen on Mairi's phone records.

According to Stuart Sinclair's first statement, she'd 'mooched around the house' on Saturday, but hadn't seemed particularly upset or out of sorts. He'd spent most of the day in his bedroom, though, and had only really seen her when she'd shouted him down to eat. He'd had headphones on, and had been talking to people online, so it was possible she'd gone out for anything up to three or four hours without him realising. Neighbours hadn't seen her come or go, though, and there was no other evidence to suggest she'd gone anywhere.

Stuart hadn't heard her go to bed, and the last interaction he'd had with her was the following morning, at three minutes past eleven, when she'd said she was going out. She'd then either walked or driven to a nearby Spar shop, taken ten pounds from the ATM, and that was where the trail went cold.

At some point shortly after that, she'd been taken to the works hut at the Falls of Foyers, tortured, mutilated, then murdered. Her body had been wrapped in plastic sheeting from the hut, tied up with a rope matching the one taken from Christopher Boyd's office, and—an educated guess—dumped over the railings into the tributary below, where the fast-flowing water carried her out into Loch Ness.

"Aye, that's about the size of it," Ben said. He looked around at the rest of the team. "Anyone have anything to add?"

"Why did she stop texting?" Logan wondered. "We've seen her records, she was never off the bloody thing. Why the big hole from Friday afternoon until she was killed?"

"Still waiting for the rest of the records to come though, sir," said Hamza. "But based on what we've got, it looks like she texts into the competition on one of the Saturday morning cooking shows every week. She didn't that day."

"Bad mood, maybe?" Tyler guessed. "Time of the month?"

"Jesus," Caitlyn muttered.

"What? It affects the mood, doesn't it?" Tyler protested.

"It doesn't stop your fingers working," Caitlyn said, miming tapping out a message on a phone.

"No, but she might've just been, you know, in a huff, or whatever."

Logan sucked in his bottom lip. "It's an extreme behaviour change, whatever the reason behind it. There's something there. We should dig deeper."

"Uh, sir."

The voice was an unexpected one, and it took Logan a second to place its source.

DS Joyce sat up straight behind her desk, one hand on her mouse, both eyes fixed on the screen.

"Yes, Detective Sergeant?"

"Message just in, sir. It's Mairi Sinclair's phone."

She looked up at him over the top of her spectacles.

"It's just been switched on."

CHAPTER TWENTY-NINE

MERKINCH—OR THE FERRY, AS IT WAS KNOWN LOCALLY—
had a reputation as being one of the rougher areas of Inverness.
A reputation that, as anyone who'd had the misfortune of
finding themselves there after closing time would attest, was
well-deserved.

Originally home to Inverness's ship-building industry, the
area had steadily declined over the past couple of decades to
become the husk of a place it now was. On the drive over, Tyler
had described the place as 'Dundee, without the good bits,' and
now that he was here, Logan felt the DC had done Dundee a
great disservice.

It must once have been a thriving area, but now it was all
bookies and charity shops, plus a wide selection of takeaways
that each looked as toxic as the one before. Evidence of its
industrial past still shone through in the architecture, but the
buildings were faded and tired, and no amount of mobile phone
accessory shops could disguise it.

It was the feel of the place that struck Logan most, though.
He knew places like this all too well. Places where desperation

oozed from the fabric of the buildings. Where the evidence of deprivation wasn't just there to be seen, it was hanging around in the very air itself to snag at the back of the throat. A tangible *thing* that blighted the landscape and the lives of everyone within its boundaries.

Logan had never set foot in the area before, but he already felt he knew it like the back of his hand.

The Ferryman was what might be described as 'a working man's pub,' although only by someone with a keen sense of irony. It was standard enough fare from the outside—faded red frontage, hand-painted sign, and frosted glass windows that were too caked with grime to see through.

An attempt had been made to tart the place up a bit by adding some uplighters just beneath the sign, but the effect had been somewhat counteracted by the crude picture of an ejaculating cock that had been scrawled in marker pen across the wall.

It was a shitehole. No two ways about it.

And whoever had Mairi Sinclair's phone was somewhere on the premises.

"Everyone else in position?" Logan asked. "Back way covered?"

"Yeah, boss," Tyler confirmed.

They were sitting in Logan's car thirty feet past the pub, watching the front door in the side and rear-view mirrors. A couple of jakey-looking bastards were hanging around out front, smoking tight rollies, the fags hidden in the cup of their hands whenever they brought them to their mouths.

"Hamza and DS McQuarrie are out back. Uniform are on standby but keeping their distance until we give the word."

"And it's still in there?"

Tyler gave a nod to confirm. "Last pinged three minutes ago. No one in or out since then."

"Right. Good. OK, then."

Logan put a hand on the door handle.

"Like we planned. Give it a couple of minutes after I go in, then phone."

He started to move, then hesitated.

"And don't fuck it up."

Tyler pulled a 'come on,' face. "What do you take me for, boss?"

Logan opened the door.

"Trust me, son," he said. "You do not want me to answer that question."

THERE WAS something of the Old West saloon about *The Ferryman* when Logan pushed open the heavy door and stepped over the threshold. It wasn't so much the design of the place as the atmosphere. The way the music seemed to quieten, and the punters sitting gathered around their little round tables all turned and scowled in his direction.

A man in his mid-fifties stood behind the bar, polishing a glass with a dishcloth. He'd been in good shape once, Logan guessed. You could still just make it out in his frame. The bulk of him had slipped downwards, though, and now gathered around his middle like a big rubber ring.

His face was pale and pasty, like he hadn't seen the sun in years. Given the state of those windows, this would not be much of a stretch. His hair was an obvious dye-job, too black to be natural. He'd touched up the eyebrows, too. Between the coal-black hair and sickly white face, he bore an uncanny resemblance to a—

"Badger!" called a voice from one of the booths in the corner. "Gonnae bring us another drink, eh, man?"

The barman, who had been watching Logan from the moment he'd opened the door, continued to study him. "Gonnae get up off your arse and get it yourself?" he suggested. "I'm no' yer mum."

No one else in the bar had spoken. Instead, they all watched Logan. Some of them were sneaky about it, peering at him over the top of their pint glasses, or squinting through their whisky-haze. Others were more brazen, sitting up straight and eyeballing, trying to scare this stranger off.

Logan's instinct was to study the faces, to see how many he recognised, and figure out which of them would have a knife, or a gun, or a big bag of pills stashed somewhere about their person. It was habit for places like these, and it took a concentrated effort for him to ignore the punters and make for the bar.

He reached for his inside coat pocket, and saw the barman bristle. Badger was clearly anticipating a warrant card, and appeared momentarily surprised when Logan produced a wallet with a couple of twenties poking out of the fold.

"Pint, thanks."

Badger kept polishing his glass. "Tennent's do you?"

Logan nodded, then watched as Badger gave the glass he was holding a final wipe with the cloth, blew inside it to blast all the little fluffy bits away, and started to fill it from the Tennent's tap.

The smell of it swirled up Logan's nostrils, filling his head and making something that had lain dormant there stir back into life.

He'd been expecting this, of course. He knew himself well

enough to know this was always going to happen. The conflict. The internal battle. The little voice telling him that a sip would be a fine. A sip wouldn't do him any harm. A sip would be *necessary*, in fact, to set everyone's minds at ease that he wasn't here to lift them.

He could still feel their eyes on him. Watching him. Accusing him of being something he most definitely was.

The amber liquid glugged into the glass, foam creeping up the sides.

He didn't even like Tennent's—no one actually *liked* Tennent's—and yet he could feel his tongue rasping across his dry lips, and a prickle of anticipation on the back of his neck.

Over in the booth, a phone rang.

Thank Christ.

Logan could see the guy reflected in the bar's mirror. He was a lanky scrote in a hoodie that had once been white but was now an atlas of colourful stains. He glanced around before fiddling with the phone, eventually silencing it.

The foam reached the top of the pint glass. There was a *clunk* as it was deposited on the bar in front of him.

"Two eighty."

Logan fished three pound coins from his pocket and dropped them on the bar. "Keep the change," he said.

The glass was icy-cold as his fingers wrapped around it. He could feel condensation forming already, hear the faint *pop-pop* of the foam bubbles bursting on the pint's head as he carried it over to the booth in the corner.

A few eyes were still on him, but a low murmur of conversation had returned to the pub. He wasn't a 'kent face' locally—not yet—and while the hackles had gone up when he'd made his entrance, he could feel the tension easing in the air.

"Alright, pal?" he asked, arriving at the booth. It was a horse-shoe-shaped number, with leather seats that were more holes than actual material. The only way out involved sliding around the table to one end of the curved bench. Either one was a simple side-step away from Logan's current position.

Bloody amateurs. Wouldn't last five minutes down the road.

The scrote on the other side of the table looked up, his brow furrowed, eyes filled with the glassy gaze of someone who'd been dished out their methadone prescription in the past few hours. He was young—late teens, early twenties—and sported a beard so patchy it could've been put together out of sweepings from a barber shop floor.

"Eh?" the scrote asked, his eyes narrowing. Logan couldn't tell if this was an attempt to look threatening, or if he was just making an effort to focus. "Fuck you say?"

"Nice phone. Where'd you get it?" Logan asked.

The pint glass was heavy in his hand. Heavier than it should've been.

He was more aware of it than he should've been, too. Part of his brain was focusing exclusively on the weight of it in his grip. The feel of it in his hand. The thought of it in his mouth.

He forced himself to focus on the phone, instead. It was sitting on the table between them, much closer to the younger man than it was to Logan.

Still, given the state of the guy, Logan fancied his chances.

"Fuck's it to do with you, eh?" the scrote hissed.

"Nothing," Logan admitted. He leaned over and placed the pint down next to the handset. "Here. Bought you a drink."

"Fuck you do that for?"

Logan picked up the phone. By the time the streak o' pish on the other side of the table noticed, he was examining the screen.

The phone was an older model than he'd been expecting.

An Alcatel, with buttons on the front and a screen not much bigger than a postage stamp.

"Here! Gie's ma phone back."

A burner. That's what this was. A burner.

At a table somewhere behind the DCI, another phone began to chime.

Ah, shite.

Logan turned. His eyes met those of a dead-eyed thirty-something wearing a baseball cap and a tracksuit. He had a phone in his hand, and a look on his face that told Logan exactly what was about to happen.

"Don't even think about it!" Logan roared, but the guy was already up on his feet. He toppled the table in the DCI's direction, then was off and running, weaving past the other punters and launching himself out through the double doors.

Logan set off in pursuit, shouldering past a couple of the runner's cronies who tried to get in his way and slow him down. He hit the doors just as they swung shut, throwing them wide and barrelling out onto the street.

He heard, but didn't acknowledge, the shout of, "Ma phone! 'At's ma fuckin' phone!" as the doors closed behind him again, and then he was off, powering along the pavement, his coat swishing behind him.

Tyler was out of the car and running, on a direct intercept course with the fleeing bam.

"Police! Stop where you are!" he bellowed, and Logan was almost impressed by the lad's authoritative tone.

Almost.

The bam was considerably less so. Ignoring the DC completely, he dodged down a side street and set off at a fair clip, knocking over a couple of wheelie bins and spilling recycling across the road behind him in an effort to slow his pursuers down.

"Get after him," Logan ordered, letting Tyler take the lead. Logan was a big man, but had a turn of speed about him when he really needed to.

Still, Tyler was younger and faster, and had more chance of catching the bastard. And, ultimately, why have a dog and bark yourself?

Catching his breath, Logan took out his radio and watched as Tyler threw himself into a controlled sprint, bounding over the scattered cans and newspapers, and already starting to close on the target. There were a few other openings to side streets ahead, though, and probably a network of alleyways that would offer multiple escape routes for someone who knew the area well. Tyler was gaining ground, but not quickly enough. The bam would reach a side street any second and be out of sight.

"He's running," Logan barked into the radio. "Down..."

He looked up, searching for a street name.

"Brown Street. Repeat, target is fleeing down Brown Street."

Suddenly, Hamza was in front of the guy, skidding around a corner just in time to make a grab for him. The scrote barrelled into him, shoulder-first, and Hamza's attempts at interception became a clumsy scramble to stay on his feet. He hit the wall backwards, the force of the double-impact knocking the air out of him, and forcing him to cling to the wall for support.

"Shite," Logan hissed, as the suspect set off again, Hamza barely having slowed his escape.

There was a screech of tyres and a black Ford Mondeo backed into the street directly in front of the runner. He hit the back of the car at speed, rolled up and over the boot, then hit the ground on the other side with an impact so loud that Logan heard it all the way back at the corner.

DS McQuarrie was out of the driver's seat in a heartbeat. Logan watched as she raced around the front of the car just as Tyler reached it and ran around the back.

It's alright, sir," said Hamza's voice from the radio. He pushed himself away from the wall, rubbed his lower back, and raised a thumb in Logan's direction. "We got him."

CHAPTER THIRTY

LOGAN STOOD AT THE BACK OF INTERVIEW ROOM THREE, out of sight of the whining wee bastard in the chair.

He'd demanded to be taken to hospital with the light graze he'd sustained to the palm of one hand when he'd hit the ground on the other side of the car. Logan had refused, and not particularly politely, and they'd placed him under arrest.

DI Forde had recognised him on sight. Chris Hamilton, well-known local irritant with a long list of petty—and some not so petty—offences to his name. He'd waived his right to a solicitor, almost certainly on the basis that having one had never helped him before.

Ben sat directly across from him, the recorder running. He was playing it 'disappointed father-figure,' rather than 'hard-nosed polis.'

Logan would handle that role.

"Come on, son. We're going around in circles here," Ben told him. "Where did you get the phone?"

Hamilton shrugged. He had a facial tic that made him wrinkle his nose and draw up his top lip every few seconds, revealing a horror-show of mahogany teeth so worn down there were gaps between each one.

"I telt ye already, man," he said. His voice was slurred and nasal, like it couldn't bring itself to go via those teeth. "A guy."

"What guy?"

"I don't know, do I? A guy, man. Just a guy."

"So, some random guy just gave you an expensive phone?"

"Aye. That's what I've been tellin' ye. Just some guy."

Ben looked past Hamilton to where Logan was leaning his back against the wall. "There you go. Just some guy. We happy with that, Detective Chief Inspector?"

"No."

Ben turned his attention back to Hamilton.

"No. Apparently we're not happy with that, Chris. You'll have to be a wee bit more specific," Ben said. "What guy?"

"He was like... You know."

"We don't know. That's why we're asking."

"Like *a guy*. What else d'ye want me to say?"

Logan was across the room in two big strides. He slammed the flat of a hand on the table. The *bang* raced around the room, with a little shriek of fright from Hamilton in hot pursuit.

"Fuck's sake, man! What was that for?"

Ben glanced at the recorder. "For the record, DCI Logan struck the table, not the suspect."

"I'll tell you what else I want you to say, Mr Hamilton. I want you to say, 'I confess to the murder of Mairi Sinclair.'"

Hamilton's eyes blinked independently of each other for a moment. His tic stopped for a few seconds, like processing what Logan had said was drawing too much brainpower to keep it going.

When it returned, it was more frequent than ever, determined to make-up for lost time.

"Eh?" was the best response Hamilton could come up with.

"Mairi Sinclair," said Logan. "Body was found recently."

"Murdered, like?"

"Mutilated by some sick wee bastard," Logan said. "And you were found in possession of her phone."

"Eh? Naw. Wait."

Ben sucked air in through his teeth. "Doesn't look good, son."

"Naw. Hang on. I didn't murder anyone," Hamilton insisted. He was twitching so hard now he inhaled sharply up his nose each time it scrunched up.

"Aye, you did," Logan told him. "You've got her phone. You must've."

Hamilton shook his head vigorously. "Naw. I told you, I got it from—"

"There was no guy," Logan barked. "Don't say you got it from 'some guy.' You abducted Mairi Sinclair, you killed her, then you disposed of her body."

"You'll be put away for life for this, son," Ben said. "Nothing I can do about it."

Hamilton's head whipped left and right, tick-tocking from Ben to Logan and back again. "I didn't... Naw. I'm no'..."

"Last chance," Logan said. "Where did you get the phone?"

The tic was near-constant now, one every half-second. It was exhausting to even look at.

Hamilton's voice was a dry croak. "I telt ye, man. It was—"

Logan turned away from the table. "Interview terminated. Chris Hamilton, I am arresting you on suspicion of the murder of Mairi Sinclair. Anything you—"

"A car!"

Logan stopped.

"I got it from a car. Alright?" Hamilton said. "I didnae kill nobody."

Logan approached the table again, leaned both hands on it, and drilled a stare right between Hamilton's eyes.

"*What* fucking car?"

LOGAN STOOD in the car park of Raigmore hospital, watching a man and a woman in white paper suits carefully check over the exterior of a light blue Citroen C3. The car was near the back of the parking area, tucked between a people carrier and one of those stupid wee city cars that were barely big enough to hold one person and two days' worth of shopping.

"Can't believe it's been here this whole time," Logan muttered. "How did we not find this?"

Ben gestured around at the car park, and the thousand-odd cars crammed into its white lines. "Busy place. Hospital's always got folk coming and going. Then, there's all the arseholes who chuck their car here in the morning and get the bus into the city centre. Treat it like a Park & Ride. Meanwhile, people wanting to use the actual hospital facilities are stuck circling around and around, trying to find a space."

Logan shot him a sideways look. The DI cleared his throat. "Aye. Well. I'm just saying. It's out of order."

"What's out of order is that this car has been here for a week, and we didn't notice," Logan said. He sighed. "Hoon's going to lose the rag. And rightly bloody so."

Ben checked his watch. "He'll be making his press statement soon. Maybe we can slip this past him without him noticing."

Logan raised an eycbrow.

"No," Ben sighed. "You're right. There's hee-haw chance of that happening."

"Get uniform asking questions. Has anyone in the hospital noticed the car sitting here? If so, when?"

"Caitlyn's already co-ordinating," Ben said. "Can't say I'm overly hopeful, though."

They watched the SOC officers do their stuff. A fine drizzle had started to fall, and they'd had to work fast to erect a little tent over the car to try to keep it dry. A futile gesture at this stage, Logan thought. By all accounts, it had been lashing down for three days solid earlier in the week.

"How's Hamza doing?" Logan asked.

"Pride's hurt, more than anything."

Logan nodded. "He panicked. I could see it in the way he moved. He's lost confidence."

"Can you blame him?"

"No. It's a miracle he came back at all."

"It's a miracle his wife bloody lets him," Ben said. "He pulled me aside when he got back to the station. He's feeling pretty bad about messing up. Reckons he should've caught the guy."

"It happens," Logan said.

"Aye. That's what I told him. He'll get back in the saddle sooner or later. Until then, every day we send that boy home in one piece is a good one in my book."

A black Audi drove past behind them, engine purring as it made its way between the rows of parked cars. Logan turned to wave it on, and it immediately sped up, pulling past the scene and continuing quickly along to the end of the row.

"See what I mean?" said Ben.

Logan frowned. "What?"

"Poor bugger's been circling for the past ten minutes trying to find a space. That's the fourth time he's passed us."

Logan looked back in the direction the car had gone, but it had already rounded the corner and was lost to him somewhere between the rows.

One of the Scene of Crime officers pushed back her hood as she crossed to the detectives. "We've got what we can from the outside."

"Not much, I'm guessing."

"No, sir. Not a lot. Confirmed the forced entry, though, and looks like the clothes hanger he used is still inside. We want to bring it in to do the interior. Permission to arrange a recovery?"

Logan nodded his approval.

"We'll have to get some of the other cars shifted," the SOC officer said.

"Give the registrations to one of the uniforms," Logan instructed. "They can check with the hospital, see if they can find any of the owners."

"And if they can't, then just break the windows and shove them out of the way," Ben said, rubbing his hands with glee. "Park & Ride bastards."

CHAPTER THIRTY-ONE

FOR A FOUL-MOUTHED ANGRY OLD BASTARD, HOON HAD A real knack for press conferences.

He shared Logan's contempt for the media, but managed to hide it better than the DCI did. Of course, he actually made the effort—something Logan had never bothered to do.

Hoon had always had a knack of knowing when a camera was pointed at him, and could slip effortlessly into the media training Police Scotland had started inflicting upon its senior officers over the past few years.

Logan himself had been booked into three of the training sessions over the past six months, but had always been able to dream up some excuse that got him out of it at the last minute.

The Superintendent opened with a prepared statement thanking the public for their interest and help with the case, then revealed some of the less-juicy details about the manner of death, focusing mostly on the stabbing and the bit where Mairi Sinclair had been tied up in plastic sheeting—two things that would be difficult to achieve with a pair of monster-sized flippers.

He also spoke about her family, about the son she'd left behind, and the children she had taught. Marion Whitehead and her PISS pals had turned Mairi's death into a joke, with the press only too happy to deliver the punchline. In a few concise sentences, Hoon had made her human again, and the gag suddenly didn't seem so funny.

After that, he put out an appeal for information on the whereabouts of Robbie Steadwood. He didn't say why, but the 'do not approach' disclaimer would paint enough of a picture for folk to come to a reasonable conclusion.

Between the statement and the shout-out, Hoon had neatly turned the press from an enemy to an ally. Robbie Steadwood's face would be everywhere by morning. There'd be nowhere for the bastard to hide.

Logan watched him take a couple of questions from the floor, then turned the TV off.

"Aye. He's got a knack for it," he said, turning away from the screen.

Ben Forde nodded his approval. "He's a better man than I am."

"Not exactly hard, boss," Tyler called from his desk.

Ben smacked his lips together a few times. "Anyone else thirsty?" he asked. "I could just go a nice cup of tea."

Tyler groaned and got to his feet. "Fine."

While Tyler took the tea order and set off to make it, DS McQuarrie filled them in on Christopher Boyd's movements.

He'd been at his climbing wall in the Eastgate that afternoon, had met a young blonde woman for lunch in the food court, then had headed home at just after four. He was still there now, although a report had just come through of a different woman turning up at the house, and being very warmly greeted at the front door.

"I'd say he's a player," Caitlyn said. "His relationship with Mairi Sinclair doesn't seem to have held any particular special meaning for him. Certainly moved on quickly enough."

"If it was him who killed Mairi, these women could be in danger," Ben remarked. "We should think about bringing him in."

Logan mulled this over. "Hamza?"

Over at his desk, Hamza looked up from Mairi's mobile phone. It had been checked for prints and other forensic evidence, then given back to the MIT for further investigation. Unfortunately, the phone was locked. Hamza had taken a few stabs at pincodes based on the dates of birth of Mairi and her closest family, but had come up blank.

"Still struggling to get into it, sir," he said. "Might have to turn it over to the tech bods, see if they can do something. Could take a while, though."

"Let's have a look," Logan said, approaching the desk and holding a hand out.

Hamza passed over the phone, and Logan regarded it with something between curiosity and suspicion. He gave the screen a prod, examined the message that appeared, then nodded and slipped the phone into his pocket.

"I might know someone," he said, heading for the door. "Give me twenty minutes."

"Don't tell me you know a phone hacker in Inverness, Jack," Ben said.

Logan paused briefly by the door. "Something like that."

"THIS IS SO WRONG. This is a whole other level of wrongness. Is this even allowed? Legally, I mean?"

Logan gave the coroner an emphatic nod. "Oh, God, aye. It's practically standard operating procedure."

Shona Maguire wasn't buying it. That much was clear from the look on her face. She stood with one hand on the handle of the drawer in which Mairi Sinclair's remains currently rested.

"Morally, then?" she asked.

Logan sucked in his bottom lip. "Morally, it might be a greyer area. But what would she want?" he asked, gesturing towards the drawer. "I think she'd want us to find who killed her, don't you?"

Shona conceded that point with a tilt of her head.

"And it's no' like I'm asking you to cut one of them off. I just need to borrow a finger for a few seconds, and job done. No one will ever know. And least of all her."

With a sigh, Shona moved to pull the handle, but then stopped.

"Fine. But you owe me one."

"Fair enough," Logan agreed. "Next time you want access to one of the dead bodies in *my* fridge, you'll be more than welcome."

"Or, you could buy me lunch."

Logan glanced at the clock. It was now comfortably past dinner-time.

"Not today, obviously," Shona said. "But sometime."

"Oh. Right," said Logan. "Lunch."

He looked down at the phone and tapped the screen. "Maybe I can guess the code."

"Funny," said Shona. The drawer *ker-thunked* as she pulled it open. "*Really* funny."

BEN HAD ACCEPTED the fact that his dinner would now almost certainly be inside some dog or another, but he hadn't even mentioned heading back to the house. The phone was a major breakthrough, and that buzz was in the air. That feeling that something was about to fall into place. That something that had been holding them back was about to give.

Alice would have a moan. Of course she would. But she understood. After all these years, she understood.

"Still a lot to go through, sir," Hamza said, after Logan jarred him about the phone's contents for the third time in as many minutes. "She's quite prolific when it comes to texting. I haven't even started on the emails."

Tyler entered from yet another tea run, balancing a tray laden with mugs. He'd made a point of bringing a half-open pack of Digestives, knowing they'd only send him back for biscuits if he turned up empty-handed. His face was a picture of concentration as he made his way across the Incident Room, trying not to spill a drop.

"Overfilled some of these," he said by way of explanation for his cautious creep from the door.

Ben glanced his way, rolled his eyes in a vague sort of disapproval, then turned his attention back to Hamza.

"Voicemails all deleted, except a couple of old ones from her boss about school-related stuff," DC Khaled continued.

"Don't tell me what we haven't got, tell me what we *have*," said Logan, growing impatient.

"Right, sir. Aye. Sorry," Hamza said. He consulted his notes. "Big headlines, then. She was sleeping with Robbie Steadwood. It had been going on for a couple of weeks, from what I can tell. There's not a lot of interaction between them, but what's there is... revealing."

"He wasn't sending dick pics, too, was he?" Caitlyn groaned.

Hamza snorted, then shook his head. "No. Not revealing like that. He was supplying her with cannabis."

"So, he was her dealer," Ben said.

"Aye, but, there's more to it than that," Hamza said. "It's like she's blackmailing him. Like she's holding some sort of secret over him. It's never specified what, but he warns her not to say anything. I quote: 'Blab, and you're a dead woman, Mairi. A fucking dead woman.' Only, without the punctuation, and half of it is spelled wrong. But you get the gist."

Ben sucked in a breath. "Not looking good for our Mr Stead-wood, is it?"

"Not looking great, no," Logan agreed. "Be handy if he hadn't vanished off the face of the Earth."

"Press coverage should help."

Annoyingly, Logan had to concede that it might.

"Aye. What else do we have?"

"Shayne Turner's story seems to check out," Hamza revealed. "There are an insane number of texts from her, but almost all of them are shite. Inspirational quotes, mostly about feminism. Links to quizzes—'Which Hogwarts House are you in?' sort of stuff."

"Harry Potter," said Ben, displaying his in-depth knowledge of the franchise once again.

"Uh, yeah. So, that stuff, some jokes. Lots of jokes, actually, none of them very funny. Some chain letter type shite—'Forward this to five friends or you'll go blind' or whatever—and a couple of genuine work questions which Mairi replies to. Mostly just noise, though. Nothing incriminating. The text Mairi sent on Sunday morning was a reply to a meme Shayne sent a few minutes before."

"A what?" Ben asked.

"Like a funny picture, sir," Hamza said. "She just replies, 'Good one!' That's it."

Tyler set the tray on the desk and started passing out the cups. "So, the teacher's in the clear, then?"

Logan took his tea and blew on it. "Looks like it, aye. She was never exactly up there as a suspect, though."

"Someone should phone her and let her know," the DC suggested. He passed Ben his mug and offered up the Digestives. "Want me to do it?"

"I'll do it," said DS McQuarrie.

"It's hardly DS work, that," Tyler said, smiling eagerly. "Honestly, I can do it. I don't mind."

"No, son," Ben said. He gave Caitlyn a solemn look. "This looks like a job for Bitch Cop."

He regarded the offered biscuits. "But *Digestives*? Is that the best you could do?"

"There were a pack of Kit-Kats, but CID had put a sticky label on the front with their name on it."

Ben tutted. "Bastards," he said, then he glumly helped himself to a couple of the stale biscuits.

"There's some back and forth between Mairi and her sister, mostly about Stuart. The son."

"What about him?" Logan asked.

"Nothing major. Looks like he stayed at Michelle's house a few times. Reading between the lines, I'm not sure Mairi was all that happy about it, but I'm purely surmising," Hamza said. "Their messages feel a bit standoffish, though. If I didn't know they were sisters, I wouldn't have been able to figure it out from those."

"Parents said they were close when they were younger, but drifted apart when Mairi hit her Robbie Steadwood phase,"

Logan explained. "If Michelle suspected he was back on the scene, that could explain it."

"One story that doesn't check out is Christopher Boyd's," Hamza continued.

There was an almost-audible change to the tone of the room. Logan set his mug down on the desk beside him. "Do tell."

"It's mostly what he said. The texts between them are flirty all week. There's also the now-infamous penis photograph, of course."

"Let's have a look," said Tyler.

Hamza turned the phone DC Neish's direction. Tyler regarded it for a moment with a mixture of horror and wonder, then swallowed and shrugged. "Not that impressive."

"Do you mind?" Logan snapped, glaring at them both in turn.

Hamza quickly set the phone back down on the desk.

"DS McQuarrie has already seen all this on Boyd's phone. I thought you had something new?"

"Aye, sir. It's a message he sent after she cancelled their meeting," Hamza said.

"I saw the messages he sent after," Caitlyn said.

"I think maybe he deleted one," Hamza said. "There were four messages asking why she couldn't come, if he could see her later, if everything was OK. That sort of thing."

"I know. I saw them," Caitlyn reiterated.

"And then, there's the fifth message," Hamza said. He circled something on the top page of his notepad, turned the pad around, and slid it across the desk.

Caitlyn read it in silence, then looked up. "That's the full thing?"

Hamza nodded. "Word for word."

Logan reached past her and took the pad. His face darkened as he read it.

"Well? What does it say?" Ben asked, standing on his tiptoes to see over the DCI's shoulder. "For God's sake, man, don't keep us in suspense!"

CHAPTER THIRTY-TWO

CHRISTOPHER BOYD LOWERED HIMSELF ONTO THE MIDDLE seat of the couch, two glasses of wine in his hand. After these, they'd have polished off the whole bottle. He had a second one on standby, but the way things were going, he wouldn't need it.

He loved the single mothers. Always a cheap date.

This one was in her early-thirties, but could've passed for younger if she put a bit of effort in. She'd tried tonight, bless her. The make-up had been applied a little clumsily, the foundation inexpertly blended in around the neck.

A mother, maybe, but also a child playing dress-up.

He'd endured all her stories about her little boy. He was nine now—"Not so little anymore!"—and sounded, if Chris was being honest, like a right wee prick. He didn't tell her that, of course.

He never told them that.

Chris smiled as he handed her the glass, their fingers brushing together as he passed it from his hand to hers.

"Thanks," she said, mirroring his smile with one of her own. "I probably shouldn't, but..."

He clinked his glass against hers, and what little resistance was there, melted away. The *chink* the glasses made rang like a ringside bell around the living room.

Seconds out. Final round. Soon, he'd be moving in for the kill.

He watched her take a big sip. She winced, just a little, at the taste of it. He could hardly blame her. It was some Lidl shite. Cheapest of the cheap.

Good enough for her.

"Is it just me, or is it really warm all of a sudden?" she asked, blowing upwards onto her face, and making her fringe twitch.

Chris was sitting half-turned to face her, one elbow propped on the back cushion. He swirled his wine around in the glass, watching her. He'd set the heating timer to click on half an hour ago and rapidly ramp up the temperature. They usually blamed it on the wine.

"No. I'm alright," Chris said, his voice soft and low, like the *Best of Motown* album currently streaming from the living room Smart Speaker. "Want me to open a window?"

She pulled the collar of her shirt away from her neck and wafted it back and forth. "No. It's OK." She blew on her reddening face again and smiled at him. "Probably just the wine."

He clinked their glasses together again and took a drink, compelling her to do the same. They each had a gulp left.

Wouldn't be long now.

"I'm usually too cold. David's usually moaning that I've always got the heating on," she babbled.

He laughed falsely, trying not to show his irritation. Another David story. How *wonderful*.

"Kids," he said.

"You can say that again."

He sipped.

She sipped.

Soon. Very soon.

He slid a little closer, bringing the arm that was propped up on the back of the couch, right behind her head. She stiffened, but tried not to show it, as he idly curled a finger in her hair. She reddened further, her eyes gazing straight ahead, and brought her wine glass back to her lips.

"You have beautiful ears," Chris said, and she snorted a laugh into her glass.

He grinned, polished off the rest of his own drink, and set the glass on the coffee table.

"Do I really?" she asked, turning to face him.

Chris nodded. "Totally. The swirly bit. The sort of... dunkle thing. The *lobes*. Sweet Jesus, the lobes."

"I have good lobes?" she asked, smirking at him behind the rim of her glass.

"You have *exceptional* lobes," he told her. "I mean, sure, not as good as mine, but still. First class."

"You don't even have lobes!" she giggled.

"What? Yes, I do!" Chris protested. He felt his ears, his eyes widening in panic. "Shit. Where did they go?"

She laughed at that, the sound reverberating around inside her glass. She drained it, and he took it off her, sitting it on the table so it was touching his own.

He felt her tremble when he went back to toying with her hair. She was looking at him now, but it was taking an effort on her part. She was an introvert. He'd seen that at their first lesson together. He'd also seen the curve of her arse as he'd guided her up the wall ahead of him, and had been planning this moment ever since.

And not just this moment, of course, but all the moments to come over the next hour or so. He'd thought about those *a lot*.

It hadn't taken much to get her here. A few jokes. The odd compliment. A tiny bit of attention that didn't start with, *"Mu-um..."* That was all it took. That was all it ever took.

Pathetic, really.

He slid closer still, until his knee was touching the side of her leg. The jeans were from ASDA. He recognised the brand. They looked new.

Bless her. She was trying. Between the new outfit and the make-up, she really wanted to make an impression. She really wanted this to *work*.

And it would work. He'd make sure of it.

Tonight, at least.

She exhaled, and spoke in a fast whisper, as if confessing some deep, dark secret.

"It's been ages since I've done this."

She followed up with an embarrassed smile, like she couldn't quite believe she'd shared that information.

"Me, too," he told her, fingers still tickling down the back of her hair.

Her eyes went wide. Doubting, but hopeful.

"Really?"

"Mm-hm," he said, pressing the lie.

"Bullshit!" she scoffed. "I bet you do this all the time."

He shook his head, his eyes still fixed on hers. "Nm-mm. No."

She still looked doubtful, but he'd convinced her enough. Not that she'd needed much.

He heard her breath catch in her throat as he leaned in, still holding her gaze. His hand slipped onto her thigh. She closed her eyes, painted cheeks flushing with embarrassment, or arousal, or some heady mix of the two. Her lips were soft, welcoming.

Grateful.

His hand caressed her thigh, fingers kneading the flesh. She'd kept in shape. Total fucking personality vacuum, but she'd kept in shape. He'd give her that much, at least.

She didn't fight him as his hand slid down between her thighs. Didn't protest as he moved it upwards. Didn't resist as—

There was a knock at the front door.

No. More than that. A thumping. A hammering that threatened to shake the thing off its hinges.

"What the hell?" Chris said, reluctantly pulling away from his conquest.

The hammering came again, even louder this time than before. Who was out there knocking? A fucking gorilla?

"Alright, alright," he said, jumping up. He hurried past the coffee table, then stopped and picked up the bottle, holding it by its neck.

"What's going on?" asked the woman on the couch.

"I don't know. Wait here. Don't go anywhere," he instructed.

Another round of thumping filled the hall as Chris crept through it. He quickly and quietly slid the door security chain in place, tucked the bottle down beside him so it was out of sight, but ready to swing, and turned the snib of the lock.

"What the hell's the matter with you?" he demanded, pulling the door open until the chain went tight.

A bear of a man in a long overcoat stood on the step, two uniformed police officers flanking him a step behind. A police car was parked right outside his gate, the flashing blue lights licking across the fronts of the buildings on either side, picking out half a dozen faces that watched from around their curtains.

Chris recognised him at once. He'd met him just the day before.

"Christopher Boyd," said DCI Logan. He held up his warrant card, presumably in case the man on the other side of the door needed a refresher. "You're under arrest on suspicion of the murder of Mairi Sinclair."

CHAPTER THIRTY-THREE

DS McQUARRIE SLID A SHEET OF PAPER ACROSS THE TABLE until it was directly between Christopher Boyd and his solicitor, Lawrence Cairns, who had been brought in while Boyd was being fingerprinted and photographed.

The page showed a blown-up screenshot of a single text message from Mairi Sinclair's phone, with the sender's name above it, and the date and time below.

Christopher's gaze flicked over it far too quickly to have read it. "What's this? What are you showing me?"

Caitlyn eyeballed him across the table. "You know what this is, Mr Boyd. It's a text message you sent to Mairi Sinclair the day before she went missing. For the benefit of the tape, can you please read the message aloud?"

Christopher's gaze went from the DS to the page and back again. "I don't... I don't want to."

"Well, I'm asking you to," Caitlyn said.

She edged the paper closer to him.

"For the tape."

Christopher licked his dry lips. His eyes were bleary, and he held himself like someone suffering from an early onset hangover. He looked to his legal counsel, and Cairns gave a tiny shake of his head. The solicitor had a face like thunder on him. Clearly, this was not how he envisioned himself spending his Saturday evening.

"He doesn't have to read it out loud, Detective Sergeant. We both know that," Cairns said.

The chair beside Caitlyn's creaked as Logan leaned over and snatched up the paper. "Fine. I'll read it, then," he said.

He cleared his throat, and read the message in a flat, matter-of-fact voice.

"'What the fuck? You ungrateful cunt. What are you fucking playing at? Don't fucking ghost me, or you'll be fucking sorry. You fucking ungrateful slut.'"

Logan didn't look at Christopher yet. Instead, he turned the page so it was facing the solicitor. "Mr Cairns, can you confirm what I read is what is written on this printout?"

Cairns slid his glasses up the bridge of his nose and regarded the message on the paper. "Yes. That's what it says," he said. "But we don't know if that's an actual message that was sent to the victim. And, even if it was, anyone could have sent it."

"Oh, it was a real message, alright," Logan confirmed. "We have Mairi Sinclair's phone, and the phone records back it up. We've got the bods going through Mr Boyd's phone now. I'm sure they'll be able to confirm he deleted this message some time after it was sent."

In fact, Logan had no idea if they'd be able to confirm that or not. Still, it seemed to put the wind up the bastard, and that was the main thing.

"Even if it was sent from my client's phone, again, there's no saying he was the one who sent it," Cairns said. "It is entirely possible that someone else used his phone to send that message."

"Possible, I suppose, aye," Logan conceded. "Not exactly likely, though, is it?"

"It doesn't matter what you consider to be likely or not, Detective Chief Inspector. It matters what you can prove," Cairns said. "And I defy you to prove that my client sent that text message."

He smiled, showing off a set of teeth far too white and regimented to be natural.

"Now, unless you have something else, I think we'll be bidding you both a good evening and being on our way."

Logan glowered at the brief. "Well, then, looks like you won't be going anywhere for a while," he said. He let his gaze creep across to Boyd, who tried very hard not to wilt under the weight of it, but failed. "Because that's not all we've got. Is it, DS McQuarrie?"

"No, sir," said Caitlyn, adding her own stare to Logan's. "It is not."

"Where was it you said you were on Sunday, Mr Boyd?" Logan asked.

"I told you."

"Aye. I know. But I want you to tell me again."

"Aviemore," Christopher said. "There was a climbing talk. Bookshop organised it."

Logan leaned back and nodded. "Right, right. I remember now. A group of you went, didn't you? Who was it who drove again? John someone?"

"Maitland. That's right. He's in the Mountain Rescue."

"How was the talk? Good?" Logan asked.

Christopher's brow creased. He could sense a trap approaching, but had no idea how to stop himself walking straight into it.

"It was alright."

"About height or something, wasn't it?" Logan said. He flipped a page on the notepad in front of him. "Here we go. Highest vs Tallest: The Case for Redefining the World's Great Summits."

He folded his arms and looked to Caitlyn for her thoughts. "Sounds fascinating, eh?"

"Not really, sir," DS McQuarrie countered.

"No. No, I see what you're saying," Logan agreed. "Still, if you're into that sort of thing, I'm sure it's fascinating. Right, Mr Boyd?"

Christopher looked to his solicitor for support, but Cairns looked as much in the dark as his client.

"Yeah. It was interesting."

"You know what else is interesting?" Logan asked. "You know what else is *very* interesting indeed?"

Christopher shook his head and swallowed, sensing the trap was about to be sprung.

"We checked with the bookshop. They confirmed the talk took place. Someone there even checked that you were there. Found your ticket, confirmed it had been used."

Boyd almost giggled with relief. "See! I told you."

"The previous Sunday."

The words hung in the air between them. Logan let them settle in, enjoying the way the expression of glee that had briefly inhabited Boyd's face was now crumbling.

"N-no," Christopher said. "What? Was it?"

"Sunday fourteenth of July," Caitlyn said. She presented a

printout of an Eventbrite page showing details of the event. One week before the murder of Mairi Sinclair."

Boyd snatched up the page, hands trembling.

"You know what this means, don't you, Mr Boyd?" Logan asked. He waited until Christopher had lowered the page and raised his eyes to meet the detective's gaze. "Your alibi's a load of old shite."

Across the table, Christopher massaged his temples with the index and middle fingers of each hand. "Wait. Wait. It was... I just got mixed up. I'm sure it..." He inhaled, his breath a shaky quiver in his throat. "Give me a minute."

"Take your time," Logan said. "We've still got... what? Twenty-three hours until we have to charge you. Thereabouts. No rush."

He held a hand out to Caitlyn. She placed a clear plastic evidence bag in it without saying a word. A nurse, passing the surgeon his tools.

Logan deposited the bag on the table. "Can you tell me what that is, Mr Boyd?"

Christopher's eyebrows danced up and down on his forehead as he stared at the bag.

"It's a rope."

"You're right. It is a rope. Well done," Logan said. "It's the rope I took from your office yesterday, to be precise."

Boyd regarded it again, then gave the faintest of shrugs. "So?"

"It's also an exact match for the rope used to tie up Mairi Sinclair's body," Logan continued. "And I mean an *exact* match. They compare them both very close up, I'm told. Magnifying glass, probably. I don't know the science."

"Microscope, sir," Caitlyn corrected.

"*Microscope!*" said Logan, folding his arms and leaning

forward so they rested on the table. "Hear that, Chris? A *microscope*. Amazing what they can do these days."

He clicked his tongue against the roof of his mouth. The *pop* sound it made was enough to make Boyd jump in fright.

"So, what have we got?" Logan said. "Motive? You were evidently angry at her for cancelling your date. You could argue —and believe me, we will—that the message you sent her was a threat of physical harm. The fact you deleted it suggests a measure of guilt on your part, but we'll come back to that.

"Alibi? Fuck all. That's gone," the DCI continued, waving a hand. "Opportunity? You knew where she lived, you haven't been able to tell us what else you were doing on the day she went missing, and you've got a fancy motor with a big boot. So, I'm going to say 'yes' to that one."

He tapped the plastic bag with a finger. "And then there's this, of course. Can't forget this, can we, Detective Sergeant?"

"No, sir. Can't forget that," Caitlyn agreed.

Logan leaned further across the table and dropped his voice into a conspiratorial whisper. "And I'm betting when we compare the DNA samples we took from you with what we've found in Mairi's car, we're going to get a nice big fat match."

"Conjecture," Cairns protested.

"Overruled," Logan told him. He smiled, or maybe bared his teeth. It was hard to say for sure. "See? I know the lingo, too, sunshine. And you're in my court now."

He let Cairns stew on that for a moment, then turned his attention back to Christopher. The smile fell away as suddenly as it had appeared.

"Why'd you do it, Chris?"

Boyd shook his head. "I didn't."

"I mean, I get the crime of passion angle. You were angry. Fine. We've seen that before," Logan continued. "But fuck me.

The symbols. Her *eyes?* That was going above and beyond. What were you thinking?"

Boyd's mouth flapped open and closed. A fish out of water.

"What? I didn't do anything. What about her eyes?"

He looked to his brief for support. "What's he talking about? What about her eyes? What symbols?"

"You know fine well what I'm talking about, Chris," Logan hissed. "You mutilated her, you killed her, you tied her up with climbing rope, and then you dumped her over the falls. Right?"

"N-no. That's not what happened!"

"Oh? Then tell me how it did happen," Logan said. "Did you kill her first and then mutilate her?"

"No! I didn't do any of it! It wasn't me!"

His breathing was coming in short, unsteady gulps. His eyes were wide, the pupils dilating.

"Sunday. Sunday. Sunday," he said, the word babbling out of him over and over again. "What was I...? I must've..."

"Cut the shite, son," Logan barked. "We both know what you were doing on Sunday. You were torturing and murdering an innocent woman. You were disposing of a body. You were—"

There was a knock at the door. It opened a crack without waiting for the instruction.

"Boss?"

Logan flinched, then bit down on his lip, stopping an outburst before it could start.

"DC Neish. We're kind of in the middle of something here."

"Uh, yeah. There's a phone call. Asking for you, specifically."

"'Take a number. I'll call them back," Logan said, still not turning towards the door.

Tyler shuffled awkwardly from foot to foot. Caitlyn had turned in her chair and was glaring daggers in the junior detective's direction. It wasn't anywhere near the standard of Logan's stare, but it was still pretty damn fierce.

"You're going to want to take this one, boss," Tyler insisted.

Logan's chair creaked as he turned. Tyler smiled weakly. "Trust me."

CHAPTER THIRTY-FOUR

THE WIPERS OF LOGAN'S FORD FOCUS *THWUMPED* BACK AND forth, fighting a losing battle against the downpour that was currently launching a diagonal assault on the windscreen. The full-beam of the headlights painted two overlapping cones of light on the road ahead, and the trees that lined it on the left.

Logan tore his eyes from the road long enough to glance at his satnav. Close now. Three minutes.

Another car rounded a bend in the road ahead. Both drivers dipped their headlights until they'd passed each other, then clicked them back up to full power. Logan caught a brief glimpse of Loch Ness through the line of trees that rounded the curve in the road. Or rather, he caught an *impression* of it—a vast darkness looming beyond the tree-line, into which the car's headlights couldn't possibly penetrate.

Two minutes.

He replayed the call in his head, as he powered on through the rain. *Calls*, technically. The caller had hung up four times during the conversation, convinced he was being traced, and that this would somehow throw them off the scent.

Hollywood had a lot to answer for.

Once all the initial 'pleasantries' had been exchanged, the actual point of the conversation had been simple enough. An address and an instruction.

"Come alone."

Ben had protested about that part, of course, but Logan had given his word. He'd eventually set Ben's mind at rest by letting Hamza set up some sort of tracking app on his phone, which meant they could follow its location. Hamza, Tyler, and Caitlyn would follow a couple of miles behind, and only move in if they smelled a rat.

At least, that was the theory. But the address had led him to a phone box in the arse-end of nowhere, and the note inside had given him a second location, along with instructions to leave his phone in the booth.

There was a small wireless video camera fixed to the corner of the phone box. Logan had no idea if it was genuine, but he decided it wasn't worth the risk. He'd held his phone up to it, then placed the device on the ground before showing his hands were now empty.

That done, he'd got back in his car, programmed the new address into the satnav, and set off into the night.

"You have arrived at your destination," chimed a female voice, snapping Logan back to the present.

He clicked on the indicator, tapped the brakes, and steered the car onto the driveway of a darkened house. It was a new build. Close to being finished, but not quite done. The walls and windows were all in, but the roof was covered in black plastic, and the grounds were still mostly builder's rubble.

Of course. The address had seemed vaguely familiar when Logan had seen it written down, and now he knew why. It was one of the sites from Caitlyn's list. Its placement on the opposite side of the loch to where the body had been discovered had bumped it down the list of priorities, though, and there would have been nothing obvious from the drive-by to suggest anything about the place might be amiss.

The car's headlights shone in through the window as Logan pulled up, casting the impossibly large shadow of a figure across the unpainted wall of the room beyond.

He cut the engine. The lights stayed on when he opened the door and stepped out, only dying once he'd reached the house's front door. He entered without knocking, finding himself in a space that would eventually be a hallway, but wasn't quite there yet.

Three empty doorways and an unfinished staircase led off from it. Only one of the doorways could feasibly lead to the room at the front where Logan had seen the figure. The glow of candlelight flickering from within that room confirmed this, and Logan's feet *clumped* on the bare floorboards as he advanced in that direction.

A man stood in the centre of the room, silhouetted by the candle sitting on a stack of cement bags behind him. He was big. Well-built. Probably wouldn't need the sledgehammer he clutched in both hands, but he'd brought it along, anyway.

Logan looked him up and down for a moment, then around at the unfinished room. Finally, he put his hands in the pockets of his overcoat and gave a disinterested sort of shrug.

"Well, Mr Steadwood?" he asked. "What can I do for you?"

CHAPTER THIRTY-FIVE

"I SHOULD HAVE DRIVEN."

Caitlyn turned in the driver's seat to look at Tyler.

"Why should you have driven?"

"Well, I've done the advanced course," Tyler said.

"We've all done the advanced course," Caitlyn countered.

"I've done it twice," Hamza chipped in from the back seat.

"No, but... I know. I just think I should have driven," Tyler said. "It's technically my car."

"But it's not, though, is it?" said Caitlyn. "Not really."

"It sort of is. And I should've driven. I'm not making a big fuss about it. I'm just saying."

Tyler shifted in the front passenger seat and crossed his arms. "I think I should've driven."

They sat in silence for a while. The screen of Hamza's phone lit up as he tapped it. Caitlyn looked back at him in the mirror.

"Anything?"

"He hasn't moved in a while," Hamza replied. The light

from the phone screen picked out the lines of concern on his face. "Reckon he's alright?"

"I'm sure he's fine. He can handle himself."

"Steadwood's a big bastard, though," Hamza pointed out.

Tyler turned in the passenger seat. "Have you seen the size of the boss? It's the other guy I'm worried about."

"Won't do him any good if he gets taken by surprise, though," Hamza pointed out. "Nothing you can do then."

Tyler groaned. "This isn't going to be another story about you getting stabbed, is it?" he asked.

Caitlyn smirked. "Did DC Khaled get stabbed?" she asked. "He's never mentioned it."

"No, he doesn't like to talk about it," Tyler said. "Except at every available opportunity."

"Ha-fucking-ha," Hamza said. "I'm just saying. It happens. You can be the strongest, toughest person in the world, then some wee bastard sneaks up behind you and..."

"Stabs you repeatedly in the lower back?" Caitlyn said.

"For example, aye," Hamza said. "Not specifically that, necessarily, but aye."

"Sorry, I'm still on the 'strongest, toughest person in the world' thing," Tyler said. "You weren't seriously describing yourself there, were you? Because no offence, mate, but you're not even the toughest person in this car."

"Aye, but neither are you," Caitlyn told him.

"Close second, though," Tyler said.

"Distant second."

A white van flew past, headed south past the layby they were parked in, far too fast for the road and the conditions. The speed and the closeness of it rocked the car.

"Twat," Tyler muttered.

Caitlyn reached for the keys in the ignition, the instinct to give chase kicking in. She caught herself before she could fire up the engine, and forced the urge back down. Now wasn't the time.

They sat in silence for a while. It was Tyler who eventually broke it.

"I spy, with my little eye, something beginning with..."

"Rain," said Caitlyn.

Tyler tutted. "Right. Your turn."

"Nah. You're alright," Caitlyn said. She looked at Hamza in the mirror. "Anything yet?"

His face lit-up in blue-white light as he opened his phone again. He studied the screen for a moment, then shook his head.

"No," he said. He gazed out through the side window. The world beyond seemed twisted and warped by the streaks of water meandering down the outside of the glass. "Nothing yet."

"SIT DOWN," Steadwood instructed.

"I'm fine where I am, thanks," Logan replied, but the other man was having none of it.

"Fucking sit down," he hissed, brandishing the sledgehammer. He nodded towards another stack of concrete bags. "Sit there."

Logan considered his options, starting with the bunch of keys one hand was clutching in his coat pocket, the keys themselves poking up between his fingers. Steadwood was big, but the sledgehammer was a heavy and clumsy weapon. There was a reasonable chance Logan could get in close before the other man could complete a swing.

Still, jamming a Yale into the side of Steadwood's face was hardly going to convince him to start talking. And he clearly wanted to talk, or he wouldn't have called in to set up the meeting.

Logan sat, but kept the keys in his hand and his options open.

"Right. I'm sitting. What do you want?"

"Did you come alone?"

"What do you think?"

"*Did you fucking come alone?*"

Logan sighed. "Aye. I came alone." He motioned to the darkened grounds in front of the house. "See for yourself."

Steadwood backed towards the window, not taking his eyes off Logan.

Once he was close enough, he shot a couple of brief glances out into the gloom, then returned to somewhere just beyond hammer-striking distance.

"Good. That's good. That's good. What about your phone?"

Logan groaned inwardly. Fake camera, then.

"In the phone box, as instructed. I showed it to the camera."

"Oh. Aye. Aye, right. Good," Steadwood said.

He half-turned for a moment, and the candlelight picked out some of the detail of his face. That dead-eyed sneer of contempt that he'd worn in his mugshot photo had been replaced by something raw and desperate.

Logan recognised the tell-tale signs of a man who hadn't slept properly in days. God knew, he'd seen them in the mirror often enough.

"They're saying I killed Mairi. Your lot. That's what they're saying, isn't it?"

Logan shook his head. "No. We said we wanted to talk to you in connection with her murder."

"Same fucking thing."

"You have to admit, Robbie, it doesn't look great, does it?"

Logan said. "You two don't exactly have the most auspicious past. Then, you get back together, and a little while later she turns up dead and you vanish off the face of the Earth. Tongues were always going to wag and fingers were bound to start pointing."

"We weren't back together. We shagged a couple of times, that was it."

"Oh, well that changes everything," Logan told him. "You should've just said. That would've cleared everything right up."

Steadwood looked confused. He tightened his grip on the sledgehammer's handle, as if taking comfort from it.

"I was being sarcastic there," Logan felt compelled to point out. "It doesn't change anything."

"What if I told you she was fucking blackmailing me?" Steadwood spat. "Would that change anything?"

Logan considered this. "Aye, maybe," he conceded. "But not in your favour."

He watched the other man, waiting for the penny to drop. It didn't.

"In that it would give you a pretty clear motive for killing her," he explained.

"I didn't fucking kill her! I told you!"

"Then why hide, Robbie?" Logan asked.

"Because I knew you lot would try to pin it on me. And I didn't do it. I didn't kill her."

He gripped the sledgehammer even more tightly until his knuckles turned white. He was one good swing-length away, and the odds of Logan making it to him in time were substantially worse now that he was sitting down.

"Alright. You didn't kill her. Let's go with that for the moment," he said. "Tell me about the blackmail."

Steadwood glanced to the window and the door as if to make sure no one was listening in.

"She'd been getting some stuff off me."

"Hash," Logan said.

Steadwood looked briefly surprised, but then nodded. "Aye. Just a bit here and there. Didn't want to do too much because of her job, an' that. She was pretty skint, so she couldn't really pay for it. We came to an... arrangement."

A jigsaw piece clicked into place.

"The sex."

"Aye," Steadwood admitted. "That was the deal."

"Whose idea was that?" Logan asked.

"Mine," Steadwood said, without any hint of regret. "But she was right up for it."

"That can't be what she was blackmailing you about."

"What? No. I fucking wish," Steadwood said. "She found out where I was getting the stuff from."

Another piece. Another click.

"Bosco. She threatened to tell him you were nicking from him?"

Steadwood nodded. "At first, aye. But that was just the start of it. She started getting these ideas. These stupid fucking ideas. I told her to cut it out. Told her what would happen."

"What kind of ideas?" Logan asked.

"She wanted to talk to Bosco directly. She said she was going to threaten him. Said she'd grass us all up if Bosco didn't give her a payoff."

Jesus. Obviously, the woman didn't know Bosco Maximuke.

"Did she ever speak to him?"

"I don't... I don't know," Steadwood admitted. "But if she did, or if Bosco found out what she was planning..."

He let out a shaky breath. The candlelight picked out the sudden wetness of his eyes.

"I wasn't hiding from your lot. I was hiding from him. If Bosco killed Mairi, then he knows. He fucking knows. And I'm a dead man."

Logan nodded. "Aye. Probably."

He stood up.

"Best of luck, Mr Steadwood."

Robbie blinked. "What?"

"It's late. I should be getting back," Logan said. "If I don't show face back at the station soon, we'll have a dozen armed response bastards kicking in the door before we know it."

Steadwood tensed. "What? You said you were alone. You left your phone at the phone box."

"Aye," Logan confirmed. "But I left your note, too. The one with the address on it."

Even in the dim light, he saw the other man's face go pale. It really made his tattoos pop.

"Seems like an oversight that, Robbie. Shame, because it was textbook stuff, otherwise," Logan said.

He made for the door, his hands still in his pockets, the keys still bunched in his fist.

"Thanks for the information, though. Good chat. If you start running now, you might get away before Bosco finds you. Buy yourself a week or two, anyway. Give you time to get your affairs in order. That sort of thing."

"What? No. Stop!" Steadwood warned, his voice rising. "Don't fucking move. You can't just leave me."

"Aye. I can," Logan said. "Goodbye, Mr Steadwood."

He stopped by the door. Only then did he look back.

"I'd say it's been a pleasure but, well, you're an arsehole, so I'd be lying."

He nodded, and tapped a finger to his forehead in salute. "Seriously, though. Why are you still here? You need to get going, and get going fast. If Bosco did kill Mairi, you don't want to go through the same thing. Trust me."

Robbie stood rooted to the spot, his mouth hanging open, his fingers twisting the sledgehammer handle like it was a stress toy.

"Or, you could put down the hammer and come with me," Logan suggested. He took the keys from his pocket, spun them around one finger, and headed out into the hallway.

His voice drifted back in through the doorway, and echoed around the bare room.

"Your choice, son."

CHAPTER THIRTY-SIX

LOGAN EASED DOWN ON THE ACCELERATOR, HOPING TO beat the lights. He tutted quietly when the watery splash of green on the windscreen became orange, then red.

Steadwood fidgeted nervously in the seat beside him as Logan brought the car to a stop. They were by the Abriachan junction, the steep road running up the hill to the left of the car, a wide turning area just off the road on the right.

The wipers were going full-tilt, a steady percussion of *ka-thunk-ka-thunk* as they valiantly battled the rain.

"Bloody roadworks. This time of night," Logan muttered.

"It's quieter. Everyone bitches about it being done during the day, so they try to do it at night," Steadwood explained through a mouthful of his own thumbnail. He'd chewed the nails of the other nine digits down to the quick, and was going for the full house. "Picked some night for it, though."

"Aye," Logan agreed. He tapped his fingers on the wheel and dipped his headlights in anticipation of something coming the other way. No sign yet, but presumably the sensor at the other end had picked up something approaching. "Some night."

They sat in silence for a while, waiting.

"One thing I don't get," Logan said, keeping his gaze fixed ahead.

"What's that?"

"Bosco. I've been involved in murder cases before that we suspected he had a hand in. Couldn't prove anything, though. He never did anything like this."

"What, kill a woman?" Steadwood said. "I don't think he'd have a problem doing that."

"Oh, no. He's an equal opportunity bastard, alright. No, not that," Logan said. "I mean the... voodoo stuff. Whatever it is. The symbols. The eyes."

He heard Steadwood shift in his seat, saw the look of confusion out of the corner of his eye.

"What?"

Logan spared him the briefest of looks. Steadwood's expression seemed genuine enough. He had no idea what the DCI was on about.

"Mairi's body was covered in symbols. Carved right into her," Logan said. "And her eyes had been removed."

"Fuck. What? Fuck!" Steadwood ejected. The words became a wheeze, like his airways were tightening up. "What kind of symbols?"

Logan shrugged. "Just symbols, really. We looked into them. Something to do with warding off evil spirits. Demons, or whatever."

"Jesus," Steadwood hissed. He put a hand on the dash, as if having to steady himself. "Jesus Christ. Seriously?"

"Not really something I'd joke about, son," Logan said.

He craned his neck, looking along the empty stretch of road for any sign of an approaching vehicle, but finding none.

Another vehicle had drawn up behind them. A van, judging

by the way the beam of its headlights filled the inside of Logan's car. He muttered something uncomplimentary, and angled the rear view mirror up towards the ceiling to stop himself being dazzled.

"It's about the house. That fucking Ouija board," Steadwood said.

Logan shot him a look and held it this time. "What?"

"When we were kids, we went to this house. Boleskine. Supposed to be all black magic, or whatever."

"So I've heard."

"We drove out there one day years back. Did the Ouija board. Mairi was right into it. She went all, like, Gothy, or Emo, or whatever you call it. Used to get her proper horny, too," Steadwood said. There was a wistful sort of look on his face as he trawled back through some memorable moments. "She kept saying she'd been possessed by one of the demons. Complete bollocks, obviously, but I went along with it for all the freaky shit."

The sound of the van's engine reverberated around the inside of the car. The lights were still red, and there was no sign of anything coming in the opposite direction.

The fine hairs on the back of Logan's neck stood on end.

It had been half an hour since he'd driven this road in the opposite direction. He hadn't been stopped then. Had the lights even been on?

"But it wasn't just the two of us. At the house, I mean. Doing the Ouija board stuff. It wasn't just us."

"What are you saying?" he asked, only half-listening.

"I'm saying that Bosco didn't kill her," Steadwood said. It came out like a giggle of relief. "It wasn't Bosco. And that means he isn't after me."

"Not Bosco? Then who was it?" Logan asked, turning in his seat to look in Steadwood's direction.

That was when he saw the headlights rapidly approaching down the hill.

Big. Bright. Blinding.

Close.

"Shite!"

The gearstick crunched. Logan's foot hit the floor.

Before it could move, an ear-splitting impact filled the car with glass and thunder.

The world slammed sideways.

Tumbled. Rolled. Flipped upside-down.

The horn blared—a long, continuous tone, like the mournful cry of a grieving whale.

Logan heard shouts from nearby, whimpers of pain from closer still.

He heard doors slam. Footsteps racing.

Felt blood tickle down his face.

And then, darkness rushed in, swallowing him whole.

CHAPTER THIRTY-SEVEN

LIGHTS. VOICES. MOVEMENT.

Pain.

A hand on his forehead. A pinprick in his arm. A comforting word in his ear.

Darkness again. Deeper than before.

Deeper than he'd ever thought possible.

He revelled in it for a while, licking his wounds. How long, he couldn't say, but long enough. Too long, maybe.

He kicked for the surface, latching onto a sound. Repetitive. Familiar.

Bloody annoying.

He followed it through the chasm of black that surrounded him, sticking close to it as the black became shades of grey, then white.

His eyelids fluttered. Blinked. Opened.

The coroner, Shona Maguire, leaned over him, smiling down.

"Christ. That can't be a good sign," Logan croaked.

Shona appeared momentarily confused, then it clicked.

"Oh. Yes. Haha. No, don't worry, you're not dead."

She looked him up and down. "I'm told it was a close-run thing, mind you. But you're still in the land of the living."

Logan moved to sit up. It quickly became apparent that this would be a terrible mistake on his part, and he fell back onto the pillow with the room spinning in big looping circles.

He was in a bed in a private room, assorted cables and tubes hooked up to various parts of his anatomy. He hurt. A lot. So much so, in fact, that it was difficult to pinpoint any one specific pain. Instead, his whole body felt like one big bruise, while the worst hangover he'd ever had played a drum solo inside his skull.

Over the din of all that, Logan heard the sound that had led him out of the darkness. It came from a phone that sat on the smooth plastic table beside his bed.

"See? Computer generated non-binaural audio," Shona said, following his gaze. She tapped the phone, silencing it. "Thought it was worth a go. Besides, I couldn't find *Come on Eileen.*"

"You don't find *Come on Eileen,*" Logan said. "*Come on Eileen* finds you."

It was only after he'd said this that it occurred to him he had no idea what he meant by it. Clearly, his brain had taken a fair old rattling.

He decided to gloss over it and pretend it hadn't happened.

"What do you remember?" Shona asked. She leaned in closer, studying his eyes. In a medical sort of way, he thought. Nothing more.

His initial instinct was to answer the question with *not a lot,* but then an image popped into his head. A series of them, in fact, flashing up one after the other.

Lights growing larger. A vehicle closing in. A man, silhouetted in the passenger seat.

"Steadwood!"

Shona flinched. "Aye. I've seen him, already," she said. "In a more... professional capacity."

The migraine drilling through Logan's skull made him miss the nuance of this.

"What do you mean?"

"Let's just say, he's not looking as good as you are," Shona said.

Logan spent the next few seconds cursing at the polystyrene tiles of the ceiling. This quickly tired him out and he sunk into the pillow, breathing heavily.

"You done?" Shona asked.

"Aye. For now," Logan wheezed.

"Good. He died at the scene, if you're wondering. Pretty instant. And I ate your sandwich."

Logan's eyes flicked left and right, processing everything she'd just said.

"What sandwich?" he asked.

Shona held up an empty plastic wrapper. "Nurse brought it in on a tray earlier, in case you fancied it. Didn't look like you were going to wake up anytime soon, and we did agree you owed me lunch..."

Logan wasn't sure if he had actually agreed to that or not, but he... Wait.

"Lunch? What time is it?"

"Just after half two," Shona told him.

Logan looked around the room until he found the clock on the wall.

"But, you know, check for yourself, don't just take my word for it," Shona told him.

"Half two?" the DCI grimaced. "On what?"

Shona hesitated. "Uh... On my watch?"

"What day?"

"Oh. Sunday. Twenty-eighth of July," Shona told him. Logan let out a little sigh of relief. "In the year twenty-forty-seven!" Shona concluded. "Dun, dun, *duu-uun*."

Logan looked largely unimpressed by this, so Shona shook her head. "It isn't. That was Fake News. Sorry. The accident was yesterday."

"Sleeping Beauty up and about, is he?"

Logan and Shona both looked over to the door in time to see Ben Forde chapping on its little glass window. He carried a copy of *The Sunday Post*, and looked ever-so-slightly disappointed that he might not get a chance to sit and do the crossword, after all.

"Sure is. Doctors haven't been in yet," Shona said. She stepped aside, making room for Ben to take her place. "I'll go corner one and get them to come in and check you over."

Ben nodded and smiled at her as she passed him on the way to the door. He waited until she was safely out of earshot before taking a seat on the plastic chair beside Logan's bed.

"What was she doing here?" he wondered. "Touting for business, was she?"

"Something like that," Logan said. He coughed. It hurt tremendously—a sharp, stabbing pain that cut through the fug in his head and snapped him back into some semblance of focus. "Tell me you got them."

Ben tapped his newspaper on his knee a couple of times. "Cleared off before we got there. Doused the insides and burned it out. Scene of Crime team had a look, but there wasn't much of it left."

"Shite. What about the other one?"

The creases on Ben's brow deepened. "Other one?"

"There was a van behind. White, I think, but the lights made it hard to tell."

"No sign of it at the scene. We'll get on it."

Logan knew there wasn't much point, but made some vague noises of approval all the same.

"Alright there, boss?"

Tyler stuck his head around the door, all smiles. Logan and Ben both simultaneously smacked their lips together, indicating their thirst.

"Fuck's sake," Tyler muttered, before disappearing outside again.

"He's a good lad," Ben said. "Everyone was worried about you. I told you not to go off yourself. I should've gone with you."

"Aye. You could've been in the bed opposite," Logan said. He shook his head. "Nothing anyone could've done."

Ben conceded the point with a nod. "Suppose so. We're looking out for Robbie Steadwood's next of kin. The only one we can find at the moment is Stuart Sinclair."

"Jesus. Of course," said Logan, closing his eyes. "God. He's had some week of it, eh?"

"Poor kid," Ben agreed. He shifted in the chair, opened his mouth to say something, then closed it again.

Despite having his eyes closed, Logan somehow picked up on it.

"What else?" he asked.

"Hmm?"

"What were you going to say?"

Ben puffed out his cheeks and scratched his head, as if trying to recall.

"Spit it out," Logan told him, finally opening his eyes.

"It's Christopher Boyd."

"Don't tell me he's dead as well?"

"No. Worse, maybe," Ben said. "He's got an alibi. Remembered it once you'd, and I quote, 'stopped bullying him.'"

"Bullying him? What is he, twelve?" Logan grunted. "What's the alibi?"

"Work."

"Work? That's it? 'Work.'"

Ben nodded. "Aye. Says he's been working so much lately he lost track of the days. Short staffed."

"Did we verify it?"

"Afraid so. Security cameras show he was there the whole weekend. Checked lesson logs and confirmed with a couple of the students that he'd been the one giving the lessons. All checks out."

"And the rope?"

"Same rope they sell at the climbing place. Bank statements show Mairi made a purchase there a couple of weeks ago that matches the price they sell it for."

"So, she was tied up with her own rope?" Logan sighed. "Aye, well. To be honest, I wasn't really feeling it, anyway. I think Boyd's a horrible bastard, but I don't peg him for a killer."

"So, we're back to Robbie Steadwood," Ben concluded.

Logan said nothing.

"Right?"

"Hmm? Aye. Maybe. I mean... I suppose it fits."

"But?"

"He said he didn't do it."

"Oh, well then. In that case..."

Logan rolled his eyes. It hurt quite a lot, and he made a mental note not to do it again. "It's not just that. Mairi had been threatening to grass up Bosco. She wanted a pay-off."

Ben choked on his own saliva. He spent a few seconds

coughing, his eyes almost bulging out of his head. "She threatened Bosco Maximuke? For *money*? Jesus Christ. We should get her cause of death verdict changed to 'suicide.' What the bloody hell was she thinking there?"

"Steadwood didn't think she'd actually spoken to Bosco. She was trying to do it all through him. He was understandably reluctant to be the go between," Logan explained.

"No bloody wonder. Probably didn't want to end up eating his own bollocks."

"Who's eating their own bollocks?" asked DC Neish, carrying a couple of paper cups into the room with near-super-human levels of concentration.

"Will you learn no' to fill them right to the top?" Ben tutted, watching Tyler shuffle across the floor.

"It wasn't me this time. It was the machine," Tyler protested.

Ben glared at him, aghast. "Machine? Don't tell me you used the machine."

Tyler looked from Ben to Logan and back again. In order to do this without spilling any of the tea, he stopped walking.

"Uh, yeah. Why?"

"There's a perfectly good tearoom just... what?" Ben said. "Three floors down."

"But the machine's just down the hall," Tyler pointed out.

"Aye, but the tea'll be shite from a machine, won't it?" said Logan. "Away you go down and get us some proper tea."

"And they do good cakes down there," Ben added. "I'll have something with cream in it. An eclair, maybe."

He turned to Logan. "Wee eclair?"

"Aye," said Logan. "Aye. I could go a wee eclair."

They watched Tyler expectantly.

"Well?" said Ben. He made a shooing motion. "Go on, then."

Tyler peered down at the paper cups in his hand, then back over his shoulder at the door.

"Is there something you want to say, DC Neish?" Logan asked, his voice dropping into something not far off a growl.

Tyler swallowed and squared his shoulders, pulling himself up to his full height. "No."

Ben's eyebrows drew closer together. "No? No what? No, there's nothing you want to say?"

"No, I'm not going to get more tea," Tyler said. The first few words came out slowly, then the rest all at once in a slightly panicky gasp. He held up the cups. "I got you tea. If it's not good enough, go get it yourself."

Logan and Ben both stared at the younger officer.

There was a low groaning sound as the leg of Ben's chair scraped backwards across the vinyl flooring and Ben stood up. He eyeballed the junior officer, squaring up to him as if ready to fight.

And then, Logan and Ben both brought their hands up and clapped. Tyler's face, which had adopted a sort of rabbit-in-headlights expression, crinkled in confusion.

"High bloody time," Ben said, still clapping.

Tyler looked between both men, the cups still in his hand. He looked like he had a hundred questions running through his head, but he settled on a generic, "What?" presumably in the hope that it would cover everything.

"You're no' a tea bitch, son," Logan told him. "It was high time you realised that."

"What? So..." Tyler's head continued to tick-tock between them. "What?"

Ben chuckled and both men stopped clapping. "Don't worry about it, son. Just put the cups down on the table."

"Oh. Right, yeah," said Tyler. He continued his slow shuffle, then sat the cups down. "That one's yours," he said, placing one of them nearer to Ben.

"You're alright. I'm not really a tea hand."

Tyler laughed for a moment, but then realised DI Forde was being serious. "What? You didn't want tea?"

"No. We just wanted to see if you'd go get it," Ben said. "I could murder a coffee, though."

"Ha! Yeah. Good one," said Tyler.

Ben held his gaze. "No, really. Just the machine will be fine."

DC Neish searched Ben's face for any indication as to how he should respond to this. He saw nothing there but honest sincerity.

"Coffee?"

"Black. Two sugars," Ben said. "Thanks, son."

He turned in his chair to face Logan. Tyler hung back for a few seconds, considered all his options, then backed out of the door.

"Ah well. One step at a time, I suppose," said Ben, sounding just a little disappointed.

"The truck that hit me," said Logan, steering the conversation back on track. "One of Bosco's?"

"No. Different building firm. Not related," Ben said. "We've checked driver records, but they're saying it was stolen off one of their sites yesterday evening. Shouldn't have been anyone driving it."

"Bosco always was a slippery bastard," Logan muttered. He pushed back the covers of his bed, revealing an unflattering hospital gown. "We'll see what he says when I ask him face to face."

"I think you should be staying where you are, Jack," Ben protested. "At least speak to the doctor."

Logan swung his legs out of bed. The floor felt icy cold

against his bare feet, and immediately sent his head into a spin. He swallowed down something that might have been bile and might have been vomit, then reached under the gown, feeling for the ECG pads stuck to his chest.

"I'm sure they've got my number," he said. There was a *rrrip* as he tore one of the pads free. "They know where to find me."

CHAPTER THIRTY-EIGHT

"Aha! Detective Logan. Please. Sit. Come. Sit. You do not look well."

Logan stood just inside Bosco's office, fighting the urge to lean on the door frame for support.

A flustered-looking doctor had cornered him for a brief conversation on his way out of the hospital, and had made a pretty rock-solid case for Logan taking a couple of days to rest and recover. He'd suffered three broken ribs, a few nasty head cuts, and a hefty concussion in the crash. He had no business being up and about, the doctor had insisted. No business at all.

Logan had thanked him for his concern and then gone ahead and checked himself out. He elected not to mention the neck stiffness, shoulder pain, or the way his right knee now *clunked* whenever he tried to straighten the leg.

He could cope with it. Most of it was fine, in fact, provided he didn't make any sudden movements. The ribs were just a dull ache as long as he stood perfectly still and didn't do anything stupid.

Like breathing, for example.

Larger movements made pain burn through his left side—a kettle-full of boiling water that poured from his armpit down to his waist, and made him hiss through his teeth. He'd sneezed earlier. That had been an experience he had no desire to ever repeat again.

"What happened to you?" asked Bosco. He was sitting behind his desk, fiddling idly with a stress ball shaped like a single breast. "Was it accident?"

Logan shook his head. Something in his neck went *twang*. He ignored it.

"No."

"Oh?" Bosco looked him up and down. "Someone did this on purpose? But who would wish to hurt you?"

"I'm pretty sure we both know the answer to that."

Bosco stuck out his bottom lip and looked blankly at him. "No. No, I cannot imagine. An upstanding law figure like you?" He shook his head. "It is disgrace anyone would do this."

With a *haach-phtu*, he spat on the floor.

"Disgrace."

He motioned vaguely in the direction of the window. "My advice to you? You should get away. Take holiday. Rest. I would be happy to contribute to cost of this. For old time sake."

"You killed Robbie Steadwood," Logan said.

"Robbie Steadwood? Robbie Steadwood?" said Bosco, stroking his chin. He straightened and clicked his fingers. "Ah! *Robbie* Steadwood. I remember. Yes."

He adopted an expression of surprise. It was even more fake than the bastard's tan. "Wait, Robbie is dead? Oh dear. This is first I hear of this sad news. My condolence to his family."

"You knew he was going to co-operate with us," Logan said. "You knew he was going to tell us about the drugs."

"Was he? I guess we will never know," Bosco said. "Besides,

he is murderer, yes? He killed bitch-whore woman. I am respected businessman."

He thumped a fist against his chest. "I am Bosco Maximuke! It is my word against his, I think my word is winner, yes? And I say there are no drugs here. No drugs anywhere I go. Clean. Yes? Spotless clean. No drugs anywhere."

Bosco got up from his chair, gave the stress-boob another squeeze, then set it on the desk. He hummed quietly as he approached the cabin's single window and looked out at the yard. Four police cars were spread out across it, lights flashing. He could see half a dozen uniformed officers in high-vis vests. A couple of them followed spaniels on leads, the dogs' noses pressed to the ground as they zig-zagged left and right.

"Aw. Puppies," Bosco remarked. "So cute and adorable."

He turned away from the window. "They will not find anything. You know this. This is legitimate business. There is nothing to find."

Bosco looked so unconcerned, so unshakably full of confidence that Logan knew he was right. They were wasting their time. The bastard had already covered his tracks.

"I'm going to be watching you, Bosco," Logan warned. "You won't be able to blow your fucking nose in this town without me hearing about it. It'll be just like the old days."

"No. Not like old days. You are new to city, detective," Bosco said. "Me? I know many people. I have many friends. Everywhere, the eyes and the ears. Some within your own organisation."

He beamed and held his arms out at his sides. "I am popular man. What can I say?"

The smile fell away. "You? You have nothing. No car. No family. And I hear even the apartment you were due to rent has fallen through."

Logan bristled, his eyes narrowing.

"Oh. You did not know? Shame. Someone outbid you, I believe." His smile returned, broader than ever. "I wonder who that could have been?"

Bosco sat down in his chair, interlocked his fingers, and rested his hands on his belly. "You look tired. Take a holiday, detective," he said, the chair complaining loudly about his weight. "And, I suggest you do not come back."

CHAPTER THIRTY-NINE

THE GENERAL CONSENSUS BACK AT THE STATION SEEMED TO be to keep out of Logan's way. He paced back and forth across the Incident Room, muttering below his breath and occasionally letting out a grunt of pain when he turned the wrong way, or put too much weight on his injured leg.

Caitlyn, Tyler, and Hamza sat at their desks, busying themselves at their keyboards, or staring intently at documents. All of them—even Tyler—had taken one look at the DCI and concluded that now probably wasn't the best time to open their mouths about... well, anything whatsoever.

DI Forde didn't share the same sentiment. None of them could figure out if he was brave, or just stupid.

"You shouldn't be here, Jack. You should still be in hospital," Ben told him.

Logan's head snapped angrily in Ben's direction. Pain raced up the side of his neck, forcing a hiss through his teeth.

"See? You need to get some rest. You're doing yourself no favours."

"I need to solve two murders, is what I need to do," Logan bit back.

"Aye, well. We can handle that, until you get back," Ben said. "Besides, as far as Hoon's concerned, we've already cracked one."

Logan stopped pacing. His knee and ribcage both thanked him for it.

"What?"

"He's looked over what we have. Reckons Robbie Stead-wood murdered Mairi Sinclair," Ben said. "He had a solid motive, history of violence, and she was killed in his hut. DNA came back showing he'd been in her car. He reckons that's enough to build a case around."

"Oh he does, does he? And what's he saying about the fact that Robbie Steadwood was just murdered?"

Ben shrugged. "Not a lot. Doesn't think the two deaths are necessarily connected. If Bosco knew you'd taken Robbie in, and thought Robbie had information he was going to share, it's no great surprise that he'd want to shut him up."

"So, Hoon knows Bosco was behind this?"

Ben shook his head. "Hoon *believes* Bosco was behind it. But you know yourself, Jack. What we believe and what we can prove are not the same thing. We found nothing at Bosco's place, there was nothing to tie any of his guys to the crash scene..."

He shrugged.

"What else can we do?"

A flush of rage went rushing through Logan, but caught in his throat before it could come out as a lot of angry ranting.

What was the point? Everything Ben was saying was right. Infuriating, but right.

Bosco had done this sort of thing before, and always managed to get away with it. Even if they could link one of his men to the scene, they were fiercely loyal to the Russian. The chances of getting one to talk were so slim as to be almost non-existent.

His shoulders sagged. The worst of the pain, which adrenaline had been keeping at bay, came rushing in to fill the gaps his fading temper left behind.

He thought about retreating to his office, but it seemed ridiculously far away. Instead, he hobbled to the closest available chair, and practically fell into it.

For a while, he just sat there, saying nothing. The only sounds in the Incident Room were the tap-tap of Hamza's keyboard, and the slow, rhythmic flicking of Tyler looking through a bundle of photographs.

These were joined by another sound, when Ben fished his car keys out of his pocket.

"Come on. I'll take you back into Raigmore. You look like shite."

Logan showed no signs of resistance. He gave a sigh that whistled as it came out of him.

"Give me a minute," he said.

DS McQuarrie briefly glanced up at him, then went back to studying a report. DC Neish briefly paused in flicking through the photographs, opened his mouth as if to speak, but thought better of it.

"We'll handle everything while you're gone," Ben said, picking up his coat. "Caitlyn can get the report done. I'll talk to the family."

"Aye," was all Logan had to say.

His chair *squeaked* as he used his feet to rotate it in the direction of the Big Board. He stared at it in silence for a while, taking in the information that had been assembled there.

It made sense, right enough. Steadwood. Sure, Christopher Boyd had been a distraction for a couple of hours, but Steadwood had always been almost the most likely suspect. It fit. *He* fit.

And yet.

"If not him, who else?" Logan wondered aloud.

Ben hesitated, his coat half on. "Eh?"

"Assuming it wasn't Steadwood. Who else?"

Ben regarded the board, then shrugged. "No one obvious. Everyone else has alibis for Sunday. Could've been some randomer, I suppose."

Logan shook his head. The jolt of pain cut the movement short. "I don't think so. If she was randomly snatched, why the change in behaviour? Why cancel the date with Boyd? Why stop texting everyone? Why take ten quid out of a cash machine she's apparently never used before?"

With some difficulty, he stood up, his attention still focused on the board. "Something was different. Her behaviour was different. It was like she knew something was coming. And, if she knew that, then she knew her killer."

"Which brings us back to Robbie Steadwood," Ben reasoned. "She was blackmailing him, Jack. She was killed in his hut. He has a history of violence against women. Against that specific woman, in fact. I know nothing's ever open and shut, but this feels pretty damn close."

"Boss?"

If Logan heard him, he didn't let on.

"It's the manner of death, though. What he put her through. There's nothing in his history that's anything like that," the DCI reasoned. "It's not his style."

"It's not really anyone's style though, is it? None of them has exactly struck me as some sort of devil worshipper."

Behind them, Tyler stood up. "Boss!"

With a grunt and a fair amount of difficulty, Logan turned. "What?"

DC Neish thrust a photograph towards him. "You're going to want to look at this."

Taking the picture, Logan studied it. It was ever so slightly out of focus, but showed a big stretch of Loch Ness. The angle of the sun and the colour of the light suggested it had been taken early in the morning.

"It's one of the photos that mad old bat brought in. The Nessie-hunter," Tyler explained. "What was her name?"

Logan tore his eyes from it long enough to shoot the junior officer a questioning look.

"You not seen it yet?" Tyler asked, looking annoyingly smug.

Logan flicked his gaze down again, and this time he spotted it immediately. A shape in the loch, twenty or thirty feet from the shore. A green hump, just cresting above the glassy surface.

"Jesus Christ," he muttered. "No way."

He squinted, bringing the photo closer, then moving it further away as he tried to better focus. "Is that... Is that what I think it is?"

"I reckon so, Boss," Tyler said. "I can get some bigger copies made, but... aye."

"Well? Don't keep us hanging on. What is it?" asked Ben. Hamza and Caitlyn were both watching the DCI, too, Hamza's fingers poised on his keyboard and Caitlyn's report held open, as if they had both been frozen in place.

Logan held the photograph up for the others to see, then tapped the spot where the shape broke the surface of the water.

"What am I looking at?" Ben asked, doing a more exaggerated version of the squint Logan had been doing. "It's no' the monster, is it?"

"Green tarpaulin," Logan said. "Pretty sure I can make out a rope around it, too, which means—"

He stopped talking as he read the studious handwriting on the back of the picture. Had there been any colour left in his face that wasn't just black-and-blue, it would almost certainly have all drained away.

"Clocked it, have you, boss?" Tyler asked.

The DC rocked back on his heels and looked around at the others, determined to take at least some of the glory for himself.

"That photo was taken on Sunday morning. Just after seven," he said.

He gave them a moment to digest this, before following up with the clincher.

"Five hours before Mairi Sinclair disappeared."

CHAPTER FORTY

"I DON'T CARE IF YOU HATE GETTING YOUR PICTURE TAKEN. It's happening. Sinead, would you?"

Michelle Sinclair handed Constable Bell her phone, then put an arm around Stuart's shoulder and pulled him in close. He was several inches taller than she was, and although he made a few vague grumbling noises, he didn't physically resist.

They were all gathered in Michelle's living room, gearing up to make the drive to Foyers for the birthday service the school had organised. Michelle hadn't changed out of the clothes she'd worn to church that morning, and looked dressed for a funeral.

Stuart wore jeans and a hoodie, which Michelle had resigned herself to being the best she was going to get out of him. At least it was clean and freshly ironed, she'd reasoned.

"Right, do I just...? I've got it," said Sinead, studying the buttons on the phone's screen. She lined up the shot and fired off a couple of snaps, then rotated the device. "We'll do a tall one. Cheese."

Michelle let her arm drop down to around Stuart's waist.

He was angled towards her a little, and she put the other hand on his chest.

"Cheese."

Sinead tapped the screen and passed the phone back. "You might want to check them. It's not my strong point," she said.

Michelle swiped through the pictures. "Oh, these are lovely. Look, Stuart. Look. Are they not lovely?"

Stuart nodded, but in a way that made it clear he couldn't really care less. "Don't put them on Facebook," he said.

"Oh, but—"

She caught the look on his face. There was no winning this argument.

"Fine. Fine. I'll keep them for my *personal collection*."

She winked at Sinead, laughing, then checked the time at the top of the screen. "Oof. We'd better get going. Did we decide who's driving?"

"I can do it," said Sinead.

Michelle gave a little wince. "Would you mind if I do it? I get travel sick on that road as a passenger. Something about the windy bits. They go right for my stomach."

"Inner ear," Stuart corrected.

Both women looked at him, which instantly made him visibly uncomfortable.

"It's the inner ear that gets car sick. Not the stomach."

"Oh. Right. Well... that's handy to know," said Michelle. She rolled her eyes at Sinead, then smiled. "So, OK with me driving?"

"No problem at all," Sinead said.

"We really appreciate you coming with us," Michelle said. "It's going to be a challenging day. We've both grown very fond of you, Sinead. Haven't we, Stuart?"

Stuart appeared to become even more uncomfortable with this, and just sort of shrugged in response.

"It's no problem, honestly," Sinead said. "Anything I can do to—"

The buzzing of her phone interrupted her. She checked the screen, and saw DCI Logan's name emblazoned across it. "Sorry. Just one sec, OK?" she said, retreating out into the hall. "I have to take this."

Logan started speaking before Sinead even had a chance to offer a greeting.

"Are you with the boy?"

Sinead glanced at the living room door. She could hear Michelle and Stuart's voices in there, low and quiet.

"Uh, yes. Why?"

"I need you to double-check something for me. Don't make a big deal of it," Logan said. "I need you to ask him when he last saw his mum."

"Sunday morning, wasn't it?" Sinead offered.

"Aye, that's what he said, but things have come to light. I need you to ask him. Now. While I'm on the phone," Logan said. "Can you do that without arousing suspicion?"

"Uh, yeah. Aye. I think so. Hang on."

At the other end of the line, Logan waited. He had his phone on the desk in front of him, the speakerphone activated. The rest of the team had gathered around to listen in silence to the conversation.

There was a rustling sound. Movement.

Sinead's voice came again, more muffled this time.

"Stuart? Quick question. Sorry. I know this is the last thing you need, but they're just finishing up some paperwork and need to double check when the last time you saw your mum was."

Stuart Sinclair's voice was indistinct, but just possible to make out. "About eleven."

"On Sunday?"

Silence. Logan presumed a nod.

"Right. Thanks."

"Ask him if he saw her. Actually *saw* her," Logan urged.

"And you actually saw her then, yeah?" Sinead asked.

There was a pause. Logan held his breath.

"You mean *saw* saw her? Like actually saw her?" Stuart asked.

Logan stared intently at the phone, like he could somehow see through it into Michelle Sinclair's living room, if only he tried hard enough.

"Tell him yes," he said. "Or did he just hear her?"

"I mean did you see her, or just hear her? Did you say you were in bed?"

"Um... Yeah. I just heard her, actually. She shouted up."

Logan leaned both hands on the desk, supporting himself as the conversation he'd had with the victim's mother, Elaine Sinclair, came rushing back to him.

Even on the phone, you can never tell who's who, she'd told him.

They sound so much alike.

There was more rustling from the phone, then Sinead's voice returned sounding much closer again.

"He says—"

"We got it," Logan told her. "Are you somewhere out of their earshot?"

"One sec."

More rustling.

"Do you two want to head out to the car? I'll just be a minute."

"Everything alright?"

That was Michelle Sinclair's voice. The concern was clear for all to hear.

"Aye. I just messed up a report. I need to explain a few things on it."

"Oh. Well, don't let them give you a rollicking," Michelle said. Her voice grew louder, and Logan could picture her leaning in closer to the phone. "She's doing a very good job, I'll have you know. She's an asset to the force."

"Thanks," Sinead told her. "I won't be long."

"I'll leave the keys in the door," Michelle said, her voice fainter and farther away. "Come on, Stuart."

There was silence for a few seconds, then Sinead spoke again.

"OK. All clear," she said. "Now, what's up?"

SINEAD HAD BEEN UPSTAIRS in Michelle's house a few times, but only to use the bathroom. She'd already identified Michelle's room by the 'Rise Up and Pray, Luke 22:46' embroidery fixed to the door in a round frame.

The spare room, where Stuart slept, was directly across the hall. Sinead took a quick check in there first, and was surprised to find the bed pristinely made. Michelle's doing, she thought. No way Stuart would've bothered his arse.

This room was at the front of the house, and Sinead risked a look out through the window. She could see Michelle and Stuart standing beside Michelle's car a little along the street. From this distance, it looked like they were arguing about who was sitting where.

Sinead quickly leaned back out of sight when Michelle

started to look back in the direction of the house. She crept hurriedly out of the room and pulled the door closed behind her.

She crossed the hall, hesitated just briefly at the door to Michelle's room, then pushed down the handle and slipped inside.

If Stuart's room had come as a surprise, Michelle's was even more so.

Not the decor. That was exactly what Sinead would've imagined. It was done out in floral print wallpaper, with various religious images artfully set out around the room.

The most striking of these was a large portrait of Christ on the cross. Down at the bottom of the image, at the foot of the cross, various dark, long-limbed creatures writhed together in what looked like some sort of orgy. Sinead didn't imagine it was the sort of image that would be conducive to a good night's sleep, but it felt 'on brand' for Michelle Sinclair, and Sinead didn't think it was particularly noteworthy.

What was surprising was the mess of the place, which starkly contrasted the room across the landing. The bed was unmade, the duvet all bunched up in a big knot. There were clothes on the floor. Jeans, one leg turned inside-out. A t-shirt. Underwear.

None of it Michelle's.

The curtains were still drawn, painting the room in a gloomy half-darkness that made the Jesus painting feel even more oppressive.

The top pillows on either side of the bed were crumpled, suggesting they'd both been used. The sheet backed that up, both sides creased, and partially untucked from beneath the mattress.

From the placement of the clothes on the floor, Sinead

worked out which side Michelle had been sleeping on. She moved around the foot of the bed until she reached the other side, and eased open the drawer of the bedside table.

A box of condoms sat in a nest of silky underwear. Opened.

There was something else in there, too. Something white, right down at the bottom, almost completely hidden by the underwear.

Taking her pen from her pocket, Sinead used it to move the garments aside. A notepad was revealed, the top page covered in drawings of strange shapes.

No. Not shapes, she realised.

Symbols.

Downstairs, the front door opened. Sinead quickly closed the drawer and turned. As she did, her foot caught something under the bed.

Three books came sliding out onto the floor in front of her. Sinead wasted a moment reading the title—*Wisdom of Eosphoros: The Luciferian Philosophy*—then hurriedly shoved the books back out of sight with her foot.

She made it back out onto the landing, closed the door, and had just opened the door to the bathroom when Michelle appeared at the top of the stairs.

Sinead summoned up the most natural smile she could. "Hey. Sorry."

Michelle regarded her in silence for a moment, then her eyes crept to her bedroom door. She looked it up and down, minutely adjusted the tapestry hanging from it, and then looked back at Sinead.

"Everything alright?"

"Yes. Sorry, I just had to run to the loo before we set off," Sinead said.

Michelle peered past her through the open door of the bathroom. "Oh," she said. "Right."

"Didn't want to stop on the drive down," Sinead said.

"No," Michelle agreed. She looked at her door again, then back into the bathroom. "I didn't hear it flush."

"Hmm? Oh. God. Sorry," said Sinead.

She turned and entered the bathroom, flushed the toilet, then returned to the landing.

"So rude of me. Sorry," she said, then she motioned past Michelle to the stairs. "Shall we?"

Stuart was sitting in the front passenger seat when they reached the car.

"I told him to get in the back," Michelle muttered.

"It's fine," said Sinead. "I'll sit in the back."

She already had her phone in her hand, ready to fire off a text to DCI Logan.

Michelle blocked her as she reached for the handle on the car's back door.

"Actually, Sinead, would you mind if I let you drive, after all?" She wrinkled her nose. "Not really feeling up to it."

"Uh, yeah. Yeah, OK," said Sinead. "What about the travel sickness, though?"

"I'll be fine."

"Don't you at least want to sit up front?"

Michelle opened one of the car's back doors. "It's fine," she said, squeezing into the car directly behind the driver's seat. "I'll be good right here."

Sinead stood outside the car, rolling her phone over in her

hand a few times as she tried to think of a way to send a message without being noticed.

She had just concluded it was going to be impossible when Michelle rapped on the window with a knuckle.

"Come on, then," she urged. "We don't want to be late."

With a final glance at her phone, Sinead slipped it into one of the pockets of her uniform, opened the door, and climbed in behind the steering wheel.

Adjusting the rear view mirror, she saw Michelle in the back. Half of her face was hidden by the driver's seat headrest, and one eye stared back at Sinead through the reflection.

"Take the back road," Michelle instructed.

"The back road?"

"Out past the hospital, then down by ASDA."

Sinead took out her phone, spying an opportunity. She shot a glance across to Stuart, but he was engrossed in his own phone, not paying any attention.

"I'll find the postcode and programme it in," Sinead said, opening the messaging app.

"No need. I'll talk you through it."

A hand appeared over the back of Sinead's chair, and she quickly clicked out of the app before Michelle leaned forward.

"Straight on, and right at the end of the road," Michelle instructed, her voice close by Sinead's ear. "I'll have us there in no time."

CHAPTER FORTY-ONE

LOGAN CHECKED HIS PHONE. AGAIN.

Nothing.

Where the hell was she?

"She was supposed to be in touch before now," he said. "She told me five minutes."

He looked up at the clock. Almost twenty minutes had passed since he'd told Sinead to have a quick snoop around in Michelle Sinclair's room. She'd assured him it was safe, that she had the perfect opportunity.

So, where the hell was she?

"Should we phone her?" Tyler asked.

Logan shook his head. "No. She'd have been in touch if she could talk to us. Phoning might put her at risk."

"You don't think she's dangerous, do you, boss? Michelle, I mean."

Logan scowled. "Well, there's a very real possibility that she gouged her sister's eyes out and drilled holes in her skull, so I'd say she's no' without risk."

"Yeah, but I mean she's not going to kill one of us, is she? She wouldn't be that mental."

"You didn't get an up-close with the body," Logan grunted. "Trust me, the photos don't do it justice."

"We could get uniform round to the house." Ben suggested.

Logan sucked in his bottom lip. "I don't want her getting spooked. We don't have enough on her yet."

"To be fair, sir, we've barely got anything on her," Caitlyn pointed out. "It's all speculation."

"That's why we need PC Bell to hurry up and get back to us," Logan said.

He checked the phone again.

Still nothing.

"I could take a drive by," suggested Tyler. "Low key, like."

"They know your face," Logan pointed out.

"They don't know mine, sir," said DS McQuarrie.

"No, but you've got Polis written all over you," said Tyler. He cleared his throat when Caitlyn glared at him. "That's... I meant that as a compliment."

Logan straightened, ignoring the series of stabbing pains the movement brought with it.

"Hold on. What day is it?"

"Sunday, boss," said Tyler, grateful for the change of subject.

"The service."

"What service, sir?" Hamza asked.

"They're doing a service thing for Mairi's birthday. Down at the campsite in Foyers," Logan explained. "A load of kids from the school are releasing a paper boat or something."

Ben's face contorted in a sort of shocked horror. "Where her body was found? Who thought that was a good idea?"

"Aye, I did wonder the same thing myself," Logan replied. "It's on at four."

He glanced at the clock.

"We can still make it. Ben, you swing by Michelle's house," Logan instructed. "Take Hamza. See if anyone's still there. If not, head down the road and meet us."

He gestured to Tyler and Caitlyn.

"You two, get your coats. You're coming with me."

"Sir," said Caitlyn, already on her feet and ready to go.

Everyone else began to move, too, reaching for jackets and hunting pockets for car keys.

"Tyler, we'll take your car. Mine is—"

"In fucking ruins, boss?"

"*Out of action.* So, we'll take yours," Logan said. He held a hand out. "But I'm driving."

Tyler took the keys from his pocket, but didn't hand them over. Instead, he looked the DCI up and down. "You sure you're fit enough, boss?"

"I'm fine."

"My arse you're fine," Ben said, giving a derisory snort. "You can barely walk, man. Can you even see out of that eye? You're not driving anywhere."

He turned to DC Neish. "Don't give him your keys. That's a direct order. I don't care if he trumps me, give him those keys and you won't just be directing traffic, you'll be bloody washing it."

Tyler spun the keys around his finger like a cowboy with a six-shooter, and grinned. "Nice one. Looks like I'm finally in the driver's seat, boss."

"Give them to DS McQuarrie," Ben concluded.

"Aw, what? But—"

Caitlyn snatched the keys from him as she walked past.

"Thanks for those," she said, marching over to the door. She stopped there and shot a look back at Logan and Tyler. Tyler was still staring sadly at his empty hand. Logan was trying to summon the energy to argue with Ben, but his injuries were very much siding with the Detective Inspector.

"Well?" said Caitlyn. She twirled the keys around her finger, exactly like Tyler had done, only with substantially more panache. "We going to arrest this bitch, or what?"

CHAPTER FORTY-TWO

LOGAN ARRIVED AT THE SERVICE JUST IN TIME TO CATCH the percussion interlude. The head teacher, a prissy-looking man with burgundy trousers that immediately marked him out as a dyed-in-the-wool Tory voter, stood by the water, addressing the assembled onlookers.

Miss Sinclair had been instrumental—pun intended, Logan thought—in getting the class band project off the ground, and so he'd thought it appropriate that the band give her a send-off in 'their own inimitable style.'

Logan wasn't sure it technically qualified as 'a band' if every instrument was a drum or a shaker of some description, but the kids were all seven or eight, so he wasn't about to split hairs.

He'd clocked Sinead as soon as he'd pulled up. She stood with Michelle and Stuart down near the front of what was a surprisingly large audience. There were fifty to sixty adults gathered by the water's edge. Mostly parents, probably, although he saw the teacher, Shayne Turner, and Mairi's parents there, too.

He'd indicated for Tyler and Caitlyn to spread out and try

to blend in with the crowd. This was partly so they could better keep an eye on Michelle Sinclair, and partly because Logan couldn't be arsed listening to Tyler anymore.

It had been a long drive down.

The crowd watched on, smiling appreciatively, as the band began to hammer and shake their instruments. It sounded, Logan thought, like a kitchen being turned upside-down. If Mairi Sinclair was responsible for this, then maybe there *had* been something demonic about the woman, after all.

He told himself off for that one. Or rather, he imagined Ben telling him off for it.

Inappropriate, Jack.

From his vantage-point at the back, he watched the family. Mairi's parents stood on Sinead's left, a few feet away. Michelle was on the constable's immediate right, one hand on Stuart's shoulders, her fingers kneading at the muscle. The boy stood with his head down, staring at his feet. Occasionally, he'd draw his sleeve across his eyes, but otherwise he wasn't moving much.

He saw Sinead turn and look across the crowd. She spotted Tyler first, and relief briefly painted the lines of her face. She twisted further until she found Logan. They exchanged almost-imperceptible nods, then she faced front again just as what was presumably the chorus kicked in and the clumsy crashing became even louder and more insistent.

And then, mercifully, it stopped. There was no warning, or anything to suggest the tune had reached any sort of conclusion. Ninety-percent of the band just stopped playing, with only a couple of stragglers left embarrassedly shaking their maracas in the silence that followed.

The performance was met with a round of applause that sounded infinitely better than any of the instruments had, then

Shayne Turner stood up to make a speech. It was short and to the point, and she spoke with emotion choking her voice.

She spoke of a much-loved teacher, and a considerate friend. She told a few funny stories about things that had happened in various classes, about all the parts of the job that Mairi loved, and touched on how much she'd be missed by everyone who had known her.

By the end of it, there was barely a dry eye in the house. Mairi's pupils were all in ruins. Their parents, too. Stuart's face was buried in his hands, and Michelle's shoulder-rub had become a full on hug.

With the speech done, the head teacher invited the children down to the shore. They went armed with little origami boats, some enthusiastically, others hanging back with their parents for a while, summoning the courage to make a move.

With some encouragement and corralling from the school staff, the children all gathered at the water's edge, boats clutched close to their chests.

They'd all written messages, the head explained. Private thoughts. Things they wished they could say to their teacher. Some had drawn pictures of her favourite things.

One had written an acrostic poem using the letters in 'Miss Sinclair.' He'd apparently used 'Super Teacher' three times, which the head suggested was a testament to how well thought-of she had been. Logan suspected it was more a testament to a lack of imagination on the boy's part, personally.

Still, the thought was there.

Once the children were all lined up, the head invited Mairi's family down. Elaine and Malcom were quick off the mark, and soon joined the children at the shore. It was hard to tell for sure from the back, but they seemed genuinely touched when Shayne handed them both a paper boat. They locked hands and stood together, gazing out across the loch.

Stuart wasn't so keen. He stood shaking his head, not looking at the offered boat. Michelle was doing her best to cajole him into taking it, but his feet were planted and he had no intention of going anywhere.

Logan watched Sinead whisper something in Michelle's ear. After a moment, Michelle unhooked her arm from Stuart's shoulders, and accepted the offered boat. She joined her parents at the shore. Without a word, her dad pulled her in for a hug, and kissed the top of her head.

Elaine Sinclair turned to Stuart and reached a hand out for him. He kept his head down, his shoulders heaving as he sobbed.

"Poor bugger," Logan muttered. Stuart didn't know about his father yet. And that was only the second biggest bombshell he was likely to be hit by today.

"Would anyone else like to release a boat for Miss Sinclair?" the head asked, casting his gaze across the crowd.

A few of the parents looked at each other, hesitant and uncertain. One voice rang out confidently, though.

"I'll take one."

Logan's head whipped around at the sound of DC Neish's voice. Tyler approached the front through the crowd, all heads turning his way.

"What the hell is he doing?" Logan spat. He caught the eye of DS McQuarrie, but she just shrugged in response.

Tyler stopped beside Sinead, touched her briefly on the arm, then leaned past her and said something to Stuart. The boy shuffled from foot to foot, saying nothing.

And then, to the visible delight of his grandmother, he

stepped away from PC Bell and followed Tyler down to the water's edge.

Once there, they both took boats from the head teacher. Tyler looked back over his shoulder and shot Logan an apologetic look. Logan wanted to be angry. He really did. Instead, he sighed and nodded.

And then made a mental note to give him a bollocking about it afterwards.

Tyler wasn't the only one looking at Logan. Michelle Sinclair was staring at him, too. There was a look on her face that Logan couldn't quite place. Confusion, certainly, but something else, too. Betrayal, maybe.

Michelle shot a look at Sinead, and Logan realised the constable wasn't necessarily out of danger yet.

He moved through the crowd, picking his way across the rocks the way he and Ben had done on his first day here. His injuries slowed him a little, and it took him almost half a minute to reach the front.

"Thanks," he said, accepting a boat. He offered up a thin smile to Mairi's family. "We wanted to pay our respects."

"Oh, that's very kind of you," said Elaine Sinclair. "Isn't it, Malcolm?"

"Very kind," Malcolm agreed. His voice was raw and hoarse. "Thank you."

A few parents came forward to collect boats. The teachers all produced their own. Soon, a long line of adults and children had formed along the shoreline.

"Ready, mate?" Logan heard Tyler whisper. Stuart's reply was a wipe of his eyes and a nod.

A breeze tickled along the back of Logan's neck, and sent ripples rolling across the surface of the water.

"Perfect timing," Michelle said, glancing skyward.

The head teacher gave the word, and everyone knelt, bent, or crouched. The boats entered the water one by one, the breeze catching their pointed sails and rocking them out into the loch.

There was silence then, broken only by the occasional sob from the children, and the calling of the gulls far overhead. The boats drifted along, an unsteady armada venturing across the waves. One by one, the currents caught them, guiding them first into groups, then into individual explorers all striking out on their own.

There had apparently been a song planned to finish, but none of the kids were much in the mood to perform, and so it was agreed—to everyone's visible relief—that it wouldn't go ahead.

Instead, some final words were said by the teachers, Malcolm and Elaine Sinclair struggled through some words of thanks, and then the whole thing was drawn to a slightly anti-climactic close.

Logan stood back with Sinead during the Sinclairs' speech. Michelle glanced their way a few times, but they were too far back and she was too close to her parents for her to hear anything of what Sinead was saying.

"Well done," Logan mumbled, once Sinead had finished telling him what she'd found.

Sinead shook her head. "I should've seen it."

"No one saw it," Logan told her.

"No one else was in the house with her all week."

"Aye well, that's true, right enough," Logan conceded.

Sinead flinched, like the words had physically stung.

"I'm kidding. You've done well. You couldn't have known."

"Thanks." Sinead shot the DCI a sideways glance. "Mind if I ask what happened to your face, sir?"

"Wind changed and it stuck like this," Logan said. "My mother did warn me."

Sinead smiled, sensing that was all she was going to get out of him right now.

They both watched Michelle sidle up to Stuart again. Tyler had been standing by the boy, but gave him a pat on the back and tactfully withdrew when his aunt joined them.

"Did you send him to talk to Stuart?" Sinead asked.

"Did I hell," Logan spat. "I told him not to get himself noticed."

"Oh."

Sinead chewed her tongue for a few moments.

"Nice of him, though," she said. "I think Stuart would have really regretted not doing it."

Logan groaned, but had to concede the point.

"Aye. I suppose," he said. He shot her a sideways look. "And I suppose you could do worse."

Sinead's face turned a shade of deep pink.

"Not *much* worse, granted," Logan added. "I'm actually struggling to think of anyone worse, off the top of my head who isn't currently in jail. But theoretically, I mean. You could theoretically do worse."

Sinead's face was a shade of beetroot now. She cleared her throat and kept her eyes to the front. "I don't know what you're talking about, sir," she said.

To her relief, DS McQuarrie appeared beside them and immediately steered the conversation back on track.

"What's the plan, sir?"

The audience was thinning now, the parents leading their children back up towards the campsite's car park. Michelle was hugging her parents, then Stuart was forced to reluctantly endure the same treatment, this time accompanied by some kissing from Elaine, and a gruff, "Your mum would've been very proud," from Malcolm.

"Sinead, there's a cafe up at the top of the path leading down to the falls. You and Tyler take the boy there. Get him something to eat."

"What about Michelle?" Sinead asked.

Logan gazed down the shore at Michelle Sinclair. He flexed his fingers in and out. One of them *clicked* painfully.

"Leave her to me."

CHAPTER FORTY-THREE

THE PATH WAS HARDER GOING THAN LOGAN REMEMBERED.

Of course, the last time he'd walked it he hadn't been sporting broken ribs and a knee injury. Now, every breath was like a blast of fire filling his chest and scorching him from the inside-out. His knee had stopped *clunking* and was now making an audible *crack* every few steps. He wasn't sure if this was better or worse.

It felt worse.

It didn't help that Michelle Sinclair whinged even more than Tyler had. Mind you, in the woman's defence, Tyler hadn't done the walk in heels and a skirt.

DS McQuarrie was hanging back, close enough to listen in, but far enough away that she didn't seem to be part of the conversation.

"Sorry, what is the point of this?" Michelle demanded, leaning on a wooden handrail as she heaved herself up a rocky incline. It was mostly downhill, but the path occasionally climbed to get over some unmovable boulder or other obstacle. "I should be with Stuart. He needs me."

"It won't take long, Miss Sinclair," Logan wheezed. "Believe me, I'm enjoying it even less than you are. But, there's something I need you to see."

She shot a look past him at the path ahead. Trees leaned down over it, an ever-moving canopy of green that sent shadows scurrying across the rocky ground. Michelle's words and tone may have been angry, but it was worry that was written in that look.

"Can't you just tell me?" she asked, stopping dead. "I don't... I don't want to go down there."

Logan stopped, too, grateful for the breather.

"Why not? Do you know what's down there?" he asked. His stare bored into her. Shrank her.

She shook her head. "N-no. I just... It's a long way."

"It's not much further," Logan assured her. He set off limping again. "Almost there."

He looked back up the slope at her.

"Won't be long now."

TYLER LOOKED up from the menu, a big smile on his face. "They do Coke Floats! I haven't had one of them in years."

Across the table, Stuart searched the menu. It was lying flat on the plastic tablecloth in front of him, the effort of holding it apparently proving too much.

"What's a Coke Float?"

"What's a...? You've never had a Coke Float?" Tyler gasped. He looked to Sinead, who sat on his right, between him and the boy. "He's never had a Coke Float!"

"I've never had one, either," Sinead said. "It's the ice cream thing, isn't it?"

"Jesus," Tyler said. "You're both in for a treat. It's Coke, right, then a big dollop of ice cream on top, then..."

He thought for a moment.

"Actually, that's pretty much it. But it's amazing."

"It sounds horrible," Stuart said.

"What are you talking about?" Tyler said, the volume of his voice rising enough to draw looks from the handful of other people in the cafe. "It sounds brilliant. And it is. That's it decided. Three Coke Floats."

Sinead and Stuart exchanged wary looks.

"Don't pull that face! Trust me, you're going to love it."

Sinead raised her eyebrows. "What do we think? Do we trust him?"

Stuart looked deeply sceptical, but then gave a nod. "Fine. I'll try it."

"That's my boy," Tyler said, high-fiving the boy across the table. "Constable Bell? You joining the Coke Float Club?"

"Are you paying?"

"No, he is," said Tyler, jabbing a thumb in Stuart's direction.

"Wait, what?" Stuart asked, straightening.

"I'm kidding. Yes. My treat."

He stood up, reaching for his wallet. "Three Coke Floats it is. Then we'll see about food."

Sinead and Stuart watched him approach the counter, swaggering like he owned the place. They didn't catch what he said to the grey-haired woman behind the counter, but from the way her face lit-up it was clear he'd turned on the charm.

"He's pretty funny," Stuart remarked.

"He has his moments," Sinead agreed.

Stuart's eyes went to the cafe's front door. It was mostly glass, and looked out over the road to where a steep path led down to the Falls of Foyers.

"Where's Michelle?"

Sinead hesitated, then smiled. "I'm sure she won't be long."

She tapped the menu in front of him. "Now, what do you fancy for eating?"

MICHELLE SINCLAIR HADN'T SPOKEN in almost a minute. Hadn't grumbled. Hadn't complained. Hadn't uttered a single, solitary word.

Instead, she just stood perfectly still, eyes locked on the nondescript workman's hut that stood at the end of the path, overlooking the falls. A mist of moisture swirled in the air, as the water crashed like thunder just a few dozen feet away.

"Something you'd like to tell us, Michelle?" Logan asked and, for a moment, it looked like she might.

But then she shook her head, pulled herself together, and looked the DCI right in the eye. "What is this?"

Logan shrugged. So, that's how she wanted to play it.

"This? This is where Mairi was murdered," Logan told her. He gave the nod to Caitlyn, and she cut the *Police: Do Not Cross* tape that had been cordoning the place off. The ends fluttered briefly on the breeze, then fell to the ground.

"Robbie Steadwood was working out of this hut," Logan continued.

Michelle tried to keep the relief from showing on her face, but did a very bad job of it.

"Oh. Was it? And, so..." She swallowed. "This was where he killed her?"

"'This was where she died, yes," Logan said, side-stepping the question.

He opened the door, stepped inside the gloomy hut, then beckoned for Michelle to follow.

"No. I don't want to," Michelle said. She shot Caitlyn a pleading look, but found no comfort there. "I don't want to go in."

"It's very important, Miss Sinclair. It won't take a second, but it'll help your sister get justice."

Michelle looked at the shadowy shape of Logan inside the doorway, then across the front of the hut. Even from this distance, Logan could practically see her skin crawling backwards, trying to pull her away from the place.

"Have you found him yet? Robbie, I mean," she asked.

"We have. I took him into custody myself last night," Logan confirmed. "Turns out Mairi was mixed up in some bad business with one of the local thugs. She was playing a very dangerous game."

"Oh. God. I had no idea," Michelle said, but she looked emboldened by the news, and took a step closer to the hut. "Do you think they did it? Or Robbie?"

"We have a few theories at the moment," Logan told her. "That's what I could use your help with. Please."

He disappeared into the hut. Caitlyn gave Michelle an encouraging nod, then gestured for her to follow Logan inside.

The hut's chipboard floor dipped a little under Michelle's weight as she stepped inside. The only light in the place seeped in around her through the doorway, the lack of windows meaning most of the hut was lost in shadow.

Her breathing echoed off the wooden walls, fast and erratic. She wrung her hands together, and even in silhouette, Logan could see how uncomfortable she was to be standing there in the half-darkness.

"Do me a favour, will you, Miss Sinclair?" he asked from the other end of the hut. "Stick the light on."

Michelle seemed almost grateful as she reached up and pulled the cord. There was a *ka-klack* from the ceiling-mounted switch, and the hut was flooded with light.

Logan sucked in his bottom lip. "Detective Sergeant McQuarrie. Did you see that?"

"I did, sir," said Caitlyn. She was standing in the doorway at Michelle's back, looking in through one of the gaps.

"See what?" asked Michelle.

Logan gestured to the three cords that hung by the door. Michelle was still holding onto one, like a child with a helium balloon.

"You knew which one to pull," Logan said.

Michelle frowned, then looked at the cord she was holding. She released it immediately, like it had just given her an electric shock. It swung back and forth, entangling itself around the others.

"What? What do you mean?"

"You knew which one was the light," Logan said. "How?"

Michelle's mouth flapped open and closed. "I mean... What do you mean, 'how?' I just... I just guessed."

"That was lucky. First time I was here, I pulled the other two first," Logan said. "They just look more, I don't know, inviting, I suppose. The one for the light is sort of hidden at the back, isn't it? Looks the least likely. And yet, you managed to pick it out. First time."

Michelle said nothing. Her face went through a range of expressions but couldn't settle on any one in particular.

"But then, it's not your first time here, is it? You were here last week," Logan said.

"You were here the day you killed your sister."

CHAPTER FORTY-FOUR

"IT WAS YOU, WASN'T IT, MICHELLE?" LOGAN ASKED. "YOU were the one who went to Boleskine House with Mairi and Steadwood. You were with them when they did their... occult whatever."

"What? No. No, I'm not... I didn't kill her. I don't know what you're talking about," Michelle said. "I'm not... I don't have to listen to this. I want to go."

She tried to leave, but DS McQuarrie blocked the doorway.

"Get out of my way, I want to go!"

"That was the night everything changed, wasn't it?" Logan pressed. "Your parents told me. You'd been close before then, the two of you. But that's when you started to drift apart."

"No. No, this isn't... It's not..."

"The three of you went up to Boleskine and you did the Ouija board together. I'd imagine that must've been pretty scary, considering your age at the time."

"How did you...?" Michelle began. She shook her head. "I didn't want to. They said it'd be funny. They said I was being stupid, but... I didn't want to."

"Afterwards, she told you there was a demon in her," Logan continued. "That's right, isn't it?"

A sob. A nod.

"A load of shite, obviously, but how old were you at the time? Ten? Eleven? You believed her, didn't you? You believed what she was saying."

Michelle clenched her jaw, her eyes filling with tears.

"You thought she was telling the truth. Didn't you, Michelle? You thought she really had been possessed, or whatever it was she was claiming," Logan continued. "Is that where all the holy-moly stuff comes from? Your parents aren't religious, but you are. Is that why? Was it to protect you from her?"

Michelle shook her head. "N-no," she said. "Not from her."

Her voice became a whisper. "From *it*."

"It?"

"The demon!"

Michelle looked around at Caitlyn, then back to Logan. There was a resignation to the way she moved now, an acceptance of what was to come.

"I know what you're thinking. It sounds crazy," she said, her voice flat and measured. "And it does. I know that."

"What sounds crazy?" Logan asked her. "Tell us what happened."

Michelle drew in a shaky breath. "Everyone keeps saying she changed back then, like it was a phase or something. But it wasn't. She didn't change."

"What, then?"

"She *left*. That thing took over. It... it... swallowed her, so that it wasn't her anymore."

Michelle took a step further into the shed, her eyes wide and blazing. "It looked like her. It sounded like her. But it wasn't her. Not really. She wouldn't do those things. Mairi wouldn't be like that."

"Like what? What things?" Logan asked. "Get pregnant? Do drugs? I hate to break it to you, Michelle, but plenty of teenagers do those things without the need for any demonic intervention."

"Not those," Michelle snapped, her pitch rising. "That's not what I mean."

"What, then?"

"Nothing. Forget it."

"What did she do?"

Michelle was shouting now. "I told you, it wasn't her! It wasn't her! Mairi wouldn't have done that!"

"Done what?" Logan demanded, raising his own voice to match.

Her scream shook the walls of the hut.

"She wouldn't have let him touch me!"

The words echoed in the silence that followed. Even Michelle seemed shocked by them, flinched away from them, like she hadn't heard them spoken aloud before.

"Mairi wouldn't have let him do those things," she said, her volume a fraction of what it had been just a moment before.

"Steadwood?" Logan asked.

Michelle made no move to answer. She didn't have to. The look on her face said it all.

"It couldn't have been her. Even after, when everyone else thought she was back to normal, it couldn't have been her."

Her voice was a whisper, so low that Logan could barely hear the words.

"Because she never even said she was sorry."

She jammed the heels of her hands against her eyes and

screwed them in, like she could physically manhandle the tears back into her eyes.

"I actually thought she was back, for a while. She almost had me fooled," she whispered.

She snapped her hands down to her sides, clenching her fists and stamping a foot. "And then she started to see him again! After everything he did. To her. To me."

Despite everything, despite what she'd done, Logan almost felt sorry for her.

"And that's when I knew. That's when I knew I had to do something. I had to get rid of it! I had to get it out of her."

"So, you phoned up Bosco pretending to be Mairi and found out where Steadwood was working, then you brought her here and killed her. Why here? Did you hope you could frame him for it."

"That wasn't... I didn't..." Michelle said, shaking her head. "I was trying to cure her. I just wanted it out of her. Before her birthday. I couldn't stand the idea of that... that *thing* being in her skin longer than she was."

Logan shot Caitlyn a look and could tell the DS was thinking the same as him. Insanity plea. No question.

"I wanted her back, that was all. I just wanted my big sister back," Michelle continued, the words punctuated by deep, throaty sobs. "There are methods. *Proven* methods. Rituals that work, that actually do work. You can read about it. It's in books. Rituals that would've saved her. Would've brought her back. It's real. It's all real!"

"I could maybe buy that, if it was just the Exorcism stuff," Logan told her. "But you stabbed her through the heart, Michelle. There's no coming back from that."

Michelle shook her head, her whole body trembling. "N-no."

"You did. You stabbed your sister through the heart," Logan insisted.

"No! I didn't!"

"You killed her, Michelle. You murdered your own sister right here in this room. Didn't you?"

"No! I didn't! I *didn't!*" she screeched. "That wasn't my idea. That wasn't me! I didn't want to!"

Logan hesitated. "What? Then who? Not this demon you keep talking about? Why would it want you to...?"

She shook her head, tears tripping her. Her expression told him everything.

Logan's words died in his throat. His stomach tightened. His heart sank.

God. No. Not a demon. Not a monster.

A man.

A child.

"Shite!" He looked past Michelle to DS McQuarrie. "Caitlyn!"

Caitlyn had her phone out, her fingers already stabbing at the screen, having come to the same conclusion that Logan had.

"No signal," she said.

"Christ. Well then, don't just stand there," Logan spat. He pointed out the door, towards where the path climbed steeply up to the road half a mile above. "Fucking *run!*"

CHAPTER FORTY-FIVE

"SEE? WHAT DID I TELL YOU?" ASKED TYLER. HE SWIRLED
the foamy white dregs at the bottom of his glass around with his
straw. "Was that, or was that not, the best thing you've ever
tasted?"

"I wasn't a fan," Sinead said.

Tyler held a hand up, blanking her. "You don't count. Your
opinion is wrong," he said. "Stuart? Back me up here. You
enjoyed it, right?"

"It was alright, yeah," Stuart said. There was a *shlurp* as he
sucked up the last half-inch of liquid. "It was pretty good,
actually."

"*Pretty* good? Or the best drink you've ever had?" Tyler
pressed. He scowled briefly in Sinead's direction. "Don't let her
influence you. Ignore her. She's an idiot and a liar."

Sinead flicked the end of her straw at him. "Bit harsh!"

Tyler sighed. "Fine. An idiot *or* a liar. Better?"

"Not really, no!"

Stuart looked between them, idly fiddling with his straw.

He glanced up when a shadow passed over the table, then quickly cast his eyes down at the menu again.

"Who's ready for a wee bite to eat?" asked the waitress. She was a different woman to the one Tyler had charmed earlier, but radiated the same sort of jolly enthusiasm. She smiled down at them, notepad and pencil poised.

"Do you do just chips?" Tyler asked.

"A bowl or a basket?"

"Which one's bigger?"

"The basket."

Tyler returned the smile. "Then I'll have a basket."

"Anything else?"

"No, that's me. Sinead?"

The waitress turned her attention to PC Bell. "Can I get the ham and cheese toastie?"

She looked up from the menu at Tyler. "Can I steal some of your chips?"

"Absolutely not," he told her, but she chose to ignore it.

"I'll steal some of his chips. That's fine."

The waitress scribbled her note. "And for you?" she asked, turning to Stuart. She gave a little start. "Oh! Hello again."

Stuart didn't look up.

"Hiya," he replied. "I'll just have chips, too."

"Basket?"

Stuart nodded.

"No cake today?" she asked.

Sinead looked from Stuart to the waitress and back again.

"He was in a week or so back. Friday or Saturday, wasn't it? Red Velvet, you had. That's right, isn't it? Last piece, too. I remember, because I'd been eyeing it up myself."

She laughed and gave Stuart a little nudge on the shoulder.

"I'm kidding. Last thing I need to be doing with my figure is eating cake."

Sinead and Tyler's eyes met across the table.

"You were here last week?" Tyler asked.

"With your mum and auntie, wasn't it?" the waitress said. She rocked back on her heels, looking satisfied. "We must've made a good impression!"

She tapped her pencil on her pad, then winked down at them all. "I'll go get this sorted. Just shout if you need anything else."

"Uh, yeah," said Sinead. "Thanks."

Neither of the police officers watched her go, their attention instead entirely focused on Stuart. He didn't make eye contact, just sat there fiddling with his straw and staring at the pattern on the plastic tablecloth.

"Stuart?" Sinead asked. "Is there something you want to tell us?"

The waitress appeared again, a rack of condiments in one hand, and some cutlery in the other. She set them down, then placed a steak knife in front of Sinead.

"For the toastie," she explained. "It's fresh bread, and a bit tough."

"Thanks," Sinead said, not taking her eyes off the boy.

They waited for the waitress to leave again before resuming their questioning.

"Mate?" Tyler asked. "Is that right? Were you in here with your mum and Michelle last week before your mum... Before everything happened?"

Stuart shrugged. "Don't remember."

Tyler crossed his arms on the table and leaned closer. "What do you mean? How can you not—"

The glass smashed against the side of his head, showering

him in Coke-foam and backwash, and sending him tumbling to the floor, blood already beginning to pour.

Stuart had the knife before Sinead could react. They were both on their feet at the same time, but he caught the underside of the table and flipped it towards her, forcing her back and blocking her path. Around them, the other diners sat frozen in shock. They were mostly elderly, aside from a woman with a toddler, and mercifully none seemed like have-a-go hero types.

"Stuart, calm down," Sinead said, holding her hands in front of her. "Put the knife down, OK? Let's talk."

"Fucking stay back!" Stuart warned. "I'll kill you, I mean it. I'll fucking do it! I'll kill everyone in here!"

There was some commotion then, as a couple of the elderly patrons and the woman with the child got up and made for the door.

"Don't fucking move!" Stuart screamed at them, spinning and slashing at the air with the knife. His knuckles were white on the handle, his hand trembling.

He yelped in shock when Tyler caught him by the legs and got a shoulder in at the back of his knees. There was a *thud* as Stuart went down, his forearms slamming into the floor.

Sinead struggled to manoeuvre the table aside, but the space between it and the furniture on either side was tight, and it was a slow process. Before she could reach him, Stuart had kicked a leg free. He drew the knee up and brought his foot down, first on Tyler's shoulder, then on the side of his head. Once. Twice.

Stunned, Tyler lost his grip and Stuart launched himself to his feet like a sprinter off the blocks. He flew at the door, threw it open, and went stumbling out into the world beyond.

After finally managing to get out from behind the table and scattered chairs, Sinead dropped down by Tyler's side.

"You OK?"

"Get after him," DC Neish groaned.

Sinead sprang upright again. "Make sure he's OK," she ordered the rest of the cafe in general, then she hurried to the door and raced on out after Stuart.

There was no sign of the boy outside, and too many directions to choose from. Across the street, the path led down to the waterfall. Another path led off to the left of the cafe, tucking in behind it before joining a track that led up into the woods behind. The road itself curved out of sight just a few dozen yards on the left. Part of the cafe building and an old-style red phone box blocked the view of the road to the right.

The boy could've gone anywhere.

A figure appeared at the top of the path over the road, hair wild, breath coming in big, frantic gasps.

"DS McQuarrie!" Sinead hollered.

Caitlyn put a hand on her chest, as if she could hold her racing heart steady. "Stuart. It's Stuart," she wheezed.

"Aye, we know," Sinead told her. "He's legged it."

Caitlyn put her hands on her knees, gulping down air. She straightened again almost immediately, and jabbed a finger off along the road to her left. "There."

Sinead jumped the steps in front of her, caught the edge of the phone box, and skidded out from the shadow of the building.

Stuart had a big head start, and was powering ahead. DS McQuarrie launched herself into a run, but the steep climb from the falls had taken its toll, and Sinead passed her almost immediately.

She thought about shouting, calling after him, pleading with him to stop, but he was in full-on fight or flight mode now, and seeing sense was unlikely to be on the cards.

Instead, she ran, throwing herself forward and hoping her legs would keep up. Stuart was younger, fitter, and had a solid head start, but...

Actually, there was no 'but,' she realised. The chances of catching the little bastard were tiny. She'd just have to hope he tired out before she did, or pray for some kind of miracle.

"Hmm. I don't know. Is that the spicy one?" asked DI Forde as he dropped a gear and guided the car toward yet another winding bend in the road.

"Piri Piri? Aye. It's fairly spicy," Hamza confirmed. "Nice, though."

Ben scrunched up his face. "I don't mind spicy, but Alice wouldn't like it."

"They do milder ones," Hamza said. "You can get just plain chicken, if you want.

Ben perked up. "Oh? She could have that."

"Aye, and you could try the—"

He hissed and gripped the handle above the side window as Ben rounded the curve and swerved to avoid someone sprinting past at the side of the road. He saw a uniformed officer running towards them, and the brakes screeched as Ben brought the car to a stop.

The gearstick *crunched* as Ben slammed it into reverse, then twisted around, one arm stretched across the back of Hamza's seat. Hamza gripped the handle tighter as the car whined backwards unsettlingly quickly. He saw the reflection of the running boy in the wing mirror and caught a glimpse of his face as the kid shot a look back over his shoulder at the car.

"Is that Stuart Sinclair?" Hamza asked, recognising the boy from his photo.

"Christ knows," Ben said. He accelerated past the boy, then swerved the car in front of him and skidded to a stop.

Stuart collided with the bonnet, rolled up onto the windscreen, then landed heavily on the driver's side of the car. DI Forde was already unfastening his belt, and after a momentary hesitation, Hamza did the same.

Both men jumped out of the car just as Stuart hauled himself back to his feet. Far behind the boy, the uniformed officer—PC Bell, Hamza realised—was shouting something, but she was still too far away for him to hear properly.

"Whoa, whoa, whoa!" Ben urged, blocking Stuart's path when he attempted to run. "Easy, son. What's going on? What's the big hurry?"

Hamza hurried around the car to block the boy's retreat. As he did, PC Bell's voice reached them, suddenly loud and clear.

"Knife!"

Hamza looked down. Light glinted off a sliver of metal in Stuart's hand as he drew it back, the blade pointed at DI Forde's stomach.

Panic ground the world into slow motion and turned Hamza's limbs to lead. He saw the blade begin its upward swing. Saw the exact moment of realisation on Ben's face, the tightening of the jaw as he braced himself, the fear in his eyes.

Hamza lunged, grabbed, caught, twisted. Stuart cried out in pain and shock and frantically tried to yank his arm free, but Hamza slammed it, wrist first, against the edge of the car door. The knife clattered across the windscreen and thumped onto the bonnet.

Stuart roared in pain and frustration. He grabbed for

Hamza, but the DC twisted his arm up his back and shoved him against the side of the car.

"Let me go! Let me go, or I'll fucking kill you!" Stuart spat.

"Aye, good luck with that, son," Ben told him. He gave Hamza a pat on the shoulder and winked at him. "Bigger men than you have tried."

CHAPTER FORTY-SIX

DCI LOGAN LEANED ON A GATEPOST BY THE SIDE OF THE road, watching as Stuart and Michelle were bundled into different cars. A crowd had been drawn by the flashing lights, and Sinead had been leading the effort to keep everyone back until a few more uniforms had turned up, and Logan had called her over to join him and DS McQuarrie.

"How's our boy?" he asked, and Sinead's eyes were drawn to the ambulance where DC Neish was—in the most literal sense —currently having his head examined. DI Forde and DC Khaled stood at the open back door, laughing and joking with one of the paramedics.

"Aye, he'll live. It's going to need stitches, though."

"Don't suppose they can do his mouth at the same time, can they?" Caitlyn asked.

Sinead shook her head. "No. I already suggested that. They were having none of it."

They all watched a couple of uniformed officers climb into the front seats of their cars. A constable pulled the cordon tape aside and stood back until both cars had passed. Michelle

Sinclair had her head buried in her hands in the back of one car. Stuart sat in the other, staring blankly out at the world.

He briefly met Sinead's eye as he passed, but there wasn't so much as a flicker of recognition from him.

"I still can't believe it," she said. "I mean..."

"Aye. Takes some getting used to, this sort of thing," Logan said.

"But you do," DS McQuarrie added. "Unfortunately."

"But, I mean... Why? She was his mum!"

Logan shrugged. "I don't know. We'll find out. From what Michelle said, Mairi had found out she and Stuart were sleeping together. Understandably, she was less than impressed and put a stop to it. Or tried to, anyway. We know how that panned out."

"He killed his mum so he could shag his auntie?"

"That's fourteen year old boys for you," Caitlyn said. "Horny wee bastards."

"And I'll bet Michelle had been filling his head with all her demon shite for years," Logan added. "That can't exactly have helped with his mental stability."

"Think she believed it? The demon stuff?" asked Caitlyn.

Logan puffed out his cheeks. "Who knows? Maybe. Aye. She was a kid herself when it all happened. Sounds like it was the only way she could process what Mairi let Steadwood do to her."

Caitlyn nodded. "Better to blame a monster than your own big sister, I suppose."

Sinead's brow furrowed as she tried to make sense of it all. "So... when did they kill her?"

"Late Saturday, from what I can gather," Logan said. "They all came down here together on Friday, a nice wee family jaunt, then they took a walk down to the falls and imprisoned her in the hut. They used her phone on Saturday to cancel the date with Boyd, and when the text came in from Shayne on Sunday they replied. I suppose they didn't realise it was out of character for her. Then, Stuart took money out of the cash machine to make us think she was still alive, but she was already dead by then. They left the phone in the car, thinking that if we found it the texts would help back up their story."

"Why dump the car at Raigmore, though?" Caitlyn asked.

Logan shrugged. "Big car park, always busy."

"Easy bus back into town," Sinead added. "I sometimes park there and take the bus into work."

"For God's sake, don't let DI Forde know that," Logan said.

As if sensing his name being mentioned, Ben came away from the ambulance, and he and Hamza sauntered over to join Logan and the others.

"Alright there, Slugger?" Logan asked.

Hamza grinned—not proud, exactly, but something else. Relieved, maybe.

"Not bad, sir, thanks for asking."

"Ben?"

"Aye, I'm grand, Jack," DI Forde said. He put a hand on Hamza's shoulder and squeezed. "I phoned Alice and told her what happened. She's invited DC Khaled over for dinner."

"Aye, well they say no good deed goes unpunished, right enough," Logan remarked.

While Ben leapt to a half-hearted defence of his wife's cooking, Sinead found her eyes drawn back to the ambulance. This did not go unnoticed.

"PC Bell, will you do me a favour?" Logan asked.

Sinead turned, the formality of Logan's tone immediately straightening her shoulders. "Of course, sir."

"Will you accompany Detective Constable Neish to the hospital?"

Sinead cheeks reddened a fraction. She gave a little cough, clearing her throat.

"Of course."

"Thank you. And look after him, will you? He's one of the good ones."

"Yes, sir. Will do."

Logan caught her by the arm as she turned to leave.

"But for Christ's sake," he hissed. "Don't tell him I said that."

CHAPTER FORTY-SEVEN

LOGAN SAT IN ANOTHER CAFE AT ANOTHER TIME.

Waiting.

He'd been waiting for a while now. Twenty minutes. Thirty? He couldn't bring himself to check.

He sat with his hands around his mug, but there was no warmth there now. A thin puddle of tea lay at the bottom of the mug, the pot already drained dry. He'd resisted the little plastic-wrapped biscuit for the first ten minutes or so, but that was now long gone.

His phone buzzed on the table, the screen lighting up. His daughter's name filled the screen, along with a photo of her from ten years ago.

"Maddie. Hello!" he said, picking up the handset. The cafe was half-empty, but he kept his voice low. He couldn't stand people who shared their phone conversations with the rest of the world, and he was buggered if he was going to join them. "Everything alright?"

"Um, yeah. Fine," she said. "I just... Listen, I heard what happened. The accident."

"Ben," Logan said.

"Ben," Madison confirmed.

There was an awkward silence. Logan couldn't leave her floundering in it.

"I'm fine," he told her. "No harm done."

"Really?"

"Really." He traced his fingers across a cluster of little scabs on the side of his forehead. "I mean, I think my modelling days are over..."

She laughed. It was music, lifting him.

"But aye, I'm fine. I promise."

"Right. Good. That's... good," she said.

There was another silence, but a little less awkward this time.

"I'd better go," Madison said. "I just wanted to check."

"Right you are, sweetheart," Logan said. "Thank you. I'm fine."

"Good," she said again. "And, well, I'm up in Nairn in a couple of weeks. With work."

"Oh?"

Logan felt himself holding his breath.

"If you're free, maybe we could..."

"Aye. I'd like that."

"Right. Well. OK. Me, too," Madison said. "But I better run. I'll... I'll call you."

"I'll look forward to it."

"Bye, Dad."

"Bye, sweetheart."

The line went dead. Logan took the phone from his ear and looked at the screen, watching until Madison's photo was replaced by the phone's home screen. He raised his eyebrows in surprise, gave a little shake of his head, and had just sat the phone down on the table when the cafe door opened.

A woman entered, a gust of wind and a spray of rain shoving her inside.

"Sorry! Sorry! Traffic was terrible," gushed Shona Maguire, once she'd spotted him. "Am I late?"

"Cutting it fine, maybe," Logan told her.

The wind had made the pathologist's hair stand on end. She took a moment to smooth it down, then blew a raindrop off the end of her nose.

"You look happy," she observed.

Logan gave this some consideration.

"You know," he remarked. "I think I might be."

"Wow. Really?"

"In that neck of the woods," he said. "Don't worry. I doubt it'll last."

Shona wiped a hand across her brow. "Phew. Had me worried there."

She took the chair across from him. "You eaten yet?"

Logan shook his head. "No."

He passed her the menu.

"Decided what you're having?"

"About an hour ago, aye," Logan said.

She pulled a face at him. "Just for that, I'm going to take ages to choose." She tapped a finger against her chin. "What to have? What to have...?"

Her eyes met Logan's over the menu. She grinned, stuck her tongue out, then went back to reading.

Logan looked out through the cafe's big window at the street beyond. Academy Street. One of the few in the city he could name.

That would change, though, soon enough.

The rain was battering down. He watched pedestrians zig-zagging through it, dodging the spray from cars and buses that trundled through the puddles lining the road. Even the Chinese tourists weren't stopping to take photographs, which was practically unheard of.

"Right. I think I know what I'm..." Shona began, then she discovered the other side of the menu and shook her head. "Wait, no. I take that back. Give me a minute."

Logan was about to reply when his phone buzzed again.

Ben Forde.

Across the table, Shona patted her jacket pocket, then reached inside.

They both brought their phones to their ears at the same time.

"Ben? What's up?"

"Got a stoater for you, Jack. Just been called in," DI Forde said.

"Where?" asked Shona, pressing her phone against one ear and jamming a finger into the other one.

"Murder, I'm guessing," Logan said. His eyes met Shona's. She smiled grimly back at him, and they both stood up.

"No bother. On my way," the pathologist said.

"Text me the details," said Logan. "I'll be right there."

They both hung up.

"So, something's come up..." Shona told him.

"Aye. Snap," Logan said.

His phone buzzed. A text message flashed up. An address. Local.

"Another time?"

"Cool, yeah. Another time," Shona confirmed.

She looked down at her own phone as it bleeped, then jabbed a thumb over her shoulder.

"Race you there?"

Logan gestured to the door. "Ladies first," he said.

He followed her to the door, they said their goodbyes, then Logan stepped out onto Academy Street. The shops and restaurants that lined it were strange and unfamiliar to him. Even the buses weren't the same, or the people hurrying along the pavement. This wasn't Glasgow. This wasn't his city.

But it would be, soon enough.

Logan pulled the collar of his coat up around his neck. He fished in his pocket for his car keys.

And with that, he set off into the howling Highland summer, and to whatever lay lurking ahead.

JOIN THE JD KIRK VIP CLUB

Want access to an exclusive image gallery showing locations from the books? Join the free JD Kirk VIP Club today, and as well as the photo gallery you'll get regular emails containing free short stories, members-only video content, and all the latest news about the world of DCI Jack Logan.

JDKirk.com/VIP

(Did we mention that it's free...?)